4 May 14
24 May 14
25 June 14

2 3 MAR 2015

R 2 M

2 2 MAR 2016

MRS B
MRS H
19/2/19

CAN

T

Please return on or before the latest date above.
You can renew online at *www.kent.gov.uk/libs*
or by telephone 08458 247 200

CUSTOMER SERVICE EXCELLENCE

Libraries & Archives

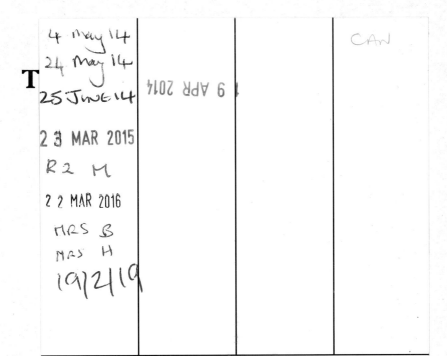

Kent
County
Council

00884\DTP\RN\07.07   LIB 7

D0308730

THE STRANGER FROM HOME

FREDERIC LINDSAY

ISIS
LARGE PRINT
Oxford

First published in Great Britain 2008
by
Allison & Busby Limited

Published in Large Print 2008 by ISIS Publishing Ltd.,
7 Centremead, Osney Mead, Oxford OX2 0ES
by arrangement with
Allison & Busby Limited

British Library Cataloguing in Publication Data
Lindsay, Frederic
    The stranger from home. – Large print ed.
    1. Meldrum, Jim (Fictitious character) – Fiction
    2. Police – Scotland – Edinburgh – Fiction
    3. Detective and mystery stories
    4. Large type books
    I. Title
    823.9'14 [F]

ISBN 978–0–7531–8084–6 (hb)
ISBN 978–0–7531–8085–3 (pb)

Printed and bound in Great Britain by
T. J. International Ltd., Padstow, Cornwall

For
Eilidh

BOOK ONE

A STRANGER FROM HOME

CHAPTER
ONE

After only three months in the United States, Betty Meldrum, who had chosen to revert to her maiden name, could tell herself that she had been lucky. She had a job, a place to stay and a friend. The Borders bookshop in the prosperous Washington suburb of Bethesda was a pleasant place and paid its assistants enough to get by. Not long after she'd started there, she'd seen an advertisement for a room in a house about twenty minutes away shared by three other women, all in their early thirties, one of whom, Lori Allingham, acted as landlady since her father owned the property. From the beginning, she and Lori, a sharp-featured blonde who caught the metro each day into the government agency where she worked as a secretary, had got on well, as much because of as despite their very different backgrounds.

Lori was from North Carolina and one lazy afternoon when the two of them had the house to themselves told how as a young journalist not long out of college she'd been sent to interview this old woman, one of the town's founding aristocracy. "It was a beautiful house, but faded, a rich family in decline. They'd had a lot of servants, but she was reduced to one. The old lady went from one room to another as she talked to me, and in each one she rang the bell for the maid, who would turn up flustered every time because of course she'd gone to the room where the bell rang, but every time it was the one we'd just left. The maid was called Beauty. Looking at her, the old woman said to me, 'Her family called her Beauty — a joke as it turns out.' Not long after, the old woman was killed in her bath — it was on the front page of the paper. The black maid had done it, and her name *was* Beauty. Can you believe that?"

On another afternoon they split a bottle of wine and Lori told of how she and her sister had found a pathology book in her grandfather's library and pored over its horrors together. At fourteen, with grandpa asleep on the porch, she showed it to a boy cousin. "We looked at the pictures and got quieter and quieter until suddenly we were making out right there on the old leather couch."

It was that same afternoon she'd invited Betty to her wedding, which was going to be held in the small town in Texas to which her parents had retired ten years earlier. "Lucky little me that they did. I was there on a visit, when I met Matt."

As it happened by the time the big day arrived eight weeks later, their friendship had cooled perhaps because try as she might Betty couldn't bring herself to share confidences about her own life. The invitation wasn't rescinded, however, and since Betty by that time badly needed to get away somewhere, anywhere in fact, she went to the wedding.

CHAPTER
TWO

"In Texas," the man with the blue eyes said, "a vegetarian is someone who eats small steaks."

She had been attracted by his accent, though he was a stranger like everyone else in the room.

"You're Scots," she said.

"Don't sound so surprised. We get everywhere. You should know that."

"I didn't catch your name."

"Wilbur Conway." He said it in an American drawl and laughed at the expression on Betty's face. "But you can call me Bobbie."

"Bobbie Conway?"

"You can call me —" He paused as if thinking. "Macleod."

"Bobbie Macleod? What *is* your name?"

"Wilbur Conway — but I thought you didn't like it."

"It doesn't go with the accent."

"So call me Bobbie."

She was slightly drunk, which wasn't one of her vices, but she had plenty of excuses. The taxi had taken her to the wrong terminal at Baltimore-Washington and by the time she got to Concourse A/B and found the gate for Southwest Airlines she had been late, which meant inevitably that she'd been picked for a more onerous check before being allowed to board. As a result, she was separated from the others going to the wedding, which made no difference to them since none of them knew her but for her meant spending a long flight wedged between a fat man with a sweet body odour and a woman going to Texas to bury her son who'd been shot by a small-town sheriff. Bewildered as any European by the culture of the gun, the woman, a native New Yorker, kept explaining how her son was a student of physics who'd gone to Texas to visit a friend. "They went for a drink and had way too much. I'm told they were both high. But weren't they entitled? They'd worked so hard, got their qualifications, they had the whole world at their feet. Outside the bar, this sheriff, he was only five foot high, started to shout at them and Danny jumped on his back. He was laughing when the little guy pulled his gun and shot him dead." It had been a long flight and at San Antonio the groom's brothers who had volunteered to pick them up were late. That first night she'd slept badly in a hotel, wakening unrefreshed and lying for what seemed like hours listening to hot water pipes butting floor beams in the dark

At the wedding rehearsal in the Baptist Church, which was the biggest in town, she spent time contemplating the banners interweaving the names of bride and groom hung behind the altar. At night they had dinner in a barn, one end still occupied by agricultural machinery, the other with living quarters two storeys high built against the end wall. Despite this, there was ample space left in the middle for tables to accommodate all the guests. Family and friends had done the catering, barbecued steak on paper plates the staple of the feast, though a fountain of chocolate also caught the eye. Afterwards, Betty was told, the older women would tidy up. Looking for something better to do, having in mind hen nights she'd gone to the night before weddings back home, she questioned the willowy blonde seated next to her who said, "You'd be welcome to come along if we go on a drag."

"What's that?"

"We get in our cars and drive around and —"

Interrupting, the woman on her other side, another friend of Lori's dating back to first grade, laughed and explained, "We drive around and every time we see a flag we haul down the windows and yell *Yee-haw!*" Since they were women in their thirties, Betty's first thought was that they might be joking.

Sensing her hesitancy, the first woman said pleasantly, "Or we could toilet roll somebody's house. That would be fun."

When she learnt that the groom and his friends were going to The Mill — "You have to bring your own bottle but it's a good old place, I've seen the Catholic priests there, I tell you those boys like their liquor" — the choice between it and the drag was no contest. The place turned out to be noisy and crowded and the group she was with were friendly and made sure she had plenty to drink and, although if she had wanted to see a priest falling into sin there wasn't one in sight, as consolation at some point she found herself talking to a tall man with a familiar accent and the bluest eyes she'd ever seen.

CHAPTER
THREE

As he ate his meal with his fingers straight from the paper wrapping, Meldrum pondered on how long it was since he had actually relished a fish supper rather than stoically feeding scraps of fish and lengths of cooling chipped potato into his mouth. An old Italian had told him that fish suppers had never tasted the same since concerns for health had led to the replacement of lard for frying with vegetable oil. Since Italians in Scotland had always made the best fish suppers, he was prepared to believe it, though it was also possible that the ones he remembered had been enjoyed so much because he was young.

The ringing of the phone startled him. As he went over, he rubbed his face as if to squeeze the need for sleep out of it.

"It's about Betty," the woman's voice said.

He hadn't spoken but she'd known he was there and launched into the conversation without preamble. Some things didn't change.

"Carole?"

"Yes, it's me," she said impatiently, though they hadn't spoken for months.

"What about Betty? She's not ill?"

"She's got married."

"What?" His first reaction was disbelief, but his heart lurched all the same as it had done since his daughter was a child in need of protection.

"It's true. I didn't believe it myself at first. She met someone in America, and they got married."

"What does he do?"

"Oh, that's such a policeman's question." No, he thought, a man's question, a father's question. "His name's Bobbie."

"She didn't say what he did?"

"No, she didn't."

"That's a good sign," he said mournfully, meaning the opposite.

"Why won't you trust her? She needs to be trusted. That's why I just listened. I had questions, but I didn't ask them. After all that's happened she needs us to trust her. There'll be time to find out more." He let the silence go on. At last, Carole said, "She only phoned last night."

After his ex-wife hung up, he stood with the phone forgotten in his hand. The knowledge bruised him of how little he figured now in his daughter's thoughts and feelings. They had been close once.

Back in his chair, he watched the traffic flowing from Princes Street down the broad artery of Leith Walk, its sea murmur punctuated every so often by the ululation of a police car or the lament of an ambulance. As he crumpled the fish supper wrapping and leant forward to put it in the wastebasket, he jostled the table and the picture frame fell over with a clatter.

He set it upright and rubbed a thumb over the undamaged glass. The picture had been taken before Betty married Sandy, before the young couple had a child who died as a toddler, before she'd had a one-night stand and got pregnant, before Sandy left her. She looked very young, laughing in the garden of the house they'd lived in as a family, standing beside her mother. But then Carole looked young as well, and as he stood behind the camera taking the picture he supposed so would he. Still married and happy, he and Carole would both have looked young. He laid the photo over again face down and stared out unseeingly at the Edinburgh night traffic until something flickered at the corner of his vision. He registered the image of a mouse scampering along by the skirting board just as it flickered out of sight under the sideboard. With a sigh, he fished the wrapping out of the basket, took it through to the kitchen and forced the greasy handful into the rubbish bin.

He started to pour water into the kettle and, bent over the sink, glanced down into the side street. As he was closing the tap, a figure emerged from the close that stood almost opposite his own. Hard to tell what caught his attention. Perhaps nothing more than the heavy cloth coat, which even from above had an expensive look. What was a man wearing that kind of coat doing coming out of that particular close? Although some of the closes were coming up in the world, as flats were refurbished and sold, the close opposite wasn't one of them.

As the man made his way towards the main street, he passed the local pub where three youths loitered in the lit entrance. As he came level with them, he broke step and turned his head sharply, as if one had said something to him. Perhaps he said something in reply since as he stood all three began to gesture at him.

Watching, Meldrum shook his head. In this district at night, a stranger was stupid to respond to a challenge. Though the man stood head and shoulders above the tallest of the three, if they were carrying blades his height and breadth only made him a better target. There was something about the group, too, that suggested the youths were on some kind of high.

As the confrontation continued, Meldrum muttered aloud, "For God's sake, man." Almost as if he had heard, the man made a gesture of dismissal and began to walk away. As he did, the tallest of the three followed for a couple of steps, head jutted forward, obviously mouthing off after him.

Whatever the excitement, it seemed to be over and Meldrum put the kettle on its base and switched it on. Giving a last glance, however, he was in time to see the man, who must have turned and come back very fast, lift the boy off his feet and hold him dangling like a puppet in the air before throwing him down on the pavement.

The fringe of smokers, who always gathered outside the pub since the smoking ban, turned from amused to agitated onlookers. At their shouts, people spilt out of the pub. Seemingly unflustered, the man walked half a dozen steps to where a car was pulling in at the kerb and climbed into the back. Next moment the car was gone, round the corner, slipping into the stream of traffic.

A few long strides took Meldrum back to the window in the front room that gave him a view of Leith Walk. He could see the car; it was held at the first set of lights but its number plate was hidden by the car behind it. A pair of binoculars was kept in the cupboard in the hall. He hurried out but took time to locate them, since they had hung there since a brief flirtation with birdwatching years before. The car was moving when he focused on it, spinning the wheel to get the sharpest image. By then it was almost at London Road and he lost his chance as it turned on to the roundabout and went out of sight.

By the time he'd walked back to the kitchen, a police constable had joined the crowd around the boy on the pavement. There was no point he decided in going down since there was nothing he could add to the testimony of those who had witnessed the incident. Shortly afterwards, an ambulance arrived with an attendant police car.

It was after eleven and a wave of tiredness overtook him. When he went to bed, however, he lay for a long time and his sleep was uneasy when it came at last. An angle as the crowd parted had given him a view of the boy just before he was lifted from the pavement. His legs had lain at an odd angle as if the ankles or knees had been snapped by the impact of being hurled down. An attack with fists and feet might have been as brutal, sudden, violent, but this assault had been in some odd way impersonal, an expression of contempt as much as anger.

Perhaps what was troubling him, Meldrum thought as he lay trying to sleep, wasn't the attack alone but not going down to help. What would have been the point, though? He hadn't got the number plate of the car, he hadn't had a look at the man's face; based on a view from above any account he might give of height and build could only be imperfect.

Forget it, I could pass him in the street and not recognise him, Meldrum decided, and fell asleep wondering if that was true.

CHAPTER
FOUR

They were in the car. When it rains in Scotland, it can be serious business. An outburst drummed so hard on the roof that it swamped the end of her sentence.

"Only a complete bastard would have —"

Barry Croft stared at the back of the driver's head. Fortunately, he didn't have to worry about what Kevin heard. Kevin was loyal. Kevin was a wall. Big, broad. And thick.

Rachel Croft's voice surfaced again, spraying venom like water from a swimmer's hair.

". . . so angry. It's not what you say, not the actual words."

"We agreed that we'd set out at eleven," he reminded her. "At eleven I'd my coat on and then I sat for half an hour. So I told you the time."

"It's not what you say. It's the tone you use. You know you're criticising me. You make me feel worthless. You know what you're doing."

"Telling you I didn't mind if we *were* late? Saying it didn't matter all that much?"

"Why mention being late at all? I don't think we're going to be late. We've still got time."

Wind shouldered the car over until it nudged the white line.

"What a day," he said.

"*What?*" She packed the monosyllable with amazement at his obtuseness.

"It's not a day to be speeding, even in a car this size."

"Listen to yourself," she urged. "You're doing it again. My blood pressure must be 190."

"You play a lot of tennis," he said. "You get coached. You're pretty fit."

She pulled her hand away as, reaching for her wrist, he laid two fingers on the taut flesh under her thumb to check the march of her pulse.

"I can feel the blood pushing against the backs of my eyes," she said. "If I die, we'll both know who's to blame."

CHAPTER
FIVE

Phoenix was also in America. The thought amused her. Never mind country, it might have been a different continent. A dry continent. By contrast, she had been conscious of a moistness in the Washington air, a relic perhaps of the swamps on which it had been built. She remembered how Lori Allingham, one evening sitting in the porch of the Bethesda house, had jumped up and sprayed a mosquito that had found its way in through a hole in the wire mesh. That summer the mosquitoes, breeding in the capital's forested spaces, were carrying Nile Fever. Here in Phoenix by contrast there were no pests; it was too hot even for flies.

"When I first flew in here in the early Fifties," the man in the bookshop had told her, "I looked out of the plane and saw nothing but desert. Now you look out and the town is ringed with green. So many golf courses!" When she nodded, he asked, "You saw them?"

"We have a lot of golf courses at home," she said.

"I know, I played on quite a few. We had our own bus and a Scots guy as a courier. Started in Troon and finished at St Andrews. The Old Course — the home of golf, isn't that right? Played our last round on it, right near the end before we came home. If I hadn't blown up on the last green —" He shook his head. "I was a sore loser. I said to them, show me a good loser and I'll show you a loser."

He seemed to be a pleasant man and he'd offered her a job. It had been embarrassing having to go in next day and explain it had been a mistake. Her husband didn't want her to work. Money isn't a problem, Bobbie had said quietly. *If I told my wife that*, the manager said, *she'd max out the credit cards. You hold on to that guy.*

After she'd got over being upset, she'd told Bobbie about the manager's holiday.

"Of course, Scotland's the home of golf," he said. "It rains all the time in Scotland."

He'd taken her downstairs and plucked a flower from the bush that grew by the front door. Then he'd laid it at the edge of the step. "If no one disturbs it, you can come back next year and find it lying here. The shape will be different and it will have faded, but it'll still be red. That's how dry it is."

Yet Phoenix was a green city. Teams of Mexican workmen tended the gardens round the apartment block, and down town every glass and concrete tower sat back from the street in a setting of lawns and fountains. "Back home in Scotland," Bobbie said to her, "even the best buildings are crowded together so you can't see them. It's the space here that makes the difference."

"You should get a job with the Tourist Board," she said, irritated without knowing why.

"That's why the Scots make good immigrants," he said. "We're patriots of wherever we end up."

Perhaps because of the spat about the job, perhaps she speculated because both of them had been upset by it, the rest of that day went on to be one of the best they'd had together.

They took the car to Camelback, parked under the ramada and set out to climb the hill. Late in the afternoon, it was hot, something over a hundred degrees, but three weeks in Phoenix had acclimatised her and they had bottles of water to sip as they climbed. It was a well-marked trail with plenty of people going up and down. When a lean elderly man passed them on the way up, not only going at a steady trot but pumping iron in both fists, she was impressed and then amused as Bobbie scowled and described him as an old goat. When they got to the top and looked out over the city, Bobbie slipped an arm around her waist. "Happy anniversary, Mrs Conway!" They had been married for five weeks.

In the evening he took her for dinner to a resort hotel and they sipped drinks as they watched the guests on the tennis courts. "We'll catch one of the tournaments," he said. "I've seen Greg Rusedski and Mark Philippousis and Tommy Haas at Scottsdale."

"I'd like that," she said, though she had never watched a game of professional tennis.

"Venus Williams too, close up she's got legs like a prizefighter. And the bald guy — stepping round the court like a wind-up toy with his scalp white from sun lotion — what's his name again?"

She shook her head, and when he laughed she thought it was some kind of test he'd given her.

"Agassi, that's it. And we'll go see the Diamondbacks. You ever seen a baseball game? You'll enjoy it. Sit on the shady side and eat hot-dogs. It's family entertainment — down in one corner they've got a swimming pool and people round it under big umbrellas eating ice cream. Only in America, like they say."

Later they ate out on the terrace with the big stoves glowing though it was still warm and the tall lanterns shining more brightly as darkness fell.

Going in to their apartment block, she started giggling and told him it was at sight of the red flower lying in the corner of the step. "Only in Phoenix," she said. Through some oversight, the air conditioning wasn't on in their bedroom and they stripped off the cover and lay naked on the bed. After they'd made love, they lay on their backs holding hands. He touched between her breasts and licked his finger tasting her sweat. She was happy, happy enough to spend the rest of her life with him, too happy to want to have any secrets.

"Don't worry," Bobbie whispered, one hand cupping her breast. "I won't let you down about wee Tommy. I respected you for telling me about the baby."

"My husband —"

"Must have been a bastard."

"He wasn't." Thinking of Sandy something moved deep inside her, like the first intimation of pain to come or the stirring of a foetus.

20

"In my book any man that deserts his wife when there's a baby is a bastard."

And then she said it, "But the baby wasn't his."

There was a long moment of silence, long enough for her to regret the words, and then he tightened his grip gently on her and whispered, "But he'll be ours. We'll send for him like I promised and he'll be yours and mine."

Lying open in the dark, she listened to his breathing slow into the steady rhythm of sleep. She had told him about wee Sandy, her oldest son, and how his illness and death had changed everything. But she hadn't told him about her illness, how the world had grown dark and confused, hadn't told him about the drugs or the patients smoking in the hospital corridor. She hadn't told him of her private fight with despair when she finally got to come home or of the stranger she'd slept with for only one night.

So much to tell him, but he had accepted her and the baby without knowing any of it. She would tell him the rest soon. Not tomorrow, but soon. After all, they had plenty of time.

CHAPTER
SIX

"My father's a policeman," she told him on impulse. She wanted him to know about her, she hoped in time he would know everything about her, just not today or all at once.

He stopped, suddenly, just like that, so the crowd had to part around them.

"You're full of surprises," he said.

He'd taken her to the mall at Scottsdale before and she had loved it, loved the hairdresser's run by the two exotic brothers, loved the cool air flowing along the wide avenues under the glass roof, loved Saks, Fifth Avenue, names she knew from malls at home that were different here, bigger, sleeker, brighter, with tiny dresses in rows, like clothes for sexy children, the gross hamburger gobblers all somewhere else in another America. She even loved the smell of the air; though she wasn't a greedy person, it smelt like money.

Afterwards they'd walked down into Scottsdale itself, abandoning the car, ignoring the bus. "Buses are for greasers and niggers," he'd said and, laughing at her shocked expression, "Just kidding. But let's walk. It's not far and the heat won't bother us. We're Scots — we're tough, am I right?"

All the same, she was glad when they got down the hill and could walk in the comparative coolness of the streetwalk shades.

"Let's take the bus back to the mall," she said. "I'm not so tough."

He took her hand and they looked in the windows of jewellery shops and went into crowded stores that sold Mexican carvings and Indian blankets. After a time they settled down at a table in the shade and drank beers, though alcohol was a bad idea in that heat and she was annoyed when he joked about it being OK since they were Scots after all. *Enough with the Scots already!* she exclaimed to herself like a Jewish momma, one of the voices she kept for her private thoughts.

"How good is he?" Bobbie asked.

"Who?"

"Your father."

"What do you mean?"

"I'm not asking if he's a churchgoer. How good a policeman is he?"

"Pretty good, I think. He's had his name in the papers."

"For what?"

"Solving murders."

"He's been a policeman for a long time?"

"Ever since I can remember."

"What rank is he?"

"He's a detective inspector."

He sipped at the long narrow glass. "He can't be that good."

She rose to the bait. "He hasn't got the promotions he should have. I don't know why. They've something against him. He never talks about it. Something that happened a long time ago. But he is *good*, believe me."

But then she saw that he was grinning and realised he had been teasing her. She smiled and put both hands to her mouth like a schoolgirl. All the same, the surge of feeling for her father had taken her by surprise.

As they were walking back, she remembered the man who'd come to the flat.

"Give me that again!"

He'd stopped so abruptly that she had to turn to reply.

"He was just a man. I thought you must have known him."

"What the hell would make you think that?"

"He asked for you by name."

"What name?"

That was a stupid question, but she didn't feel at all like smiling.

"Wilbur — when he said Wilbur, I just stared at him, but then he said, I'm looking for Wilbur Conway."

"Why didn't you tell me this?"

"I'm sorry. You were so upset when I told you about getting a job in the bookstore and then there was one thing after another —" Having to go back and refuse the job; making up with Bobbie; the magic day they spent together; making love at night. She shrugged and tried to smile. "It went out of my head. That sounds so stupid."

24

He shook his head at her and suddenly he was smiling. "You're perfectly right. It doesn't matter. Of course, it doesn't matter." He took her by the arm and they began walking. "Truth is, I was upset at the idea of anyone interrupting our time together. If I had my way, we'd be alone on a desert island . . ." He laughed. "Speaking of which. Tomorrow I'll take you to a lake with yachts and swimming and people fishing for trout."

"Is it far?"

"Not far at all. Tempe is just up the road. It has a manmade lake. You walk along the footpath beside it, and look out at the water until you come to the end. Like coming to the end of a bathtub — there's a wall — one side's blue water, the other's dust and sand. A lake in the middle of the desert."

"It sounds amazing."

"Only in America. Almost two million gallons a day evaporate off the surface, and they replace it from the Colorado River — the one that runs through Death Valley."

"But that must be hundreds of miles away."

"They have an aqueduct. Like I say, only in America."

It was a favourite expression of his.

She found the thought of the lake in the desert offended her. It was heroic but it was arrogant. More than anything else, it seemed so heedless. Sooner or later if you went against the grain of the world, there would be a punishment. There was no way she could say any of that. When he took her to the lake, she

25

resolved, she would enjoy it with a simple heart. Any other response instinct told her would disappoint him. It had been like that with everything he had shown her in Arizona. Like a host, he had wanted her to appreciate the wonders of so much luxury in so unforgiving a place.

"Why don't we turn back?" she asked. "There's a bus stop back there. Let's get the bus. It's so hot."

The air was stifling her suddenly. She was physically weary. Not like me to be so tired, she thought, perhaps there's been too much emotion these last few days.

"Sure," he said, but in the act of turning he grinned and pointed across the street.

"The bookshop?" she asked. Nothing in their time together had suggested he would get excited over a bookshop.

He was already crossing over. As she caught up, he said, "Look at the name!"

The Poison Pen, she read.

"Guess what kind of books they sell."

Crime books, of course, shelves of them.

"We're famous," the woman told them. "Look us up on the Net."

And when she learnt they were Scots, "We had Ian Rankin in here one time. You enjoying your visit?"

"We live here," Betty said, making and enjoying a claim to belong.

"Seems like everyone in Arizona comes from somewhere else," the woman said philosophically. "I'm from Idaho originally."

The shop was empty except for them. Bobbie mooched around the shelves while she and the woman talked.

"If you'd been earlier, you'd have seen a real cop," the woman said. "Somebody stole a car from the vacant lot. He was in asking if I'd seen anything. Of course, I hadn't. Who'd expect a crime here?"

Betty wondered about telling her that the night before as they lay in bed Bobbie and she had heard guns popping faintly in the distance. That hadn't been in Scottsdale, of course, but Phoenix, which like any city had a downtown you wanted to avoid at night. It was even possible, it occurred to her, that Bobbie had been testing her credulity. As she glanced over at him, he was reading a book he'd taken from the shelf.

Following her glance, the woman asked him, "You like crime books?"

"Ones I've read don't know what they're talking about," he said.

"Not all of them! Some of the writers do a lot of research. They've got magazines too. With articles on ballistics and DNA, all kinds of stuff. And then there's some writers have been policeman or lawyers. John Grisham was a lawyer. George V Higgins, I think he was a district attorney."

"I've read John Grisham," Betty said.

"Seen the movies," Bobbie said. "I'm kept too busy to find time for reading."

Betty looked at him in surprise. Each time she'd asked what he did for a living, he'd laughed and told her money wasn't a problem. She'd left it at that, happy to live in the moment, though knowing she'd have to come back to the subject at some point. It wasn't something you could put off for ever. Now when he looked back at her, blank eyed, she felt a stab of guilt as if he had read her thoughts and she had been disloyal.

"You're from Idaho?" Bobbie asked the woman, replacing the book on the shelf. "My mother was from Ennui. That's a little town in Idaho."

"I don't know it," the woman said.

He smiled, a twitch of the lips, as he took Betty by the elbow and made to leave.

Holding the door open, he said, "Ennui — if you look it up on the map, it's just south of Bored Shitless."

Outside, she said to him, "Why did you do that?"

He shrugged. Going back the way they'd come, he moved in long strides so that she had to catch up.

"Is something wrong?" The words came in a little gasp as if she was more out of breath than she should have been. She glanced sideways at him, remembering the previous night when his lovemaking had included persuading her for the first time to "suck his dick". He'd actually used the charmless American locution. "Suck my dick," he'd whispered. She was a grown woman, but that had been a new experience. Sandy hadn't been into fellatio; and as for the only other man she'd slept with, it hadn't come up on their one night stand. She had been excited by the response she'd got from bobbing her head between his legs, but now she wondered if it had made him despise her. She knew it was a stupid thought, an old-fashioned thought, but bewildered by what he had done she couldn't help the idea occurring to her.

They turned left and at the end of the street she could see where the bus would stop. Abruptly, he swung across to where tables were set out in the shade. By the time she took a seat opposite him, he had ordered drinks.

They sat in silence.

When the drinks came, she said, "She seemed a nice woman." She knew she should keep quiet, but she couldn't leave it alone. She wanted everything to be all right again. "What you said upset her."

"You think so?"

She nodded.

He pushed away his drink and stood up.

"She seemed like a nice woman?" he said seriously, as if seeking her opinion. "You think I was cruel?"

"Not cruel," she protested. She hadn't said "cruel". "Where are you going?"

He'd taken a few steps from the table. "I'll tell her I'm sorry. You wait here. Finish your drink." Her impulse was to stand and go with him, but he held her in her seat rubbing a hand along her shoulder. "Don't miss me too little," he said.

Accompanying him was something to be done at once before second thoughts intervened. Let him go if he wanted to, she told herself. It was stupid. It was as if he was mocking her. It was cool under the awning. Let him walk back in the heat, if that's what he wanted. Five minutes passed. When she next looked at her watch, quarter of an hour had gone. She got up and went to the corner. Cars went past. The hot street stayed empty.

In the bookshop, the woman looked up and frowned. "Your husband? He hasn't been back here."

Her smile was thin and hostile.

"I'm sorry he was rude to you," Betty said.

"Didn't seem a funny joke was all. I don't suppose he meant any harm."

Betty laid her hand on the pile of books on the counter then took it away. The front cover showed a rag doll with frizzed blonde hair and its legs askew. A knife lay at an angle to the doll. Betty picked up a copy and laid it down again.

"He was coming back here," she said.

"If that's what he told you, he didn't make it. I wouldn't have any reason to lie to you."

"I didn't mean — I just can't think what could have happened to him. We were having a drink in the shade — it's so warm — and he told me he was coming back here to apologise."

"To apologise?"

"Yes."

"I can't see any need for him to do that."

She hadn't seen any need for it either. It was why she had sat on in the shade, out of the hot sun.

"Why would he say that he was coming back, if he wasn't?"

"Maybe he was joking. Seems like he had a funny sense of humour." The words having been sharp enough to relieve her irritation seemed to restore her at once to a more neighbourly feeling. In a tone of some kindness, she advised, "It's been some kind of mix up. Believe me, you'll find him waiting for you back at your hotel."

"We're not in a hotel. I told you we live here."

"So you did," the woman said.

CHAPTER
SEVEN

By the third day, though she was bewildered and frightened, it was a consolation that the police were taking her husband's disappearance seriously. A sympathetic woman detective had gone through all the possibilities with her and though there was nothing from the hotels or the hospitals she clung to the notion of some kind of memory loss. Heat stroke maybe; he hadn't been wearing a hat.

It was the afternoon of the third day that things changed with the appearance of two new officers, men she hadn't seen before. She asked after the woman detective whom she had come to rely on.

"She's not available."

They'd taken her up in a lift to a room she hadn't seen before. With the thick carpet on the floor, prints of wild horses, big windows on one wall showing segments of solid blue sky, it wasn't like an interview room but an office borrowed for the occasion. It didn't feel as if she was in a police station any more, and if the two men were policemen, as they claimed, they were a different breed from the ones she'd been dealing with till then.

"I've been through all this," she told them.

"Not with us," the smaller man said. His name was Finn. The other man must have been over six feet in height. He had broad shoulders and big hands and was meaty from the neck down, especially across the belly and buttocks. She thought he might be over twenty stone, a lot of Americans were like that, burdened with flesh. She hadn't caught his name, a stutter of consonants, Polish maybe in origin. When he spoke, his voice was soft and reasonable. "We like to get things first hand. We pick up things other people miss."

"I can't think of anything that might help. I don't know why he didn't come back to the apartment. If he had an accident, he isn't in any of the hospitals. They've been checked."

"It didn't help that you didn't know the details of the car."

"I'm not good on cars. It was red and the book I was reading was on the back seat. I know I should know the make and the number plate, but I knew where it was and I found it — because it was red and my book —"

"But he didn't come back."

"I didn't have a key and I stood beside it waiting for a long time. And then I got the bus and went back to the flat. But he wasn't there. I waited till the next morning and then I went back out to Scottsdale on the bus, but the car wasn't there. I was sure of the place but I went up and down the rows anyway." She remembered the sick emptiness in her stomach. It had been like losing him for a second time. "That's when I got in touch with the police. All I could think of was that he'd had an accident."

"You'd a key for the apartment?" Finn asked.

"Of course I had!"

"You didn't have one for the car," the man with the Polish name said reasonably.

She rubbed her forehead. She was so tired it was hard to think. She felt if she let her eyes close she would fall asleep. There was a level of tiredness where slipping into sleep was like surrendering to pleasure, giving up, drifting away, if she slept she might waken and find all this had been a bad dream.

"We haven't been married for very long," she said, as if that would make them understand. If they'd been married longer, of course she would have had a key for the car. Thank God she'd had a key for the flat. She hadn't asked for one, he'd given her it. That must mean something. Trying to explain, she said, "We'd hardly been separated. We were together all the time."

"With being just married, you mean."

"That's right."

"He must have been about due to go back to work, though?"

"I suppose so."

"What did he work at?" Finn, who'd been studying her, joined in.

"I don't know."

Now they both sat silently as if trying to make sense of that answer.

"You don't know what your husband does for a living?" the big man asked.

"I know it sounds stupid, but —"

"Unusual," Finn said judiciously. "It sounds unusual."

"We met and fell in love. Then we were married. It all happened very quickly."

"A whirlwind romance," Finn said. His tone was neutral but because he said it to the man with the Polish name not to her she felt as if she was being mocked. When she didn't respond, he asked, "Did Wilbur know what you did for a living?"

"Bobbie," she said, "he asked me to call him Bobbie. And yes, I told him about myself. And he talked to me about how he'd lived in Glasgow as a child when his parents brought him back from America. He'd been born in New Jersey. They lived in Glasgow with his great-grandmother for a while. We talked about everything, the way you do."

But when she'd asked about his work, he'd just laughed and said money wasn't a problem, and she'd left it at that. She was busy being happy, and they had all the time in the world to find out about one another, no need to rush.

They listened patiently as she tried to explain.

"And now he's gone," Finn said.

"And the car's gone."

"Not much chance of tracing him through the car, not without knowing the make and what the plate was."

"There are a lot of red cars."

They were talking to one another not to her, back and forward, letting her eavesdrop on how impossible it was.

"What about the flat?" she broke in.

"What about it?"

"The people he bought it from. Maybe they'd know where he works. Maybe he bought it from the owners of the complex. All the apartments are new." She'd been so impressed by the gardens around the neat blocks, by the exercise room with its running track and Nautilus machines, by the pool area with the palm trees round it. On her way to the pool, she'd passed the office and glimpsed more than one receptionist behind a long desk. "You can search our flat if it would help." She blurted the offer on impulse. She'd searched, but hadn't forced the only locked drawer. He couldn't blame her if the police opened it.

On the way out of the building, she saw the policewoman who had been friendly crossing the hall from the front entrance, but almost at once the woman turned her head as if searching for someone in the other direction. Maybe so she won't have to see me, Betty thought. The idea chilled her.

Pulling in to the complex, she thought they would go to the office, but instead they asked her to guide them to the flat. They walked in the sunshine past the crew of Mexican gardeners who were sweeping round the pool and watering the trees. She opened the front door and led the way upstairs. They looked at the living room and opened the doors onto the two bedrooms and the kitchen and bathroom.

"Have a seat," Finn said. "I'll go talk to the people in the office. You want to start looking around?" he asked.

The man with the Polish name shook his head. "It'll keep till you get back."

He took a seat without waiting to be asked and as Finn left said, "A coffee would be nice. If you can make it, that is. I can take tea."

"I can make coffee," Betty said and went into the kitchen.

As she filled the perc, she realised he was leaning in the doorway watching her.

"You like it strong?" she asked.

"Three spoons would be fine."

"Not strong then. My . . . husband —" Why had she hesitated before the word? He would think she was lying, but they had married, she *was* married. Perhaps she'd hesitated because it had been so recent, so sudden a decision, and now he had disappeared. "My husband Bobbie takes five spoonfuls. I make the breakfast coffee. He needs it to start the day, like kickstarting an engine, he says."

The detective said nothing, leaning in the doorway, filling the space, his shoulders brushing on either side, the swag of his belly pushed out towards her, saying nothing.

When the coffee was made she poured two cups, but picked up only one and went through into the living room, leaving him to collect his own from the worktop. Even if it wasn't much of a protest, she felt the need to make a claim to respect.

When they were seated, he sipped his coffee. She resisted the temptation to ask if it was all right.

After a while, he asked, "So you've no idea how he earned a living?"

"No." As he waited, she almost added *as I said*, but was afraid if she gave way she might scream the words. Whatever his opinion of her, people like him offered her only hope of getting back to normality.

"What about distinguishing marks?"

"What?"

"Scars, anything like that. They must have asked you."

She couldn't remember. Her first interview seemed a lifetime ago.

"I expect they did," she said. "They must have made notes. Didn't you see their notes?"

"According to the notes, he didn't have any distinguishing marks."

"Well, then." She meant, in that case why ask?

"It doesn't have to be where people could see them."

"I don't understand." But almost at once she did. "You mean if they find a body?"

"It doesn't have to be that. He might have lost his memory. A doctor could check — some way of checking it's really him."

With that, she remembered. "At the top of his left leg," she said. "He has rough skin, shiny skin, from an old burn. It happened when he was a baby. He pulled a teapot over on himself. He might have died but his great-grandmother ran cold water on it and saved him. He said the strange thing was he never liked her."

It came out in a rush, perhaps because it had impressed her at the time. They'd been lying in bed and she'd run the tips of her fingers over his skin. He hadn't minded when she asked. His voice murmuring in the dark after they'd made love. It was the kind of thing that brought people close, talking about their past; and so she offered it now as if it proved something.

As if he'd read her thoughts, the man with the Polish name said, "He shared that with you." *Shared*, Americans were big on sharing. Before she could respond, he went on, "But yet he didn't tell you what he worked at."

Before she could answer, the outer door at the bottom of the stairs banged shut. The other detective must have left it open when he went out, she thought, and in confirmation Finn's head, round as a soccer ball, rose into sight as he mounted the stairs.

Instead of offering what if anything he had discovered, he answered her expectant look by asking, "You want to come with us while we look round?"

The apartment wasn't large and the search didn't take long. It was thorough but polite, as if taking account of her feelings at every step. They asked her permission before going through the drawers in the bedroom, and when they forced the drawer in the desk it was done so professionally she had no sense of violence, and so quickly that she only glimpsed a sheaf of papers inside before Finn had gathered them up and slid them into an envelope. "We'll check these out and let you have them back," he said as if it was the accustomed routine against which there could be no argument.

All the same, she hated the whole process and perhaps it was that which made her assert herself.

"I have to go home," she told them.

"Home?" the man with the Polish name wondered.

"To Scotland. I have a little boy there. My mother was going to bring him here next week. It's what Bobbie wanted, he was happy for him to come. But now —" Her throat blocked as if with unshed tears. "I have to explain what's happened. I have to see my child, I haven't seen him for months." She was a bad mother. She saw that verdict on both their faces, but she already knew that. "I'll be back quickly," she promised.

"You planning on bringing the little guy back with you?" Finn asked. "Where are you going to stay?"

"Here, of course."

"Thing is, ma'am," Finn said, "your husband didn't buy this place. He rented it." And as if in answer to an unspoken question from the other detective added, "Just for eight weeks."

"I can't think about that," she said. It was the simple truth. Her overloaded brain, at one more problem, refused like a tired horse at a fence. "All the same, I have to go home." And then she heard herself saying, "My father's a policeman. He'll know what to do."

When she read something like mild contempt into the blank canvas of the look they turned on her, she wondered how much more they would have despised her if they could have known of her long estrangement from her father.

BOOK TWO

ARRIVALS AND DEPARTURES

CHAPTER
EIGHT

After charging the girl, Meldrum felt sick, physically sick and morally sick of the job he had to do, sick of all of it, the people he had to encounter, the sadness of the world. She was twenty-four years old, and described her mother as, "Nosy. Tell you, she went mental when she checked up what I was doing on the internet." She'd married young. Her husband was weak. Since they'd got married, they'd lived with her parents. She'd tried to work, but each attempt had ended in a breakdown caused by the stress of dealing with people. More than once she had tried to commit suicide, at least that was what she claimed. For one attempt there was outside verification; she'd stayed alone in an empty office and swallowed pills, not knowing cleaners came in at night. She had a bad back — fused vertebrae at the bottom of her spine causing pain. "I've been on seven drugs over the last four years — every one turned me into a zombie. I don't care what they say, I'm not doing that again." The father, mother and husband verbally abused her. She had longed to get away but had no money or car or qualifications. She kept thinking about getting a job but was afraid of another breakdown. It had been the last straw when her mother snooped on her. "She wanted my father to ban me from the internet. But if he pulled the plug, everything electrical in the house would crash. I fixed it so it all came in through my computer. None of the three of them can even wire a plug. I'm the one that fixed the TV." And so she visited again the sites she'd been banned from and her mother caught her again and this time her father said she had to leave the house. How could someone so afraid of people leave the house? Desperate, hopeless, angry, she had stabbed her mother. Just once was enough. You can beat someone a dozen times with a hammer and not kill them, but with a knife death can happen very easily.

No doubt if her lawyer was competent and cared to make the effort he would explain how easy it was for a knife to cause unintended harm and describe for the jury the pain she suffered and the strange life she had led in that house, but whatever he said she would spend the next part of her life behind bars.

All of which explained but didn't excuse his reaction when DS McGuigan remarked, "If only they were all as quick as that."

"Still holding the bread knife when the constable went in, you mean," he wondered sourly. "With blood on it. If she'd been really trying she'd have hung a notice round her neck."

"A notice?" McGuigan wondered as they walked back to the lift. He wasn't usually slow on the uptake, but perhaps irritation was preventing him from working it out.

"Saying I DID IT."

McGuigan grunted, and swung aside into the squad room.

No *good night*. Meldrum thought, no *fancy a pint*. On the other hand, he hadn't said *fuck you*, which is what he'd almost certainly wanted to say. There was some benefit, after all, in working within a hierarchical structure.

When he came out of his office, shrugging into his overcoat, he could hear the hum of voices from the squad room. They probably would go for a pint, even McGuigan who wasn't a sociable type. It was part of the job. Detectives liked murders to be solved, and if they were solved quickly so much the better. Not celebrating a win didn't go down well. Part of the job is welding your team together, Assistant Chief Constable Fairbairn would have said, it's called leadership. Of course, it was. They had courses on it. Not so long ago, Meldrum had sat through one. Under protest. He'd been a detective inspector for a long time. Too long. Not going for a pint was probably another reason why they wouldn't promote him.

He didn't have a residents' parking permit but as long as Hibs weren't playing a home game, he always found a place. Tonight he found one beside a van in the dead-end street round the corner on the right. It was a short walk back to the close. With the key in the entry door, he turned his head and looked at the pub across the street. Light spilt through the glass frontage. He could hear men laughing. His mouth moved in a dry tasting motion. Abruptly he turned the key in the lock and went into the close.

He began to tramp up the two curving flights that led to the second floor. At one time each stone step had been worn down in the middle by more than a hundred years of footsteps; but as part of the remodernisation they'd been coated with a salmon pink composite. As he went into the flat, the phone was ringing. He contemplated not lifting it, but it kept on ringing.

In answer to his grudging hello, a voice asked, "Is that the policeman Jim Meldrum?"

A woman's voice. An American woman.

"How did you get this number?"

After a brief pause, she said, "You're not in the phonebook." It wasn't a question.

"That's not an answer. I'm hanging up."

"Wait! I got it from your daughter."

"Why would she do that?"

"I'm a policewoman."

His heart lurched, even though he didn't believe her. It wasn't the way a genuine policewoman would have gone about things. For one thing she hadn't identified herself.

"I doubt that," he said.

She made a small sound like a sigh, which without seeing her face could have meant anything.

"My name is Sandra Foley. I'm with the Phoenix Police Department."

"So?"

"You know your daughter lives here?"

"My daughter lives in Washington."

"Not since she was married . . . You did know she was married?"

"I knew." Carole had phoned to tell him. But she hadn't said anything about Phoenix. Had she known?

"Phoenix. That's in Arizona, isn't it?" And, before she could confirm that, could no longer restrain the real question. "What's happened? Is she all right?"

"I hope so. I just wanted to pass something on. I'm not looking to get involved, right? I mean, she's *your* daughter."

"Is she in hospital? Is she injured?" I could be on a plane tomorrow, he thought. Maybe even tonight. There are flights to America from Edinburgh. New York's a hub airport. Get to New York. A thought struck him. "Has she been arrested?"

"What would make you think that? Has she been in trouble?"

"No." She's had her heart broken. She's been in a mental ward. She's run away to bloody America. "Of course not." The wife of an old detective sergeant had told him, my husband torments the kids, that's the worst of you coppers, everyone's guilty, even your own children. "If you've something to tell me, get it over with."

"It's her husband Wilbur. She's reported him missing."

"When did this happen?"

"He's been missing since mid-afternoon Monday."

"That's not a long time. What makes her think he's not coming back?"

"Newly weds," she said. "Husbands tend to stick around." He could hear her make that odd little sighing sound again. "Unless something's wrong, that is."

"You have reason to believe something's wrong?"

She grunted. "You're a cop all right. Even if she hadn't told me I'd have known."

"My daughter talked about me?" Not a policeman's question; a father's, a father who was surprised.

"The day she reported him missing. It came out in the middle of other stuff. According to her, you were the best."

"She must have been in a state."

"If you mean in a bad way, that she was."

"Would you let me speak to her, please?"

He listened to the silence. At last she said, "Thing is, it's out of our hands."

"What do you mean?"

"Let's just say a different, uh, branch has taken over the inquiry."

"A different force?" Trying to make sense of it, he asked, "State police, you mean? Police from somewhere else?" Betty had lived in Boston. "Boston police? Did her husband work in Boston?"

"We have no idea where her husband worked. Far as we can tell, neither has your daughter. We thought that was strange. You find that strange?"

"Yes."

"Far as I'm hearing, there's been no sign of him. He'd rented the apartment the two of them were living in. The details she gave that first day, she said he owned it."

Automatically he recorded that, a fact, something to build on. "You didn't tell me who these people are who've taken over from you." He needed to get in touch as soon as possible.

"I didn't and I'm not going to. These are serious people."

She had said she didn't want to get involved.

"If you feel like that, why phone me?"

"I wanted to help your daughter. I've got a daughter who's had her troubles. Your daughter reminded me of my own child. Something about her, the look in her eyes, couldn't get her out of my head. Hold it!" she interrupted his attempt to reply. "I'm going to hang up now. Your daughter gets in contact, tell her to come home, you understand? I know she wants to find her man, but tell her sometimes you have to let go. Doesn't matter how strong a woman she is, tell her to come on home. She'll be safe at home."

CHAPTER
NINE

"I wanted to thank you," Violet Terry said, smiling till it seemed her mouth would touch her ears. She had a wide mouth, generous, wasn't that what they called it, a mouth that wide? "I want to thank the whole world today. But everyone in the village will do for a start!"

"I can see why you'd be pleased," Barry Croft said.

"I'm so excited." She slid a hand into the pocket of her waterproof jacket and pulled it out empty. "I've left it! What a fool! I've left it on the table in the hall. I laid it down to put my boots on and the fish van came and when I came back with the fish I went back out through the kitchen and forgot all about the letter. I want to show it around. Do you feel like a walk? We could walk down and collect it and then I can carry on round the village. Unless you're busy? You're not working? I'm not interrupting?"

"Wednesdays I don't work," he said. "And Rachel's gone into town."

"I know," she said. "I saw her go past in the car."

He rubbed his chin slowly as he studied her. A tall slim woman with an English rural accent just discernible under what seemed to be the universal incomers' twang of diphthongs. It would be amusing to tell her she wasn't his type, but that wouldn't be a prudent way to talk to a neighbour. In any case, it wouldn't be entirely true, there being moods and days when any woman who wasn't senescent and had legs which parted was his type.

When he and Rachel had first come to the village, the traffic had been light. Now as he accompanied Violet along the main street, it was hard to talk over the vehicles hurrying south. Getting tired of it, he took her by the elbow and drew her across the road to the gate that led on to the track up the hill.

As they climbed, the roar receded to a murmur and the wind freshened in their faces.

"I don't need to see the letter to believe you," he said. "Tell me about it instead."

"Some people will want to see it." She laughed. "Not everyone's like you."

"I gather you won."

"We won. Everyone in the village. Can you imagine what it would have been like if they'd got permission to use the quarry as a landfill site? We'd have had dozens of lorries coming through the village every day. Sundays too, did you realise that?"

"I think you pointed it out. You were pretty thorough."

"Not just me. I wasn't the only one. Everyone on the committee had a shoulder to the wheel. Jack organised the petition. Tony put all the facts and figures together. Rachel took the photographs." She laid a shade of emphasis on his wife's name. "It was a real team effort."

"And you won."

"We —" she began, and broke off. "Now you're teasing me!" She laid a hand on his arm. As he kept a companionable silence, she said, "You're so detached. You float above things. Not everybody understands that, but some of us do."

"I didn't realise it was so obvious."

"Is that you teasing again?" She cocked her head to one side, studying him. The gesture, which was intended no doubt to be flirtatious, struck him as silly in a woman of her age. They walked in silence for a while, until he asked, "Are we going all the way?"

She laughed, hesitated on the edge, it seemed, of taking up the double meaning, then asked, "Why not?"

"I thought you were in a hurry to show the letter from the Department to everyone."

"It's early. Time enough to take a look at the quarry and have a good gloat."

Another hundred yards of climbing took them up the long slope of turf scabbed by patches of rock to the edge of the quarry. They stood side by side looking down at the black sheet of water that spread between the gouged face of vertical rock opposite to the steep drop under their feet. From above, it was as dark as a mountain lochan under a winter sky.

"I could never understand," he said, "why anyone would think it was suitable. They'd have had the cost of draining the water out of that end before they could make a start. There must be better sites."

"Apparently not. Maybe it's not so deep as it looks."

"Did they say that?"

"Not in so many words. Their argument was that the costs had all been factored in and it was a viable proposition. If there's enough of a demand, I suppose they could just up their charges to pay for what was needed."

"Anyway it won't happen now. Or at least not for a while."

"It shouldn't happen *at all*," she said emphatically. "We've been told that once planning permission has been refused, that's it. The environment people won't 'revisit the decision', that's the phrase they used. In confidence, we were told how lucky we were it was a small company that had come forward with the plan to use it as a dump. One of the big operators would have bulldozed the project through with high-powered lawyers and the usual purchasable experts, but since we won and the decision's been made, that should be it. The village is safe!"

They watched a car run along the road hidden on the far side of the quarry.

"You make it sound like paradise," he said.

"How do you feel about it?"

He stared down at the water, feeling her eyes on him. "Oh, glad you won, of course. It'll keep the house prices up."

"Not just about the quarry. How do you feel about living here?"

"I like walking in the hills."

"Is that what brought you here?"

"Rachel fell in love with the house."

"And that was it?" She laughed, a brief faintly breathless protest. "I'm not sure I believe you. It's always seemed to me that you were the one who made the decisions. I doubt if anyone could make you do something you don't want to do."

Idly, he ran through the possible replies and, since he wasn't interested in her sexually, chose the most neutral. "I leave that side of things to Rachel." The words were no sooner said than he heard how out of fashion they were.

"That side of things! The house and the meals, carpets, curtains, menus and what else? Holidays? Oh, and shopping, of course. An account at Jenners. What on earth could any woman have to complain of if she's given an account at Jenners?"

"I'd have thought your preference would have been for Harvey Nichols."

"Is that where Rachel has an account?" She bared her teeth at him in what might have passed for a smile, or the snarl of a bitch about to snap at a hand.

Catching her excitement, he responded, "I don't give a fuck where she has an account."

"Poor Rachel," she said, as he put his hand on her breast.

She put her own hand over his and held it against her as they began to walk back down towards the village. There was no one in sight on the bare hillside, but he had lived long enough in the country to know that was no guarantee they were unwatched. Already he was cursing himself for a fool. Before they came to the gate, he slid his hand from under hers. She kept her own hand in place on her breast, however, eyes half shut and her tongue licking across her lips. She's about ready to start without me, he thought, and decided that he'd walk her to her door but refuse if she invited him in on the pretext of seeing the letter recording the quarry protesters' victory. To his surprise, however, she turned back along the street the way they had come, away from her house and towards his.

They didn't talk. He walked slowly, lengthening his stride so that the lazy reach of his walk gave a false impression of eagerness. He thought of the times he had encountered people as he strolled through the village. They might meet the woman who lived in the old cottage at the end of the main street, the one who pushed her disabled son in his wheelchair, he couldn't recall her name, he had a bad habit of forgetting the names of people who could be of no use to him. Or the man who made violins or the one who mended clocks or the man who wrote cookbooks that combined recipes with accounts of travelling to the relevant regions, cookery and travel, a successful formula. "What a wonderful village," Violet Terry had said to him once, "so many clever people; it must be the pure air." Best of all would be to meet Tarleton whose hobby was fixing old racing bikes, who never passed without stopping for a chat, what could be more detumescent than an account of stripping out a cylinder head? They met no one. Events unspooled with the inevitability of a toy dog bowling head over heels across a carpet. She marched ahead of him round the house to the back entrance and waited as he unlocked the door.

He contributed an erection to their coupling. She managed the rest, so that she was on top of him when he glimpsed beyond the rhythm of her rise and fall the inverted exclamation mark of his wife in the doorway, the white dot of her face focused on them. He bucked with surprise, which was enough to produce an orgasm in the woman above him even as he shrivelled within her. Gripped as if in a wrestling hold, feeling the grind of her against him, he felt as alien from her passion as the spectator in the doorway. When she'd finished, and it was a tentative finish, perhaps conscious at last that something was missing in her lover, Violet Terry subsided on him with a sigh.

It was at that moment that Rachel said, "Should I have phoned to say I'd decided to come home early?"

Although her tone was conversational, almost contemplative, laying a branding iron on the naked back of the other woman could not have produced a greater convulsion. Barry Croft guessed by the thin smile on his wife's lips that she found the effect satisfactory.

"The first time Barry and I fucked," she went on, "I gave him crabs. It was a long time ago, though, so I shouldn't worry about catching anything."

CHAPTER
TEN

Philip Donald Corrigan was her husband's name. For most of her life her husband had been a man with a different name. Carole thought about Jim Meldrum as she held her grandson on her knee and let her gaze drift around the waiting area for International Arrivals. Tommy stirred and his head blindly sought comfort in the snug cleft between her breasts. A short time before he had been running from her seat to the one opposite asking, "Is that her now?" as passengers began to stream through from the Customs hall. "Mummy's plane hasn't landed yet," she'd explained, and shortly afterwards he'd climbed on to her knee and fallen asleep. Philip, she thought. Donald. My second husband. He had charmed her when they first met. She wasn't a weak woman; she had run a school and broken up with Jim Meldrum her first husband, which hadn't been easy for she had married young and loved him for a long time. Even after their separation she had stayed friends with him, something she recognised in retrospect as even less easy than working up the determination to make the break. Comforted by Tommy's warmth pressed against her, it occurred to her that the affection Jim Meldrum and she had never ceased to feel for one another might have drawn them together again. Perhaps, perhaps not. Could you ever recover something that had been thrown away? There was no way now of being sure. Anyway, one day she'd met Philip Donald Corrigan.

"Gran?"

Tommy's eyes were open.

When she checked the Arrivals board, Betty's flight was delayed by forty-five minutes.

"We'll get something to drink," she told the boy.

"Are we going home now?"

"No!" She hugged the boy against her. "Mummy *will* be here, but her plane will be later than it was supposed to be. That's all. We'll get a biscuit, too. Come on."

Instead of going to the small place beside Arrivals, she decided to distract the boy by walking back along the concourse to the main café. There was a small queue waiting to be served and as she joined it, she remarked on something familiar in the broad shoulders of the man in front and then as he turned his head slightly recognised him as John Neally, the head teacher of her old school, who had been her deputy before her resignation. He was the last person she would have expected to see, but she felt no great surprise. Random encounters were not unusual in this intimately sized city. She had no desire to talk to him, and even wondered about backing away quietly. At her first tentative step, however, Tommy protested and Neally glanced round.

"In America?"

He had insisted on buying a coffee for her and a juice for the boy. There had been an awkward moment when he had expressed his surprise at how young Tommy was and been embarrassed to learn of her older grandson's death.

"A job," Carole said. "But she's changed her mind and is coming home."

"You'll be glad of that."

"Oh, yes." Despite everything, Carole thought, whatever was wrong, glad of that and longing to see her daughter again.

"And what about her husband?" Neally asked. "What was his name? Sandy, yes, I mind he was an art teacher, wasn't he?"

Glancing at the boy who was busy trying to suck juice up through a bent straw, Carole said quietly, "Ex-husband."

Neally took it in his stride. "Modern times. I get them in the office." He mimicked, "I'd like you to meet Derry. He's my life partner. And three months later, she's back. This is Pat — my new life partner." He shook his head. "Not like when you started, eh, Carole?"

"Things have changed."

"Oh, we're still holding the line, thank God." A flicker in his eyes made her imagine he was recalling Jim Meldrum, and the pressure of disapproval she'd come under from the Church authorities when she separated from him. As if conscious of that, he bustled on, "I've a colleague in the school down the road who has to do sex education with his godless flock. He was

59

telling me this wee toe rag asked him in one of those lessons, 'Please, sir, what makes my mother shout and bawl when she's getting shagged?' He put up a hand to shield the last word from Tommy, shaping it exaggeratedly with his lips as if signing for the deaf. "Primary Seven! He knew bloody well — sorry — *really* well what he was saying."

"No answer to that," Carole said.

Neally grinned. "This chap told me — 'I just looked at him and asked, Are you a Hibs supporter? Thought you were. Imagine the centre back goes on a long run, all the way up field, beats three men and lays on a perfect pass that the right winger runs on to. Bang! It's in the net. What a goal! *Yes!!!* the wee guy says punching the air. And that's why your mother's shouting I told him.' "

"No wonder there are a lot of confused children in Edinburgh," Carole said, smiling despite herself.

"Confused about who their father is," he said. Was it her imagination or did his gaze settle on Tommy when he said that? She told herself that was impossible. He hadn't known of Tommy's existence; hadn't he been puzzled because the boy seemed too young to be poor dead little Sandy? All the same, for an instant she entertained the possibility that somehow he knew that Tommy was the illegitimate product of a one-night stand. It wasn't impossible; Edinburgh was a city of gossips.

She hated him and then remembered him as kind and harmless and hated herself. It was a relief to get away from him.

As if he sensed that this time would be different, Tommy sat quietly on the seat beside her, not getting down even when the first passengers from Betty's flight began to appear through the entrance and hurry along behind the rail into the hall of the airport.

"Watch for Mummy," she told him and his eyes observed her from a still face.

Perhaps that was what made her lift him when she saw Betty coming among the very last of the passengers. She took him up and carried him towards her daughter, assuming excitement on his behalf, imposing her anticipation on him, not putting any trust in the idea that her grandson would run to his mother.

CHAPTER
ELEVEN

They had reversed in to the track and switched off. The city spread around them and yet leaning forward the driver could see a scatter of stars. Why was that? The glow from the streets should put out the lights of the sky. It was a scattered city, of course, and there was a lot of desert over there to the left. He stared at the opening across the road, which led to the track continuing along by the banks of the canal. It was too dark now to see the water, but he knew it was there. The two of them had walked the route in the brief twilight. He remembered trying to identify the tune being played by an orchestra, faint in the distance from one of the resort hotels, and hunching his shoulders with an instinctive distaste as shapes flickered and swerved at the corners of his vision, bats swooping across the water. A show tune, from one of those Fifties musicals, full of energy and hope and know-how, the country with a war not long over, a war won against the little yellow fanatics and the Nazis in Europe, the bad guys beaten and the good times ready to roll.

He eased back his cuff and angled his wrist to catch the time. As he did so, he felt his companion stir irritably and shrugged a silent response. Sure, they'd come when they'd come. He still liked to know what time it was.

Minutes passed in silence. Other partners he'd had, they'd have killed the wait on a night like this by talking. There were men who liked to talk about sport, men who liked to talk about women, even one time he'd been partnered with a guy who liked to talk about eastern religions, which he'd thought weird at first but had got used to after a time when he was reassured that Islam wouldn't be one of the religions under discussion. He let others choose, he was an easy going guy that way, and if a partner chose silence, why then silence it was. If they'd been under observation, an observer might have decided they were two of a kind, sitting that way in silence as the hour passed. If the observer had been one of his previous partners, though, he'd have been struck by the contrast with the volubility he'd once shown. The truth was he could hide himself as easily in one as the other, words or silence.

Even when the van finally appeared, only an exchange of grunts acknowledged its coming into sight and the confirmation offered by its turning into the opening opposite. They watched its tail lights until they vanished. After a time, running on side lights, the van came back, turned on to the road again and was gone.

As if at a signal, the two men got out and crossing the road made their way along the track. The driver had a sense of the canal water at his right side. He imagined the track curving and walking straight on till the water took him. Nonsense, he told himself. He'd seen the canal run straight ahead as far as the eye could follow. His companion took out a torch and shone the pencil-thin guarded beam ahead of them. Once was enough. They'd both seen the shape of the body at the side of the track. No effort had been made to conceal it; it was meant to be found in the morning, most likely by some jogger not long after first light.

Another dozen steps took them to the body, and the driver crouched down beside it. He felt where the face should have been, then wiped his hands on a handkerchief, put it back in his jacket and zipped the side pocket carefully shut. He opened the coat the corpse was wearing and fumbled for the trouser belt, unfastening it and pulling it loose. That done, he opened the flies and tugged until the trousers slid down the corpse's thighs. With the tips of his fingers, he stroked the left thigh. He heard the click of the button on the torch and the briefest illumination showed him the shiny patch where the skin had been burnt.

He was careful to pull down and smooth the shirt, tucking it away as he pulled up the trousers. That done, he refastened the belt, slid a finger between it and the belly of the dead man and slackened it off by one hole. Working by touch, he did up the coat again.

As they started back, the driver contrived to have his partner between himself and the water. Task accomplished, it was pleasant walking back to the car; and if there were dark shapes against the stars it was only desert bats going about their business in the warm night air.

BOOK THREE

THE VIEW FROM ABOVE

CHAPTER
TWELVE

It was good to be out on the road with something to look at other than in-trays and cardboard files. A young woman hesitating on the pavement with a child at her knee caught his attention and then was gone, leaving him with unwanted thoughts of Betty and his grandson. He tried to make the effort to force them from his mind. Later, he thought, there would be more than time enough later to think about the mystery man Betty had married and what had happened to him. At the moment, he had not the slightest idea as to what he could do that might help. His call to Phoenix had been met with suspicion as to his motives, every question he'd asked being met with another in return. The only solid information he'd obtained was that no officer called Sandra Foley was presently employed in the Phoenix Police Department. Dead end.

He stared out unseeing at straggling hedges and fields at the foot of the low hills patched with standing water due to the recent heavy rain. The city left behind, McGuigan began to pick up speed.

"It feels like a wild goose chase." It was the first thing the DS had said since they set out. He was used to Meldrum's silences, and though the sharp edge of their mutual dislike seemed to have settled through habit and proximity into something milder, he found it increasingly easy to pass the time with his own thoughts. It struck him that he'd spend more time with Meldrum on a typical day than with anyone else. Had the same kind of idea ever occurred to Meldrum? he wondered. He doubted it, but then who could tell what Meldrum was thinking?

"The local man went to see him."

"Go up on his bike did he?" McGuigan enquired. He wasn't a great admirer of uniformed policemen, and even less of constables stationed in small towns.

"Name's Harrison. Come to think of it ..." Meldrum nodded as he came to a decision. "Let's see him first."

"Isn't the guy expecting us?"

Instead of answering, Meldrum checked the case notes and put in a call on the mobile. Constable Harrison promised to be waiting for them. After that, McGuigan listened to a second call as Meldrum shifted their original appointment back an hour.

"He happy enough?"

"No problem."

"Maybe," McGuigan speculated hopefully, "he has something to hide after all."

He didn't get a reply, but then he wasn't expecting one.

DC Harrison was younger than Meldrum had expected, but voices on the phone often gave a deceptive impression. He led them through into a cramped back office with a sink in one corner and a kettle on the work surface. When the three of them were seated, the room was full.

"Remind me how you got the letter in the first place?" Meldrum began.

"It was lying behind the door when I opened the place up on Tuesday morning." The station, a converted cottage, was manned only on a part-time basis. "I thought it was funny. I mean it hadn't been put through the letterbox, just shoved under the door. Then I read it and," he shook his head, "well, you'll have seen it. I knew right away it would have to be checked out. To be honest, I thought they'd send somebody — but I was told to go up and have a word myself."

In his middle twenties, Harrison was tall and slim with a narrow face and sharp blue eyes that flitted from Meldrum to his sergeant as if checking for some clue as to their assessment of his performance.

"No point," McGuigan said, "in involving us if you'd gone up and found the wife sitting at home."

"I can see that."

"Good for you."

The constable was young enough to have a telltale flush of red on his neck, but whether with nerves or in irritation at McGuigan's tone was impossible to tell.

"Anyway," he said, "she wasn't there but . . ." He trailed off, seemed to think better of whatever he had been about to say, and finished by reasserting, "She wasn't there."

CHAPTER
THIRTEEN

"He didn't like Croft," McGuigan said, as they made their way back up again towards the road that would take them to the village. "Didn't say so in so many words, but you could feel it."

"For what that's worth."

"You could see he was dying to say that he'd an instinct. I'm not a believer in instinct."

"We'll see."

And they fell silent again until at the far end of the village they turned down a side road and came to Croft's house, a substantial Twenties villa set back among green lawns. A sailing dinghy ready for towing sat at the side of the garage.

Pulling in through the gate which had been left open, McGuigan said, "Doesn't look as if money's a problem."

That perception was reinforced by the man who opened the door, a solidly built man about five-foot ten wearing a beautifully cut dark blue suit complete with collar and tie as if he was ready to set out on business the moment they were gone; and confirmed when they were shown into a big front room with pictures on every wall and tables crowded with pieces of pottery and china that struck them as expensive, not as antiquarians but policemen with an eye for what looked worth stealing.

"I've already had one of your lot in to see me," Croft said. He spoke softly in an educated accent with the falling rhythms of someone originally from the west of Scotland. "I wasn't surprised when you rang me." He waved them to a seat, but once they had sat down, got to his feet again and stood in front of the fireplace so that Meldrum was able to see both his face and the back of his head at the same time. "He said somebody had put a letter into the police station, but wouldn't show me it."

"He gave you an idea, though," Meldrum said, "what it contained?" For courtesy's sake, he gave the statement the inflection of a question. "There's no reason why you shouldn't see it."

He took out the letter in the clear plastic slipcase and handed it to him. Watching Croft's face for a response, Meldrum could recall every word of the typewritten note.

I'm not one to interfere with other people. Live and let live has been my rule. I hope you'll understand that I don't break it lightly. The man's name is Barry Croft. I'm concerned because his wife Rachel has disappeared. I hope I'm wrong but I'm very much afraid something has happened to her. You should pay him a visit. It's not a usual name — you'll find him in the phone book.

Believe me, no one will be happier than I, if you find her safe and well, but it needs checking.

Croft turned the paper over, found no writing on the back and began to scan the letter again.

Finished, he looked up and said, "That explains why your constable was so unsure of himself. He didn't even have an address."

"He did establish, though, that your wife wasn't here?" Taking it slowly, Meldrum's tone was carefully unaggressive.

"Walked out a week ago."

"And you don't know where she is?"

"If I had, I'd have told him. I suggested a couple of possibilities — her mother, her sister — oh, and a friend she made before we were married."

"A male friend?" Meldrum asked.

"Haven't you checked them? I thought that's why you were here, that you'd checked and she wasn't with any of them." Taking a cue from the brief silence, his eyes narrowed. "You haven't checked, have you? So she might be with any one of them." He shook his head. "It's not urgent, is it? An anonymous letter. I'm not surprised you have better things to do."

Meldrum studied him for a moment in silence, before saying mildly, "We've got round to it now."

McGuigan, infected as always with impatience, asked abruptly, "Have you phoned your wife's mother and the others?"

"No."

"Can I ask why not?"

"I didn't see any need to."

"Not even after Constable Harrison came to see you?"

"Harrison. I'd forgotten the name, not that I paid much attention to it in the first place. Perhaps if I'd given him more time, he'd have let the thing drop." He smiled. "I suspect he took against me because of all this." He waved a hand around the room. "Not much use explaining to that kind of man that I'd earned all of it. To be honest, I found his visit irritating. And no, I didn't rush to the phone after I'd got rid of him. Why on earth should I?"

"To find out what had happened to your wife?" Meldrum wondered.

"It never occurred to me that anything had 'happened', as you put it, to my wife before the constable's visit. Why would I change my mind because of an anonymous letter?"

"She didn't say where she was going?"

"No."

"Just walked out," McGuigan said.

"Exactly."

"Was there a quarrel?"

"I seem to remember the constable asking me that. I told him there wasn't."

That special alertness, which he'd felt so often before, tingled through Meldrum. A denial gave something to chew on. Disprove it and everything might fall into place.

Before he could frame a question, Croft went on, "That wasn't true. But I didn't feel it was any of his business. He didn't make a very good impression on me."

He nodded at Meldrum, as if confident that he would take the point.

"Let me understand you," Meldrum said. "Your wife walked out after a quarrel. Can I ask what the quarrel was about?"

"I don't think that's any of your business." Croft stood up. "In fact, I'm going to ask you to leave now. I've been pretty patient. This is the second time I've answered questions, and to be honest I can see no reason for it. My wife isn't here. She has been gone for a week, not a long time. I have no idea where she is, but she'll explain herself no doubt when she comes home. Does that cover it?"

He had made his points quietly as if concluding a business meeting. Now as Meldrum stood and McGuigan followed his example, Croft summed up, "I think that covers it."

"I'm sure you're right, sir," Meldrum said. He didn't move, however, as Croft turned to leave the room, clearly expecting them to follow. "If you would let us have those addresses, we'll be on our way."

"What addresses?"

"Your mother-in-law, I think you said. Your wife's sister. You mentioned a close friend, too. People she might have gone to after you quarrelled."

"You want their addresses?"

"I gather you don't want to phone them yourself."

Croft looked from one man to the other. "I didn't want to," he said.

74

"Why would that be?" McGuigan asked.

"I didn't want to," Croft repeated, ignoring the sergeant. "But that doesn't mean I fancy them getting a call from the police. God knows what they'd make of that. I don't think it's your job to start a lot of stupid rumours."

"Why would it start rumours?" Meldrum asked.

"Isn't that obvious?"

And then it seemed as if Meldrum suddenly caught his point, for he nodded, perhaps a shade too emphatically so that there was an element of caricature in this understanding.

"Oh, I see," he said. "You don't think your wife will be there. None of them will have any idea where she is."

"I didn't say that. Whether she's there or not, getting a call from the police would start talk. You know what people are like."

"Has your wife done this before?" McGuigan asked.

"Done what?"

"Gone off by herself after a quarrel."

"She doesn't make a habit of it."

"Would her mother, say, be surprised to see her? I mean, if she turned up wanting to stay for a week or whatever. She's already been gone a week, isn't that right?"

"I'll deal with it myself," Croft said. "I'll phone round tonight."

"Not just now?"

"I have business to attend to. I'll phone tonight."

"That would be a good idea," Meldrum said.

By this time, Croft had the door open.

Pausing on the step, Meldrum said, "And you'll let us know, of course." He took a card out and handed it over. "If you phone tomorrow morning, you might catch me. If not, leave a message and I'll phone you back."

CHAPTER
FOURTEEN

Meldrum sometimes wondered if it would have been better if he had never known about Corrigan's perversion. Finding it beside Corrigan's name in a prostitute's notebook, kept by her to jog her memory on her clients' tastes, had left him only vaguely the wiser as to its exact nature and as the years passed even that insight had grown hazy. At the time, he had established that Corrigan could be eliminated from their inquiries and had as a matter of self-respect resisted the temptation to tell his ex-wife. Since there was no risk of the prostitute betraying it, she being the murder victim in question, Corrigan's secret had remained safe. In the years between, the spirit being weak, Meldrum had speculated what Carole might have done if she'd been told about the contents of the prostitute's notebook, even on occasion daydreaming that it might have led to her breaking with Corrigan and coming back to him. The legacy of his secret knowledge had been an added edge of distaste at Carole's submissiveness to her husband. To put it another way, he had been left to contemplate the old problem why a nice woman would make a doormat of herself for a shit.

Because the spectacle was painful for him, he had kept out of the way of the presumably happy couple. After, however, Betty's marriage had broken up and she and little Tommy had been taken in by the Corrigans, he had found himself with no option but to put up with Corrigan as the price of seeing his grandson. The passage of time hadn't made it any easier. Indeed, he had a sense that Corrigan's antipathy to him had if anything grown stronger. Not able to resist, just after he'd found the notebook Meldrum had given himself the satisfaction of telling Corrigan about knowing his secret and that for Carole's sake he would keep it. No surprise then if he was hated. Corrigan might be perverse, but he had a natural human distaste for being done a favour.

All the same, on the evening of the day he and McGuigan had interviewed Barry Croft, instead of heading for home Meldrum went to the big house in the prosperous suburb of Barnton where the educational administrator with the public school accent and the inherited private income enjoyed marital bliss with his devoted wife.

"What are you doing here?" Carole asked when she opened the door.

"You don't think we've anything to talk about?"

Without waiting for an invitation, he moved steadily into the hall. The sound of music came from behind a closed door on the left, and catching Carole's uneasy glance in that direction Meldrum assumed the husband must be in there. Taking the initiative, he went into the room on the right, and found himself in a small sitting room with a television playing quietly in the corner. It seemed as if Carole must have been watching it for her glasses lay on the arm of the chair opposite the set.

"Where's Betty?" he asked.

"You can't see her just now."

"For God's sake, why not? I've got to see her." Despite his best intentions, he felt an upsurge of anger that was dangerously close to self-pity. "I wasn't even told she was going to get married —"

"She didn't tell me either! Not until it was done. And then I told you." Even in defending herself, she spoke softly as if afraid of being overheard.

"In a phone call," he said bitterly.

"As soon as I heard!"

Before he could answer, he saw a change in Carole's expression as she looked past him. Turning, he saw Betty in the doorway.

"I'm sorry," she said. "It's my fault."

But he remembered her as a child. That sometimes happened: if he hadn't seen her for a while, if she turned her head a certain way, if she used a phrase out of the past. In such moments, the years between were obliterated and all he wanted to do was cherish and protect her.

"I just wanted to talk to you," he said.

CHAPTER
FIFTEEN

"I hate it when you fight," she said. "I've always hated it."

Instead of answering, he got up and went to the bar where he bought a gin and tonic and a whisky and asked for the music to be turned down. The place was almost empty and he suggested there was no one who would suffer if they halved the volume.

Setting the drinks down on the table they'd taken in the corner, he said as he sat down again, "That's not fair. There was a time when your mother and I argued. But we never fought." He almost said they'd been too fond of one another, but stopped himself in time, not wanting to make her angry in her turn.

"Wee Tommy's all right?" he asked.

She nodded.

"He'd be glad to see you."

She stared into her glass and then said, without looking up, "I know I'm a bad mother."

Shocked, he protested, "No, you're not."

The shock was genuine, though that was more or less what he'd thought when she'd taken herself off to America.

"I was so unhappy," she said, "and Mum was there to look after Tommy. And — I *had* to get away. I was so unhappy I felt I was going to be ill again. I didn't want to be ill again."

He thought of the huddles of patients smoking in the corridors of the Royal Edinburgh Hospital, the young staff in jeans and ragged jumpers, the woman psychiatrist blandly reassuring who had nothing to recommend apart from drugs, and his heart moved for her.

"You won't be," he said. "It's all in the past. You're basically a strong person. It was because you were heartbroken after wee Sandy's accident."

"Heartbroken," she said, as if properly hearing the phrase for the first time and applying it to herself, and then, after a moment, "I was coming home for Tommy. I was going to take him back with me to Phoenix. Bobbie said that's what he wanted, the three of us together. And I believed him. I told him why Sandy left me. I told him Tommy was illegitimate. But he didn't care. I loved him for that." She stared at Meldrum with dazed eyes, and he realised how disoriented she was. "And then he disappeared."

"You've no idea why?"

"Don thinks it was what he'd always intended to do. He thinks I was lucky that he didn't turn out to be some mad killer."

"If Corrigan doesn't have anything more helpful than that to say, he should keep his mouth shut."

He expected her to protest, but she pulled a face and said, "Do you know what he said to me? I told him that Bobbie was Scots, but had an American passport as well because he'd been born there. And he asked me, Did he scrunch up the toilet paper when he wiped his bottom or fold it? British people fold it, he said, but Americans scrunch it up."

Meldrum, who rarely swore and never in front of his daughter, said savagely, "I think he must be fucking mad."

"He was joking. That's what he said to Carole."

"She was there?"

"I didn't know what to say to him. I told him Bobbie and I were only together a few weeks."

I never saw your mother use the lavatory, Meldrum thought. She never saw me. Wouldn't happen. Not ever. Not if we'd been married a hundred fucking years.

"I'll get you something else to drink," he said. "Do you want the same again?"

Going to the bar gave him time to collect himself. Getting angry and miserable was no help to anyone. Remember, he chided himself, you're a policeman.

Seated again, he waited until she had sipped her drink before making a start. "Can we get back to Bobbie?" It seemed strange to be using the name of a man he'd never met, who was his daughter's husband. "Or is it Wilbur?"

"Wilbur's the name the police used. And for the flat he rented that was the name he gave. I feel . . . stupid."

"Don't." He tried a smile. "If I was called Wilbur, I might prefer to tell a girl my name was Bobbie."

"His voice was Scots," she said. "When he spoke to me, it was like a voice from home."

"This was at the wedding in Texas?"

"Hmm. I was feeling out of things. I hardly knew the girl who'd invited me. I shared a house with her in Washington. Apart from her, I didn't know anybody and she was busy being the bride." He slid a notebook across the table to her together with a biro pen.

"Let me have her name and address."

"Lori Allingham," she said as she wrote. "But she won't be in the Bethesda house any more. Oh, and she's married!" She looked up, knitting her brows into a frown. "I can't remember his name — her husband, I mean. Matt, Matt . . . What was his second name? Matt Something."

"Leave it for the moment. It'll come back to you. Who invited Bobbie to the wedding?"

"Oh, he'd been invited by the groom. I think they might have worked together." She put her hand to her mouth. "Oh, I see. Maybe that way — if we could find where Bobbie worked . . ."

"It would be a start."

"I knew you would know what to do."

"It's routine," he said. "The police in Phoenix must have asked you the same things."

"The woman did, but I was too upset to take it in. But the two policemen later, I'm sure they didn't ask me about the wedding or anything."

"They'd have details of what you said earlier," he said, covering his own uneasiness. "Do you remember their names?"

"The policemen? One was called Finn. The other had a name I'd never heard before, maybe it was Polish, something like that. Does it matter?"

"Probably not. What about the policewoman you spoke to when you reported Bobbie missing? Do you remember her name?"

She shook her head. "I was so upset."

"It's all right. Tell you what. Would you write me a description of Bobbie?"

He sat watching as she scribbled and thought and added another few words.

"Six two?" he asked reading it over.

"I think so. He was almost as tall as you. I wish I could draw — or paint, paint would be better. His eyes were — are — are an amazing shade of blue. I've never seen such blue eyes. That was the first thing I noticed about him. No, the second. The first was his accent. Like I said, a voice from home. And then his eyes, his beautiful eyes." She stopped and he looked at her own eyes, half expecting tears.

"Is there anything else you can remember?"

"Distinguishing marks," she said.

"What?"

"That's what the two detectives called them. Any distinguishing marks? one of them asked me. And I told them he'd an old burn at the top of his left thigh. When I stroked the skin it felt hard and shiny. Can something feel shiny? It happened when he was a baby. He pulled a teapot over on himself. His great-grandmother saved his life. She ran cold water on it. Kill or cure, he said. The old bitch, he said. But then, after calling her that, he laughed and said, Just kidding."

"It's all right," he said. "Sit for a minute. I'll get us something. I feel like a coffee. I'll get us both one."

84

Pub coffee. One sip was enough, sour and too strong. Better than another gin, though. No more gin. He couldn't handle it if she broke down.

"I've been trying to think," she said. "The man who came to the flat; how would he know where to come? You see, I thought Bobbie owned the flat and had been there for a while. But if he'd only just rented it . . . How did the man know he was there?"

"Slow down! Somebody came to the flat in Phoenix looking for Bobbie? You didn't tell me that. Did he talk to him?"

"Bobbie was out. He came back not long after the man left. And because I was upset about the job, I forgot to tell him."

"Job? Bobbie had got a job?"

"No! I'd got a job in a bookstore without telling him and he got mad about that. We've plenty of money, he told me."

"This man, did he say why he was looking for Bobbie?"

"I didn't ask. I was on my honeymoon!"

At the word, he read in her face, which he knew so well, hope and hope disappointed and the fear of what might be to come. He pushed the notebook back over the table to her.

Slowly she said, "There was something about him. I just wanted rid of him. He wasn't a nice man."

"Try to describe him for me. And I want you to let me have whatever you can find in the way of addresses and telephone numbers. Anything to do with Lori Allingham, where she worked if you can find an

85

address, and anything you can find on the wedding, the invitation if you kept it — her parents, the place you stayed, anything."

Without lifting her head from the notebook, though she wasn't writing, she said, "I'm going back, you know. I can't stay here not knowing what's happened."

"I could find out from here. I could find out what's happening."

She shook her head. "I should be there."

"I don't think it's a good idea."

"All the same."

"What about Tommy?"

"I'll leave him here. Again. That's what everyone will say — *again*. I'm a bad mother."

"I don't believe that."

He tried to find or manufacture an argument that would prevent her from going back, but before he could say anything else, she leant forward and said earnestly, "He'll never trust anybody. Because I went away, and came back and then went away again. When he grows up, he'll be one of those people who always keep a little of themselves back. It's hard for people like that to be happy."

She was talking about her son, and he could find nothing to say.

CHAPTER
SIXTEEN

It took three days before Meldrum realised Barry Croft hadn't rung or left a message about his inquiries as to where his wife might have gone. There were excuses: it wasn't a major case, maybe not a case at all, just a nudge from an anonymous letter writer moved by who could tell what kind of grudge or idle mischief; the in file was full, it was always full, crime never stopped; and at the back of his mind all the time like the throbbing of a wound there was the worry about Betty.

All the same, when he did remember he was irritated with himself for failing to follow up. It wasn't something he often did, which made him feel worse not better.

"Croft," he said to McGuigan, expecting him to go through the same process and even prepared to find some enjoyment in watching him do it. For his taste, the DS took too overt a pride in his memory.

"What about him?"

"He was supposed to get in touch."

"I thought he had."

"What made you think that?" Meldrum asked sharply.

"When you didn't say anything, I assumed he'd phoned round and found his wife. As far as I was concerned that was it. We've plenty of other stuff to do, and you don't tell me everything."

McGuigan looked at him with the smugness of a man who felt himself to be fireproof. For a moment, Meldrum entertained the thought that he had known there was no call and decided not to remind him, but pushed the idea aside. McGuigan had the knack of making him feel slightly paranoid.

He contented himself with saying, "You thought wrong then."

"Maybe he's found her, and just not bothered to tell you."

"Stupid if he has."

"Not much we could do about it."

Meldrum thought about it. He'd a meeting in ten minutes, but he should be free in an hour.

"See if you can get a number for him. If you get hold of him, ask what's he's done about contacting people about his wife. Unless he's found her safe and well, tell him we're coming to see him and make a time."

"He'll be at work probably."

"So?"

"I don't know what he does."

"If you're stuck phone Harrison. Maybe he knows."

Unsaid, maybe *Harrison*, the uniformed constable who'd cycled up to talk to Croft, had done a competent interview. Not for the first time in the last few months, Meldrum asked himself if he was losing his grip. It was true that when he'd spoken to Croft, McGuigan had also been there. But then maybe the DS wouldn't be sorry to see his superior officer twisting in the wind. Just because you were paranoid, didn't mean they weren't out to get you.

When he got back after the meeting, though, McGuigan had spoken to Croft.

"How did you get him?"

"He was still at home. Just leaving when I phoned. Told him what I wanted. Then he came out with this stuff about not understanding what the fuss was about." As he remembered, McGuigan shook his head in a kind of sour disbelief. "He's a cool customer."

CHAPTER
SEVENTEEN

As they rode up on the escalator, Meldrum watched the gallery of shops come into view. Below was a central court from which a tree reached up, passing them on its way towards the glass roof. Bloody atrium, Meldrum thought. He preferred his trees in parks.

"Which floor?"

"Second."

They stepped on to the second escalator. Looking up now, Meldrum had a glimpse of the restaurants on the third floor.

Seeing the direction of his gaze, McGuigan said, "I took a girlfriend to one of those for her birthday. Cost over a hundred quid."

"I hope it was worth it," Meldrum said in the tone of a man who doubted it. He could still recall his indignation when a fish supper had broken the four-pound ceiling.

The shop they were looking for was halfway round the second floor gallery. CROFT ANTIQUES. That explains the stuff he had lying around at home, Meldrum thought. A single chair sat in the window. Beyond it, there was a view of subdued lighting and deep blue carpets separating raised areas of chests, couches, clocks, and three paintings on easels. As they went in, a woman approached them. Like the goods for sale, she looked well presented and expensive.

"Mr Croft?" she repeated. "I'm afraid Mr Croft isn't here."

"We had an appointment," Meldrum said. "For eleven."

She looked at her watch. "It's only five to."

"You're expecting him?"

She contemplated that as a possibility, then offered, "Could I help perhaps?"

"He'd want to talk to us himself." Giving up on discretion, Meldrum finally held up his identification, giving her time to take in his rank. "Wouldn't you think?"

Outside the shop, McGuigan said, "I wouldn't have minded a coffee."

"We've better things to do than sit waiting on him."

"Anybody could tell that. You'd your hanging face on."

"If he's not here in three minutes, we're off."

He leant on the rail and looked down into the court below. Most of the activity was around the periphery. Only one figure, a man moving quickly, was crossing the central area. Hard to tell what caught Meldrum's attention. Perhaps nothing more than the long black cloth coat, which even from above had an expensive look.

"Is that Croft?" McGuigan wondered.

Seen like this from above, something about the set of the man's shoulders, the way he moved, made up

Meldrum's mind. This was the man whom he'd seen come out of the close opposite his flat a few nights ago and, in response to some gibe from a group of youths outside the pub, lift one of them off his feet and smash him down on the pavement like a broken toy.

"It is Croft," McGuigan said. "See him taking a quick look up?"

The figure of the man below disappeared into the glass lift in the far corner. They watched it slide upwards and come to the second floor where the door opened. As Croft began to walk round the gallery towards them, Meldrum's face gave no clue to his mental turmoil. He knew at once there would be no point in denouncing the man. Denounce him for what? Because he'd witnessed him committing an assault; an assault he'd felt too indifferent about to report at the time? *"You were where?" "In my flat." "But he looked up, right? You saw his face?" "No, but I recognise his coat."* The fragment of dialogue sizzled in his brain. Try that on ACC Fairbairn and he'd be back directing traffic.

Croft made an apology for having been called away. It was perfunctory, but moments later they were seated in his office and it was still only a few minutes past the hour.

There was a desk with a pen set as its only furniture and a second one, its rolltop pulled down, set against the wall with an old map of Scotland framed above it. The room was big enough to hold a wide low coffee table with five narrow leather chairs grouped round it where he'd indicated he'd prefer to sit with them.

"Have you found my wife?" he asked.

"What makes you think we might have?"

"After the sergeant here made an appointment, it occurred to me that might be why. Was she upset?" When the silence went on, he asked, "You did find her?"

"We have no idea where she is."

"Then why come and see me? I'm in the middle of the working day. I don't really have time to spare."

"It was my understanding," Meldrum said, "that you were going to get back in touch with me."

"Did I say that? Damn, I did, didn't I? Apologies again. I had the chance to do a very good piece of business yesterday and it put everything else out of my head."

"Including your wife's disappearance?"

Croft shrugged. "I don't think of it like that. We had a disagreement and she took herself off. When she's ready she'll come back."

"Can I ask again what you quarrelled about?"

"You can," Croft said, with a mild stress which reminded Meldrum of an old biddy of a primary school teacher pointing out to him the difference between "can" and "may", "but I won't tell you. It was private."

"So you didn't phone your mother-in-law?"

"About Rachel? Didn't phone anyone. So there really didn't seem much point in contacting you. Nothing to tell, you see."

CHAPTER
EIGHTEEN

"You mean now?" McGuigan didn't bother to conceal his surprise. "Go and see her? Is it worth the time? We could phone her."

Croft had provided them with details of his wife's mother, her sister and her closest friend. He hadn't demurred when asked and indeed had left the impression that as far as he was concerned they were welcome to an irritating chore.

Getting no response, McGuigan mused aloud, "Maybe he likes the thought of us finding her. Hopes seeing us'll bring her to her senses. Or maybe that it'll show her how much he misses her without him having to admit it by chasing after her." He gave a sideways glance. "I hate to be used that way. The man's a bloody user."

Listening, Meldrum had an indication of how much his thinking had been affected by recognising Croft as the man he'd seen attacking the youth outside the pub. Thinking about it, he caught again the feeling he'd had of the unnerving nature of the assault, of how contemptuous and extreme it had seemed to him as an onlooker. The difference between any of his colleagues who might become involved including

McGuigan and himself was that from now on he was in possession of this piece of private knowledge that Croft was a man capable of a special level of violence, a man who could lose his temper in a moment. A man capable of murder.

"We'll try the mother first," he'd told McGuigan. "She's nearest."

Mrs Maggie Lenzie, mother of Rachel Croft, lived in Trinity on the far side of Ferry Road. He recognised the style of house since he'd been in similar ones before on business of one kind or another. Three floors with a suite of rooms at the top, used in earlier times by live-in servants, a big sitting room on the first floor flooded in summer with sun from bay windows; terraced houses leaving no space for afterthoughts such as garages, cars not having been invented when they were built; substantial houses with tiny sunless gardens at the back like guilty secrets.

Mrs Lenzie herself opened the door, and kept them at it for some time before she let herself be persuaded they should be allowed inside. She took them into a small sitting room on the ground floor and said for the second or third time, "But why didn't Barry phone me?" Adding, when Meldrum found yet another noncommittal reply, "I can only assume he's not really worried." She frowned, "In which case, why on earth has he gone to the police?"

"He didn't," Meldrum said, searching for a way into her privacy, tired of circling around, ignoring McGuigan's glance. "We went to him."

"Are you not telling me something?" Now she looked alarmed. "Are you breaking something to me gently? Has there been an accident?"

"Someone sent an anonymous letter. It claimed that no one had seen your daughter for more than a week."

"An anonymous letter? People can be so vile. I'd have thought you would get plenty of letters like that. Surely you don't waste too much time on them. There must be plenty of criminals for you to catch."

"We try not to spend more time on them than is needed," Meldrum said.

"Thing is," McGuigan added, as if taking a cue, "it seems Mr Croft's wife has left home. He suggested she might have come here."

"Well, she hasn't. She's not the kind of person to come running home to Mummy. It's ridiculous, a foolish idea. I can't imagine what Barry is thinking. They've been married for twelve years!"

She looked from one to the other as if to check that they saw the absurdity of it.

"It's not something she's ever done?" Meldrum asked sympathetically. "Even years ago?"

"Why would she? For God's sake, she wasn't a child bride. She was almost thirty when they married. And she and Barry get on well. They've always got on well."

"And you and your son-in-law — do you get on with one another?"

"Of course, we do. Why on earth ask such a question? Because he hasn't phoned? I don't understand that either. Perhaps he didn't want me to

96

know. Why wouldn't he want me to know? Has Rachel gone off with someone?"

"Mr Croft hasn't suggested anything like that."

"What has he suggested?"

"That she went off after a quarrel."

"He told you they'd had a quarrel? What did they quarrel about?"

Meldrum let a moment pass before answering. He was looking for some sign that she might know the answer to her own question, some crack in the incredulity she'd attached to the idea of a quarrel. The oddness of the situation had brought a faint flush to her cheeks. That apart, plumply prosperous, she rested in the carapace of her background.

"He refused to tell us," Meldrum said at last. "His position is that if they had a quarrel, it was private and none of our business."

"Oh, yes, that sounds like Barry." Inconsequentially, she added, "Barry was very kind to me after my husband died."

"I'm sure it would settle your mind," Meldrum said, "if you knew where your daughter was. If you do hear from her, I'd be grateful if you would let us know. I'll give you my card with a number where you can leave a message."

"My mind isn't unsettled," Mrs Lenzie said. "Apart from the idea that those two might have had a disagreement, of course. I'm going to ask Barry about that." She stood up and looked at the clock on the table by the window. "If you haven't anything else, I'm

playing golf this afternoon. I will phone Barry later —
probably tonight. I'm sure there isn't any hurry."

Meldrum delayed his reply, letting her shepherd
them back to the front door. On the step ready to go,
he said, "I hope you're right."

"Would it help if I told you Rachel has money of her
own?" Up close, the skin of her neck was firm and her
eyes were clear. She looked as if she spent a lot of time
out of doors. "If she's gone off to be on her own for a
bit, that must be what she needs and, believe me,
money wouldn't be a problem. She wouldn't need to
turn to me or anybody."

CHAPTER
NINETEEN

McGuigan expressed his reservations about going to see the missing Rachel Croft's sister obliquely.

"Her mother didn't seem too bothered," he said.

"Too busy trying to get to her golf."

"Doesn't make her a bad person," McGuigan suggested.

There had been a time when Meldrum insisted on doing all the driving. Lately — if it was a sign of mellowing, it was the only one McGuigan could detect — he took the passenger seat on occasion. Like today, on the way to see the sister, he'd yielded the driving to McGuigan, who took pleasure in the process and the mild alertness it required. He kept silent as he took the journey out into the country on the south side of the city until he came to the Haddington roundabout and ran down into the market town. The hall they were looking for was on the right. The banner strung across the front promised ART EXHIBITION.

Inside there was a cavernous space with a table at the entrance where two women were taking entrance money. After Meldrum affirmed they weren't there for the art, one of the women indicated that they would find Miss Lenzie at the far end of the hall. As they went up the middle, Meldrum couldn't resist glancing into the spaces created for the occasion along each wall by partitions on which paintings were hung. He glimpsed dogs, flowers, bridges. Nothing that would stop him in his tracks, but then he wasn't there to look at paintings. Perhaps half a dozen people were viewing what was on offer.

At the far end a small group was engaged in arranging pottery and some clay sculptures along the edge of a stage. Two men, one plump, one lean, both with the abstracted air of the recently retired, were doing the work. A tall woman with an impressive bosom and an abundance of red hair that didn't match her complexion seemed to be orchestrating their efforts.

"Now what we have to do is tell the misery elephant to bugger off," she was saying. "It's not the first year we've had a slow start."

"Miss Lenzie?" Melrdum asked. "Miss Sylvia Lenzie?"

She looked at him as if about to celebrate a convert to the visual arts, but the look lasted only a moment before a more realistic streak took over. "Of course, you're here to ask about Rachel. There's a little room in the back, which is quite private. We can talk there."

The room struck Meldrum as being just about fit for a janitor's mop store, but it had a selection of wooden-backed kitchen chairs against one wall and a small window which admitted a watery grudging light.

"Your sister has disappeared from her home. We're anxious to trace her," Meldrum said.

100

"Why come to me?"

"Apart from her mother, you seem to be her only family," McGuigan said. Meldrum, who had come to know him, was able to catch the concealed undercurrent of disapproval at her attitude. The detective sergeant was a believer in family ties.

"Her husband gave us your name," Meldrum explained.

"Let me tell you something about families," Miss Sylvia Lenzie said staring down at McGuigan, whom she topped by a couple of inches despite being in flat heels. It occurred to Meldrum that she might have a very good ear for undercurrents. "In my experience, it's not uncommon for sisters to get on badly. Often it's the parents' fault, of course, most things are. Sometimes they are just *born* to rub one another up the wrong way. Or one of them can't stand the other. I knew two sisters who shared a house — one didn't speak to the other for twenty years — didn't even say good morning at breakfast. And she didn't go to the funeral. Yet she did beautiful little watercolours. Woodland scenes, bushes in the foreground, autumn trees, just a hint of a path if you looked closely enough. What do you feel about that — Sergeant, is it? Have you any feelings about that?"

"Are you telling us that your sister and you didn't get on?" Meldrum intervened, settling for the methodical plod approach.

"Haven't spoken to her since she was married."

"That would be twelve years ago," McGuigan said.

"I suppose it is. I haven't been counting. They've no children, of course."

That last remark struck Meldrum as inconsequential. If Rachel Croft was twenty-nine when she married twelve years ago, that would make her forty-one. He wondered if this sister was older or younger. There couldn't be much in it either way, two or three years perhaps, not that he was much of a judge. With breasts like those, though, she seemed made for having children. Out of self-respect, he kept his eyes determinedly turned from their magnificence.

"So your sister hasn't been in touch with you?"

"I'd be surprised if she had."

"And you have no idea as to where she might have gone?"

"I haven't been in her confidence for many years. I'm not sure I ever was."

CHAPTER
TWENTY

James Finn turned a pen in his fingers as he listened to the voice on the phone. "I'm negative on that," he said. "It's my opinion we've moved as fast as we could. It took the police longer than we thought to make the identification. Wally was getting impatient, but I decided against pushing it — no anonymous tip-offs or any of that crap. It was better if they came to us. And finally somebody got half smart, and they did." He listened again. "Not yet. It's the middle of the night there." Another pause and he answered, "I made a judgement call. Let the police treat it as an ordinary homicide. Whatever they do should frighten her. And I'm the guy in the white hat. That could be useful if —" He stopped abruptly. "I know it shouldn't have happened. I'm in the middle of a shit storm here, trying to cope."

After a short exchange, he finally managed to hang up and sat back with a sigh.

The man who'd been listening said, "Don't tell me — he's not happy."

"He's not happy," Finn said sardonically. "He can't see why we need the corpse and that makes him so fucking unhappy."

Wally Perzynski shrugged his shoulders and heaved one ankle up on to a massive thigh. The double convulsion of flesh made the chair creak under its load. For such a big man, his voice was a surprise, very light and precise. "The corpse," he said, "is aesthetic. It gives the cops something to keep them busy — so busy maybe the bad guys will believe it. And it gives us a shot at keeping the wife back home. Maybe Conway doesn't give a fuck about her, but if he does he'd be safer in Scotland till we can pick him up. She's our contact. How else are we going to find him? Is that complicated?"

"Not for a genius like you."

"You're not wrong there, my friend."

Finn, however, had relapsed into gloom. "We've got to make this work. If we're wrong about where he's going —"

"We know he got on a plane."

"But we can't be sure he made the change in New York. The right one, I mean."

"We've got the note he left for his wife. It's worth a gamble."

"High stakes for us," Finn said. "The boss kept saying, Find Wilbur C."

"Or else what?"

"He didn't bother to say or else. Probably thought it was obvious."

The chair protested again as Wally Perzynski gestured. "There's always the pension. Keep calm. We've got time."

"Time?" Finn said bitterly. "Five weeks — you call that time?"

"That's a nice philosophical question."

"And fuck you too," said Finn, who was under a very special and personal strain.

CHAPTER
TWENTY-ONE

Later Meldrum learnt that Betty had made half a dozen efforts to contact him. She'd phoned the flat, which showed the state she was in since there was little chance he'd be there during the working day.

Calls to St Leonards weren't any likelier to work, as she should have known as a policeman's daughter. They hadn't yet set up a system on 999 that answered a Message for Daddy call. She wasn't thinking straight. Panic did funny things to people.

While all that was going on, he was taken up with a woman called Carrie Wilkie, who lived in a penthouse like a witch at the top of a tower. The witch idea got into his head because of her green eyes and the hint of malevolence he believed he saw in them.

From the couch where he sat beside McGuigan, he could see through the patio doors the Pentland Hills beyond the plants on the terrace. It was raining hard, but on a dry day at a warmer time of the year it would be a good place to sit and drink a bottle of chilled white wine and listen while a slightly husky voice wove spells in the long afternoon. The witch wasn't in fact old or ugly. She'd a long nose but it didn't bend to her chin; it was thin and straight and her chin was small under a wide mouth. He wondered if she lived alone.

"You like the view?" Carrie Wilkie asked.

"It must be quite something in the summer."

"What do you think of it?" she asked, looking at McGuigan.

"It's all right."

She laughed. "Indeed, it is. I bought this to rent, but when I saw the view I changed my mind."

Meldrum wondered if some instinct let her sense how much the sergeant disliked people with more money than they needed.

She waited a moment as if for a comment, then went on, "I bought another one for that. Not too far away. But without the view."

It seemed to Meldrum that one way or another she probably had the instinct, or perhaps she just enjoyed baiting handsome younger men.

"We'd be grateful if you could lend us a hand." As he heard himself say that, he resisted the impulse to cross his legs self-protectively.

"If I can, of course. Rachel and I are very old friends. We became close in our second year at university. People used to say we resembled one another, that we could have been sisters." In a moment of distraction, Meldrum remembered Sylvia Lenzie. She too had had that kind of wide sensual mouth. Presumably Rachel Croft had shared that with her sister, and that had been one of the points of resemblance. "We've kept in touch ever since."

"So we understand from Mr Croft."

"And Barry claims to have no idea where she is?"

"No." *Claims?* "Would you have any reason to doubt that?"

"That he would know? Or that he might not tell you the whole truth?" She smiled playfully. "He started off by selling bric-a-brac from a barrow in Glasgow, did you know that? Helping his father. I suppose you could call it the family business. Since then he's done very well. I imagine Barry has a fairly relaxed attitude to the truth."

"Shading up the price of an antique doesn't seem the same as lying about your wife's disappearance," McGuigan said.

"Lying?" Carrie Wilkie said. She looked at Meldrum and asked, "Did I use that word? I hope the sergeant isn't suggesting I did. I'd take that quite seriously."

Serious wasn't quite the word, Meldrum thought, grim would be more like it. Just for a moment she looked like a woman who might enjoy causing damage. If she did, he suspected she'd have the contacts to do it effectively. And then the look was gone, the claws were sheathed. She smiled and both men regarded her warily.

"I don't know about lying," she said, "but Barry has a cruel tongue. Where you're sitting now, Rachel has sat in tears. Sometimes what she told me he'd said didn't honestly seem too bad. Put it this way — it wouldn't have bothered me, but what does that signify? Either Rachel is more sensitive than I am, or he knew how to get under her skin."

While Meldrum considered his response, McGuigan pressed ahead.

"Was he ever physically violent?"

"Of course not!" She paused. "I dare say you see a lot of that among the kind of people you usually deal with." She paused again. "I'm not stupid. I know it happens everywhere. But they are a very civilised couple. Barry has buried the barrow boy with the barrow. Believe me, all the years I've known Rachel, she wouldn't have kept something like that from me."

"It's something we have to ask about," Meldrum said. "We're grateful to you for being so helpful."

"Here's something else you might be grateful for. Rachel was desperate to have a baby. Barry wouldn't hear of it. When I said he had a cruel tongue, I was thinking of some of the things he said to her about having children. If he'd said them to me, I'd have felt low and I don't even want a brat. With Rachel it was worse than feeling low or a little hurt."

"In what way?" Meldrum asked in a gentle, almost uninterested voice.

"Put it like this. If you'd come here to tell me that Rachel had committed suicide, I'd have been heartbroken. But not surprised. Not one little bit."

"Has she ever made a suicide attempt?"

"No. Or rather, I suppose I should say, not that I know of."

"Probably not then," said McGuigan. "I mean with you being so close to her."

"Quite."

"Can I ask you then what put the idea into your mind? If she'd no history of self-harm, why think of it at all?"

"She talked of it and . . ."

"And?"

"We were in the same hall of residence in first year at university. After that, you'd to find your own digs. We weren't really friends at that time, but we shared friends and joined them in a flat. One day I caught her self-harming. It's the right word, isn't it? You used it just now. She would cut her arms and the inside of her thighs. That's some kind of history, I suppose."

"Would you describe yourself now as her closest friend?" Meldrum asked.

"Did Barry say I was?"

He nodded.

"I think I am. Though I don't see as much of her as I did. There's a woman in the village she seems to be friendly with. Did Barry mention her? A woman called Violet Terry."

Again Meldrum wondered, yet couldn't be sure. Was what he was detecting really a gleam of malice in those green eyes?

CHAPTER
TWENTY-TWO

"That's astonishing. Where did you get this? Of course, I recognise it. It's mine all right"

As if to prove the point, Peter Tarleton read from the paper Meldrum had given him.

"*Turn now,*" he read, "*as the turning world*
Faces into the dark.
Turn your back on the dark.
Walk towards the light
And if at last
The dark overtakes you
Lift your face to where
The sun should be,
As the acrobat runs
On the turning ball of the world
And all the circus applauds."

Finishing, he folded the paper and was about to put it in his pocket when Meldrum shook his head to stop him. Reaching forward, the policeman retrieved the sheet of paper and tucked it back into the clear envelope from which he'd produced it.

Tarleton blinked, but instead of protesting or asking why, said, "A poem like that requires a special kind of voice. You'd recognise it if you'd ever heard a recording of Yeats reading his stuff. The vatic note, the prophetic mantle, same thing with Tennyson — there's an old recording of him, believe it or not. *Break, break, break On thy cold grey stones, O Sea!* You have to chant the words. *But O for the touch of a vanished hand And the sound of a voice that is still.*"

Apart from the mimicry of Tennyson, he offered this in a normal conversational tone. It was to the tone rather than the content that Meldrum chose to respond. "So it's your poem. Did you type it yourself?"

"Why not? You're not one of those people who imagines a poem should be written with a quill pen?" Since it wasn't something to which Meldrum had ever given any thought, he waited. In this kind of exchange, waiting was one of the things he did best. "A poem is a structure of words. Construct it in your mind while you're out walking. Put it down using a typewriter. Or a computer. Or a quill pen, come to that. It's still the same poem. As a matter of fact, I use an old typewriter, not even an electric one, which at this point in time almost is a quill pen, eh?"

As the confident voice rolled on, Meldrum thought, He knows why we are here.

"I wonder if you'd mind showing us the typewriter, sir."

"I'd be within my rights to refuse."

Meldrum waited.

"Why not?"

They followed him up the back stair, which was surprisingly narrow and led into a narrow passage. At the end, a door on the left opened into a small room with a dormer window set into the combed ceiling. Sitting under the light it gave was a desk with an old manual typewriter.

"Can I take a sample?" McGuigan asked. "With your permission."

"I should say no, but I'm a curious spirit. A curious spirit," Tarleton said, "can make you an Einstein, but it can disable a man in the world's battles."

Without scrutinising this too closely, McGuigan took passivity as consent. Leaning over the machine, he wound a sheet of paper into the feed and began to type, copying from a second sheet that he didn't bother to remove from the clear envelope used for storing evidence.

I'm not one to interfere with other people. Live and let live has been my rule. I hope you'll understand that I don't break it lightly. The man's name is Barry Croft. I'm concerned because his wife Rachel has disappeared. I hope I'm wrong but I'm very much afraid something has happened to her. You should pay him a visit. It's not a usual name — you'll find him in the phone book. Believe me, no one will be happier than I, if you find her safe and well, but it needs checking.

"We'll take an expert opinion," Meldrum said, "but to me it seems that the anonymous letter and the poem were both produced on this machine."

"That arse Croft," Tarleton said. "All he ever wanted to listen to was talk of motorbikes. I repair motorbikes

113

as a hobby. But my *vocation* is poetry. He could never get that through his thick skull."

"Is that an admission?" Meldrum asked.

"You never did tell where you got the poem."

"We didn't. The constable who initially received the letter —"

"Harrison. Foxy-looking type. Came once with a complaint about noise from the outbuilding I rent from the estate for the repair work."

"That must have been annoying. Since the anonymous letter had been sent to him, he took a particular interest in it. He'd been struck, for example, by that phrase at the end 'it needs checking.' A Scot would have written 'needs to be checked'. To him that indicated the letter had been written by an Englishman."

"That doesn't narrow the field much," Tarleton guffawed. "Not in this village."

"It was somewhere to start, as he put it. And then he got hold of your poem."

"Did he say where?"

"I couldn't say."

"Of course, you couldn't. There are a few copies of my poems go the rounds. I give them to friends." He shook his head. "It's not nice when people let you down."

Harrison had taken a photocopy of the anonymous letter before passing it on. The comparison he'd made between letter and poem was persuasive enough for him to draw it to their attention. It had been a smart piece of work and, as on earlier occasions, Meldrum had been amused by the coolness the clever McGuigan could display towards cleverness in other people.

"So what happens now?" Tarleton asked as they waited for McGuigan to come back from stowing the typewriter in the boot of the unmarked police car.

"It's not up to me to decide. It's quite a serious offence. It might help if you could provide an explanation for writing and sending the letter."

Tarleton shook his head. "Not something I want to go into at the moment. You know the verse: I do not like thee Doctor Fell, Yet this I know, And know full well, I do not like thee Doctor Fell? Let's leave it at that, shall we, till we see what happens?"

"The letter doesn't much concern me. The important thing is to find Rachel Croft. You'd be in trouble if you had evidence that might help us find her and failed to produce it."

McGuigan coming back in time to hear this added a nod of agreement to the pressure.

"On the other hand," Tarleton said, "it would be possible to argue you wouldn't even know she was missing if it wasn't for the letter."

"That might be your way of looking at it."

"Doesn't everyone have his own way of looking at things? A wise man called Shankarachanja said once 'The "I" is an illusion, but that illusion needs to be experienced, and it is only by experiencing it that it can be known as illusion.' Isn't that good?"

CHAPTER
TWENTY-THREE

"Fucking idiot," McGuigan said.

The sergeant didn't often swear, but as they walked along the village street Meldrum understood that he had been severely tried.

In a moment, though, McGuigan surprised him with a chuckle. "I wonder what he'd have said if I told him, here's a quote for you. 'Some circumstantial evidence is very strong, as when you find a trout in the milk.' That was an American guy called Thoreau. Teacher I'd had at school told me that when I met him in the street and told him I was going to be a policeman. Old clown thought he was hell of a funny." He gave Meldrum a sideways glance. "In the days before supermarkets, farmers used to cut their milk with water. Welsh milkmen in London did it all the time apparently."

Gurus and Welsh milkmen. It's my day for being patronised, Meldrum decided, and thought, *Fucking idiot!*, dividing the imprecation impartially among Tarleton, McGuigan and himself.

As they approached the cottage that had been pointed out as the one occupied by Violet Terry, Meldrum saw what might have been the shape of a woman move away from one of the front windows. Someone's been watching, he thought.

The woman who opened the door at the first ring was tall with little high breasts that showed their shape under a tight white jersey. She had a wide sensual mouth, which McGuigan would comment on later by saying, "She could eat a banana sideways." As a puritan, the sergeant had his own tricks for keeping lustful thoughts at bay. For Meldrum, her mouth recalled Sylvia Lenzie and Carrie Wilkie and, it seemed likely, the missing Rachel Croft also. Sisters and friends. Not forgetting, of course, bananas.

When they were inside and seated, she looked at Meldrum and asked, "Did you see me at the window?"

"That was you?"

"Strange men walking about the village." She smiled. "I shouldn't suppose I was the only one who noticed. Are you policemen? Tony thought you were."

"Tony?"

"Tony Carr. My next-door neighbour. He'd popped in for a g and t. We've been rather celebrating the last few days. Slipped out of the back door when he saw you coming."

"When he saw us coming," Meldrum repeated neutrally.

"Not that he'd anything to hide! Normal people just aren't all that keen on having to do with the police. You must find that."

"It depends. People are very good at helping with our inquiries, if there's been a burglary, say, or an assault."

"In other words, if we need you!"

"Or a disappearance," McGuigan said.

She put her hand to her mouth in a gesture that seemed theatrical. Her voice, however, trembled a little when she said, "So it's true then? Rumours have been going round the village. I dismissed it as nonsense. The police taking an interest doesn't happen. Not to people you know."

Normal people, Meldrum thought.

"I take it," he said, "that you're referring to Mrs Croft?"

"Rachel."

"I understand that you and she are close friends."

"Friends at least. I'm sure she has friends she's known for longer. I've known them both since they came to the village, but Rachel and I have seen more of each other since we formed the committee." When they looked blank, she explained, "To fight the quarry being made into a waste-fill site." She gestured over her shoulder. "On the hill behind us. Everything would have been covered in dust. Lorries day and night. Poisons seeping into the water table. We fought the proposal and we won. That's why we've been celebrating."

"And Rachel Croft was on this committee too?"

"God, yes. She was splendid. Everyone worked hard, but Rachel took these wonderful photographs. She's artistic you see. I believe her sister's a painter."

"So I imagine she'd be joining in these celebrations?"

"Well, that's the thing . . . All I could think was that she'd gone off somewhere. Perhaps on a holiday."

"When did you last see her?"

"The last committee meeting, I think. Just before the letter came telling us the proposal to use the quarry had been refused."

"But she went off before the letter came?" McGuigan asked. "That must have seemed strange to you. If she was so involved, you'd think she'd have made sure she was here for the verdict."

As the silence stretched, both men realised some chord had been struck. She blinked and wiped her tongue along her lips. "Silly of me. I can't think what made me say that. I took the letter along to show her. She was pleased."

"And she said she was going off on holiday?"

"No. I just assumed. Later I mean when she wasn't around."

"Around?"

"Around the village."

"You didn't call in at her home?"

"Why would I?"

"To ask about joining you for a drink. If you were all celebrating," McGuigan said.

"I was busy. In and out of town. Time passes so quickly. You don't realise a week's gone by."

"Was it the same thing with Mr Carr, your next-door neighbour? He must have wondered why she wasn't joining in the celebrations," Meldrum asked.

"I don't know. I suppose so."

"You didn't discuss it with him?" Meldrum let his incredulity shade the question.

"He thought she'd probably gone off for a few days."

"By herself?" McGuigan asked.

"It must have been."

"Because her husband was still here. You'd see him," he quoted, "around the village."

"His car. Going to work. He wasn't as sociable as Rachel. He joked about the committee, even when we won all he said was, that'll keep up the house prices. He was joking, of course. But he didn't have the same feeling for the village as Rachel. She fell in love with the house the day they came out to look at it. Love at first sight she called it."

She fell abruptly silent, as if feeling she was talking too much.

"Is that what everyone assumed," Meldrum asked, "that she'd gone off on holiday? Or is that what Mr Croft told people?"

"No, he didn't. Not to me at least. It was just a general feeling. I mean what else would people think — if they gave it a thought at all."

So much for the rumours she'd mentioned, Meldrum thought.

"Did you discuss where she might be with your neighbour Mr Tarleton?"

"He's the last person I'd discuss anything with!"

"You don't like him?"

"Not much." She made a face. "I know you caught me peeping out of the window. We all do. It's what living in a village is like. But Peter Tarleton takes it too far. You've heard of a degenerate gambler? He's a degenerate gossip." She hesitated, then said firmly, "You don't want to believe a word he says."

"Did he gossip about Mrs Croft?"

120

"Not to me, he'd know better. But he didn't like Barry Croft. He repairs bikes and Barry complained about the noise."

Meldrum almost let that pass; almost asked if Tarleton had gossiped about her to anyone else. Asked instead, moved by some policeman's instinct, "So he must have been working near Mr Croft's property?"

"Just the other side of the fence. In an old byre on the estate."

"So Croft could hear the noise coming from this old byre?"

"Well, otherwise why would he complain?" She allowed herself a smile.

Patronised again, Meldrum thought. Third time lucky.

"Could he see it as well?"

"It was just over the fence!"

"That would work both ways, wouldn't it? If Tarleton was watching, he'd get a good view of Croft's house."

It was as if the air had run out of her. As she deflated, her shoulders sagged and the wide mouth hung a little open as she sighed.

"Oh dear," Violet Terry said. "You know, don't you?"

CHAPTER
TWENTY-FOUR

"It didn't mean anything," Barry Croft said. He meant the sex with Violet Terry. "This came from Tarleton, did it?"

"When interviewed, he told us that he had been working in the outbuilding that afternoon. He saw Violet Terry and you come round the house to the back door."

"Little bastard," Croft said, but not with any emphasis. His tone, indeed, if the topic had been different might have been described as good-natured. "Must have been one of the rare occasions when he was working quietly."

"He kept an eye on the house and after half an hour, he thought, perhaps less, Violet Terry reappeared. He described her as dishevelled and adjusting her clothes. According to Miss Terry your wife caught the two of you in the middle of making love, but Tarleton doesn't mention having seen her."

"She must have come in the front door. I go in by the kitchen when I've been on the hill."

"So you admit that your wife did catch you with Miss Terry?"

Croft shrugged. The two detectives were sitting with him in the front room, surrounded by the expensive decorative pieces that they'd remarked on their first visit.

"As I said before, it didn't mean anything. She was on heat, and I was stupid enough to go along with it." He made a placatory gesture. "I'm sorry if that shocks you. I'm not a saint, but I love my wife. Violet Terry — I don't even know her that well — but she gives off signals. I think the damned woman is a nymphomaniac. I did my best to ignore the fact that she was interested in me. To be honest, she wasn't my type. But she was high because there wasn't going to be a dump in the old quarry. She was intending to go round the village and show the letter confirming that to everybody. Unfortunately, she'd seen Rachel going off with the car so she decided to show me first." His smile this time had an edge to it, which McGuigan found unpleasant. "She showed me everything she had."

"Your wife was angry when she caught you," McGuigan said.

Croft stared at him. "That's not what Violet said." He sounded as certain about that as if he'd been a witness to their conversation.

"How would you describe her feelings then?" Meldrum asked.

"Irritation with me. Contempt for Violet Terry. When she saw my wife, the woman leapt like a scalded cat. What did Tarleton say, that she was adjusting her clothing? I'm not surprised, she was still pulling on her knickers when she got out into the hall."

"What happened after that?" McGuigan asked. "You and your wife must have quarrelled."

"Sorry to disappoint you. That wasn't my wife's style. She went upstairs, came back down with her case packed. Told me she needed a bit of breathing space and off she went."

"How did she do that?" McGuigan asked.

"I don't understand."

"You're out here in the middle of the country. I don't suppose there's a great bus service. Did she have her own car?"

"Yes."

"Is that what she left in?"

"Yes."

"So if we went and took a look in the garage, her car wouldn't be there?"

They both sat and watched him think.

CHAPTER
TWENTY-FIVE

It was a handsome house, more than Corrigan's salary could have won for him even in an age of unscrupulous lending, but then apparently he'd been born to inherit a private income. A handsome house even with inflation, thanks to three generations that had ground the faces of the poor, Meldrum thought. With him, musings of this sort never generalised themselves into reflections on society or how it might need to be changed. His mind didn't work that way.

As he got out of the car, the last lit window on the façade went dark. He looked at his watch.

Just after ten wasn't late, but it looked as if they had all gone to bed. From memory, he worked out that the light, which had just gone out, was probably in the master bedroom. The windows on the ground floor, including those of Corrigan's study and the small sitting room used by Carole, were in darkness. Betty might be awake in one of the bedrooms at the back, but he would have to rouse the house to find out. It was a measure of how badly he wanted to speak to her that he was tempted to beat on the door; but only for a moment before common sense told him how counter-productive that would be. Reluctantly, he got back into the car.

Another half hour took him to Leith Walk. He found a parking place in the side street and walked back to his close. Somebody had failed to pull the entryphone door shut and it gave as he went to put his key in the lock. Once inside he made a point of pushing the door till the lock engaged, and as he climbed the stairs made the usual resolution to get the spring on the door repaired or at least mention it to one of his neighbours. He was climbing the second flight of stairs when some instinct made him sense a presence on the landing above. He didn't break step but readied himself, his body tensing for defence.

At the end of the landing, Betty was sitting on the stair opposite his door.

"God's sake!" he said, and felt his heart thump in his chest.

As she got to her feet, he said, "You must be frozen. How long have you been sitting there?"

He had the door open before she could answer. He waved her into the front room and turned the other way into the kitchen. He boiled a little water in the kettle and, for speed, made two cups of instant coffee. When he took them through she was standing with her back to him staring down at the traffic. He came beside her and handed her one of the cups. From the busy street, the double note of an ambulance drifted up to them.

"I kept trying to reach you all day," she said quietly. "I had to see you."

"What's happened?" Before he could stop himself, he asked, "Tommy's all right?"

"Fast asleep. I waited until he'd gone to bed."

"Do you want something to eat? There're rolls from this morning and I've got cheese or maybe a bit of cold meat."

"That was always your solution. If I cried as a wee girl, you always made me something to eat."

Impossible to tell from her tone if the recollection moved her to affection or irritation.

"I went to your mother's house tonight. All the lights were out. I wanted to see you."

"I was already on my way here. I sat on the stair waiting for you to come back." She shivered.

"It was cold."

"Stone steps. Come and sit on the couch."

She moved slowly like an old woman. "I couldn't bear my life," she said. "And so I ran away. Isn't the New World where you go to find a new life? I needed a new life. One that didn't have so much death in it." As he sat beside her, she turned her head to him with the same slow sense of difficulty. "Now Bobbie's dead," she said.

"Who told you that?"

"Always the policeman." When she said that, it occurred to him she might have wanted him to put his arm around her. "Remember I told you about the two detectives? The one called Finn rang me back."

"You'd already been on the phone to him?"

She shook her head.

"I'd never have phoned him. It was a woman I spoke to and I asked if there was any news of Bobbie and I told her I'd bought my ticket to come back to Phoenix."

"How long after that was it before Finn phoned you?"

"Not long. I was sitting with mother. She was trying to persuade me not to go. And then the phone rang."

She had come to him for help. He loved her and wanted to comfort her. When she was a child he had played with her, and held her. Why was it so difficult now?

"What did he say?"

"He said, 'I've been asked to talk to you.' He sounded irritable more than anything, as if his lunch had been interrupted. He told me, 'If I was you, I wouldn't come back. Your husband's body has been found. He'd been shot through the head. There isn't any of his face left.' That's exactly what he said. Wasn't that cruel? I've gone over and over it in my mind."

He put his arm around her shoulder. She didn't come into him, but she didn't pull away. He stayed still and after a moment asked, "How could they be sure it was your husband?"

"Identifying marks, he said." She explained, "Bobbie had a burn on his leg he got as a child."

He thought about that. "Yes, you told me. It doesn't —"

"Seem enough. That's what I said. Not enough to be sure. And then he told me the fingerprints taken from the body matched Bobbie's."

What did it mean if they had Wilbur Conway's — Bobbie's — prints on file? At one time, that would have suggested he had a criminal record, but Homeland Security must have taken the prints of a lot of Americans since the Twin Towers were destroyed.

"What else did he say?"

"It was a short call. Very businesslike. 'Your husband's dead.' I asked if he was threatening me."

"Why?" He was incredulous at the idea.

"It was when I said I'd come back for the funeral. He said there wouldn't be any point in that or don't bother. Something crass. It was the way he said it. And then he said, anyway the body wasn't released yet for burial. He said it might take some time and that he'd let me know. And then he was gone. It was as if he hadn't been there at all. I sat not able to move for a long time. I couldn't get any of it to make sense. And then I had to tell you. There wasn't anyone else who could help me."

He looked at his watch. "It'll be three in the afternoon there. Round about that. Let me try phoning him back."

He half expected that — as had happened with Sandra Foley, the woman who'd called claiming to be with the Phoenix Police Department — he'd be told they had no knowledge of Finn. It was something of a surprise on giving his name and business to be immediately transferred to another line and told that James Finn would get back to him. He gave his home number and asked if they had any idea when he might expect a call.

"He's not in the building," he said as he put the phone down, "but I'm told he should get back to me in a couple of hours."

"You'll let me know what happens?"

"You don't want to wait?"

She shook her head. "Mum will be sitting up till I get home."

He thought about the darkened façade of the house he'd seen earlier, but decided against saying anything. Maybe Corrigan had insisted Carole go to bed.

He phoned for a taxi and they stood at the window until they saw one pull into the side street. As he saw her into the taxi, he gave her a £20 note.

"That should cover it."

"You shouldn't." She didn't resist as he closed her fist on the note.

"I'll ring when I get the chance," he said, and watched until the taxi was out of sight.

CHAPTER
TWENTY-SIX

At four a.m. he went to bed and lay dozing until it was time to get up again. Before he left for work, he tried to tell Betty no call had come during the night, but when Corrigan answered the phone he hung up without saying a word.

Perversely, that morning McGuigan felt a compulsion to talk. "Makes no sense. My older brother was in his car waiting for me to come home last night. I got in and sat beside him. God knows how long he'd been there. He was frozen. I told him he should have waited inside, but he didn't want to upset my mother." Meldrum recalled that although almost thirty the sergeant still lived in the family home with his widowed mother. "He'd brought the paper in case I'd missed it. Collie Harper. Collie's father was an evil bastard who used to beat the shit out of his wife. She was a poor wee rag of a woman. Collie spent all the time he could at our house. My mother was more of a mother to him than his own mother ever was. And there it was in the paper. Killed in Iraq. A bomb at the side of the road. Blew up at the side of the lorry, but he was the only one killed. The other three were badly injured, but Collie was the one that was killed."

"If you join the army, you take your chances," Meldrum said. It was the best he could manage. Easy sympathy wasn't something he volunteered. He was irritated with McGuigan, even disappointed in him, that he should seem to be looking for it.

Unheeding, McGuigan exclaimed, "I didn't even know he was in the army! We lost touch when he started taking drugs."

Meldrum gave a grunt that suggested sympathy had just got a lot less easy. Leaning forward, he spotted Constable Harrison making his way along the pavement from the sub-station, narrow head turning on its long neck like a bird in search of seed.

"There he is."

He pulled the car in beside the constable and pressed the button to run down the passenger window. McGuigan called and a swift glance pecked them up. Harrison folded himself down to the window.

"Kevin Roche," McGuigan said.

Harrison wrinkled his forehead, then solved the puzzle. "Mr Crofts' chauffeur. At least, that's what he calls himself. I can take you where he lives. It's not that far. He's in the scheme just the other side of the main street."

"We know where he lives," McGuigan said.

"How come you do?" Meldrum asked the Constable. "Has he been in trouble?"

"No, sir, not with me. After the anonymous letter, when I went to see Mr Croft, he told me he didn't have too much time to waste. He was getting ready to go into town and Kevin Roche was there to drive him in. I made it my business later to find out what I could about Roche."

"Why did you do that?" McGuigan asked sharply.

Less thrown by McGuigan's abruptness on this second encounter, Harrison held steady. "He looked more like a bodyguard than anything else. He's a big fellow."

"So what did you find out?" Meldrum asked.

"He's not been nicked for anything far as I could find out. Somebody thought he'd been a boxer. But maybe that was because he looks the part."

Using the directions and map McGuigan had taken off the computer, they made their way up the hill into a council housing scheme. Neat semi-detached houses changed halfway along a street to four-in-a-block constructions with outside stairs leading to the two flats on the upper floor. After the usual trouble with hidden or vanished number plates, they found Roche's flat, one of two on a ground floor, different from its neighbours only in having a wild tangle of grass in place of a shorn lawn surrounded by flowerbeds.

A ring at the bell brought Roche to the door. Without a word, he turned and led the way along the lobby into the kitchen. He was a big man, a couple of inches shorter than Meldrum, with a heavy overhang of shoulders and a neck like a navvy's thigh. At their first sight of him, Meldrum had been conscious of McGuigan stiffening as if sizing the man up as an opponent. It was a reaction he'd seen before in the sergeant, in the minister of a church he'd been taken to as a boy and in other men who had the temperament of street fighters.

"I waited in like you said." Roche spoke slowly as if testing each word as he might the steps of a stair to see if they would bear his weight. By his accent, he was originally from Glasgow. "The boss doesn't need me today."

"Mr Croft, you mean?" Meldrum asked.

"Right."

"He knows we're seeing you?"

"I told him."

"How long have you worked for him?"

"Long time." He drew in a breath and thought it over. "Must be fifteen years. Something like that."

"All that time as his driver?"

"No accidents. I've a clean licence."

"What about Mrs Croft?" McGuigan asked. "Did you drive her as well?"

"She'd her own car."

"So you never drove her?"

"I wouldn't say that."

"What would you say?"

"Sometimes."

"Sometimes you drove her?"

"That's right."

"Recently?"

"Week past Monday. She phoned and I went up and drove her into the bus station in St Andrews Square. Then I took her car back to the house. The boss didn't need me so I went home after that."

"How did you get home?"

"Same way I came. On my bike. It's not far."

"You know that Mrs Croft has disappeared?"

"Don't know what you mean."

"Nobody's seen her since that day you took her into Edinburgh."

The big man frowned. "She'll have took a bus."

"Did she say where?"

"Why would she?"

Meldrum took over. "You say she mostly drove her car herself. Didn't you think it was strange her asking you to drive her into town?"

"She was going in to catch a bus," he said seriously. His brows drew together in a stressful frown. "She couldn't leave her car in the town — not if she was catching a bus."

And having clarified the difficulty, Roche leant back and his brow cleared.

BOOK FOUR

TO HAVE AND TO HOLD

CHAPTER
TWENTY-SEVEN

It would have been wonderful to go to the pictures, find a good film, a musical or a comedy, sit in the dark and find relief from her thoughts. Tommy tugged at her hand and Betty Meldrum turned from the row of posters and their promises and asked the child, "Would you like an ice cream?"

Whether or not it was good for a toddler's teeth was irrelevant to the purpose of the afternoon. She was on a mission to bond with her child, and to that end had managed to persuade her mother not to come along. She held his hand as he stepped bravely on to the escalator and they rode the same step side by side all the way down from the second floor to the one below where she ignored the smaller eating places in favour of the big restaurant space. Once they were seated, she drew his attention to the glass ceiling high above them, and tried to make him share her pleasure in the wash of light from the soaring wall of glass with its view of the harbour. "Look!" and she pointed out the towers of Platinum Point with the hills of Fife beyond them across the grey choppy waves on the open expanse of the Forth. Meanwhile, Tommy took it all in with the matter of factness of a child to whom everything was too new to be wondered at.

When she looked at her watch, it was five past twelve.

"Why don't we have lunch?" she asked. "You like pizza and we can have our ice cream at the end. Would you like that, Tommy?"

He looked at her solemnly. "You won't forget?"

"The ice cream? No, I won't forget. We'll have pizza and then I'll get the menu and you can pick the ice cream you'd like best."

It was a relief when he nodded agreement. Too bad, she thought, when your son doesn't trust you to order ice cream. But then, she thought, before dismissing it as self-pity, he hasn't had much reason to trust me or the world.

Behind her a man's voice asked, "All right if I join you?"

An ordinary voice, if anything struck her about it, it was that it belonged to someone from the other coast, from Glasgow probably, what locals commonly called "someone from the West". It was only when she turned round that she recognised Bobbie Conway, her husband who she had been told was dead.

She hardly reacted. It was as if the shock had paralysed her. She felt his hand grip her lightly by the shoulder and then he had seated himself beside her.

As if at a great distance, she heard him ask the boy, "What's your name, little guy?" and when there was no answer, "You look like a Billy? No? Charley? What about Tommy? That it? That's a good name. I used to

140

know a friend who had a little boy called Tommy. He was a good boy. Are you a good boy?"

And she heard Tommy, who wasn't outgoing with strangers, say, "Yes." And then unprompted tell him, "I'm going to have ice cream. I've to have pizza first and then we'll have ice cream."

"Sounds good to me. I think I'll have the same. I like ice cream. Wonder what it would be like if we had it on top of the pizza. Do you think they'd do that if I asked real nice?"

"No!" Tommy exploded like it was the funniest idea he had ever heard.

"Better not ask then. I think you're right. We'll have the pizza. And then the ice cream. And I'll have coffee. And maybe your mum will let you have a Coke. Tell you what. You keep an eye open for the waitress. We don't want to miss her and not get anything to eat."

There was a roaring in her ears as if she was drowning, and then as the waters subsided the voices became clearer and the noises of the restaurant rose and she heard the clatter of a knife knocked from a nearby table. She opened her mouth to say his name, and he smiled and put a finger to his lips.

"Little pitchers," he said, looking affectionately at Tommy, and she understood that whatever he had to tell her wasn't for her son's ears.

By the time the pizzas had come and been eaten, Tommy was chattering away. It seemed that Bobbie had a way with children, and this more than anything placated her. Yet when he pushed his plate away and said, "That was good. I've changed my mind about the ice cream. Have you changed your mind?" and Tommy shook his head and watched wide-eyed as he got to his feet, she too found herself standing in protest.

Before she could speak, he said with a smile, "Thanks for letting me share the meal with you. I'm on holiday and get tired of eating by myself."

"I have to —"

What? Talk with him? Of course. Get him to turn the world right side up again so that it made sense? Something like that.

But his voice overrode her, repeating how good the meal was. "I might even come back tomorrow. Don't think I'll find better company anywhere else. This is a good time to eat, don't you think?"

"Yes."

"That's settled."

Looking after him as he walked away, she understood that she had made a commitment and that there was no way she would fail to keep it.

CHAPTER
TWENTY-EIGHT

On his driver Kevin Roche, Croft was relaxed, even expansive. "He'd very fast hands and a glass jaw. All his fights were a kind of race between the two. One way or the other, they had a tendency to end suddenly. Because we were in the same class at school, I took an interest. When he started out, he didn't do badly. But when he moved up a class, he met people who were hard to hit and packed a wallop of their own. He started losing and then he started losing badly. I'd always liked him. A big good-natured kid, not a bully — even at school he used to follow me around. Before he turned into a bum, I got him out of the fight game. He's been my driver ever since."

"Sounds like he owes you something," McGuigan said.

"You think so?" Croft looked at him with dislike.

There wasn't any doubt that Roche did, Meldrum thought. Enough to lie for Croft? For an idle moment, he wondered how well the big man would stand up under cross-questioning in court. Before they could charge anyone, of course, they had to find a crime. For his part, Meldrum was very close to believing in the possibility of a body.

"You haven't heard from your wife, sir?" he asked.

"If I had, it's the first thing I'd have said. I don't enjoy this."

"You must be getting worried."

"As a matter of fact, I'm not. My wife went off in good health. She's not short of money. I keep waiting for her to walk in through the door."

"Money," Meldrum said thoughtfully. "Does she have a bank account of her own?"

After a pause, Croft nodded. His initial easiness had entirely dissipated.

"I wonder if we could have a look at it."

"There's no need for that."

"If she stays away, she'll have to lift money. That would mean she was safe somewhere. Wouldn't that settle your mind?"

"Unless she was being held and forced to sign." At the look on Meldrum's face, Croft gave an angry bark of laughter. "Stupid? Of course, the idea is stupid. But you're the one looking for trouble not me. I just want to be left in peace. And no you can't look at her account. I can imagine what she'd say if she came back to find you people had been poking through her private affairs. Even I don't know what her financial situation is."

Meldrum said equably, "If you feel it hasn't come to that yet, let's leave it for the moment. You'll agree, though, we have to find her."

"For your sake, not mine. If she needs time away, fine by me. I'll be happy to see her, when she decides to come back."

"We've checked the people you thought might help — her mother, her sister Miss Lenzie and her friend

144

Mrs Wilkie. None of them have seen her since she disappeared."

"I object to the word. She didn't disappear. She got herself driven into the bus station. She didn't disappear, she got on a bus."

"Difficulty is we don't know which one. I'd like you to think about where she might have gone. Some old friend perhaps. Maybe somebody you haven't seen for a long time. Places you've lived. Places she loved to go on holiday. People she worked with perhaps."

"She hasn't worked for years, not since we were married."

"Fine . . . Meantime, what I'd like to do is get a recent photograph of her and show it around. I think it's time we moved this up to the next level."

"I don't want any of this in the papers."

"I accept that. Let's try some inquiries at the bus station. We'll make it as discreet as possible."

"I'm not a fool," Croft said. "You start showing her photograph around and someone is going to phone the papers."

Suddenly Meldrum was conscious of McGuigan's body language. His expression was attentive and involved, but he was sitting back in his chair, not enough to remark on but perceptible once noticed. If Rachel Croft arrived back in the morning, McGuigan was making it clear that it hadn't been his idea to push things forward instead of giving her time to come home again.

"I'm afraid," Meldrum said, "that's a chance we'll have to take."

CHAPTER TWENTY-NINE

"At Ocean Terminal," Betty said.

He'd asked how she'd spent her day. Not that it mattered, it was a way of trying to calm her before they talked.

"I took Tommy to Ocean Terminal. We had lunch. Pizza and ice cream."

"That's good," he said, his mind on what he wanted to tell her. "He'd like that."

She'd made some excuse to her mother and Corrigan, she said, after he'd called and she'd agreed to meet him. He'd spoken first to Carole, hearing the television in the background, mouthing banalities to his ex-wife before asking to have a word with Betty. His daughter was a grown woman. What had gone wrong with her life that she had to find an excuse to come out and meet her father for a quiet drink?

In the middle of the evening the small lounge bar was certainly quiet enough. He turned the whisky tumbler in his fingers and said, "I started trying at midnight, but I couldn't get to Finn. He didn't ring back and they wouldn't give me a number for him. Nobody else would talk about your husband. I'm sorry."

She sipped at her glass of wine. "It's all right," she said. "It was good of you to try."

He stared at her. He hadn't expected her to take it like that. What had happened to the panic that had brought her to sit in the cold outside his door because she needed help so badly?

"Are you all right?"

"There's nothing wrong with me."

She was flushed and looked tired, but that was to be expected.

"You haven't booked a ticket?"

"For what?"

"To go back to Phoenix." When she hesitated, he went on, "It would be a mistake. Wait until I've found someone who'll talk to me. I don't want you going back at least until then."

"I'm not going back," she said. "You can stop worrying about that."

He should have been relieved, but she was smiling, and the fact she was smiling at all and something strange in the smile itself disconcerted him.

"It took me until two in the morning, but I finally got Lori Allingham."

"I can't see why you bothered."

He looked at her in astonishment. "I was trying to find out where Bobbie worked. Remember?"

"What did she say?"

"What a nice woman you were. I'm to give you her love. She sounded pretty cheerful — until I asked to speak to her husband. That's when she started asking

147

why? If there was trouble, she didn't want anything to do with it."

"So you didn't get her husband? Matt, I'm sure it was Matt."

"Matt Crais. I can be pretty persistent."

"Poor Lori," she said.

It was almost as if she was detached from what he was saying. He couldn't understand the difference in her.

"He admitted he was the one who invited Bobbie to the wedding. But when I asked him where he worked he told me that was confidential. I asked if Bobbie was a colleague. That was confidential too. When I asked if he'd heard that Bobbie was dead, he hung up." He waited for her to comment, studying her face as she sat deep in thought. "Well?"

"He wasn't much help."

"That all you've got to say?"

"Maybe he just didn't want to get involved. There are plenty of people who feel that way."

"You told me one time that Lori Allingham worked for the government."

"Half the population of Washington does. She invited me for lunch once. Big building in the middle of town."

"What department was that?"

She screwed up her forehead. "Isn't that stupid? I've always had such a good memory."

"You've been under a lot of strain."

"Something to do with Security? Or maybe not!" When she gave even the shadow of a smile, her face shed the years. "You needed to show identification

148

before you could get in. I'd forgotten my passport, but the black guard said, 'Try the next door along.' I got in there no bother, walked back and met Lori in a big hall decorated like an Egyptian temple. Try the next door along! It was nice to know America was still like that."

"Like what?"

"Easy-going. Even after 9/11."

"Doing a bad job isn't the same as easy-going," Meldrum said. He was on automatic pilot, keeping the conversation going while he tried to work out why she was behaving so differently from what he had anticipated.

CHAPTER
THIRTY

She was standing looking across the restaurant in Ocean Terminal, when she felt a hand on her elbow.

"Hello again," Bobbie said.

With the gentlest of pressures, he drew her back out into the mall.

"We can do better than pizza."

"What happened to you?"

"Not now. Let's get out of here and I'll tell you over lunch."

They were walking past Marks and Spencer. Glancing inside, she thought she would never forget the impression of orderly plenty made upon her by the neatly ranked cardboard boxes of food. She remembered the black guard who had said, 'Try the next door'; and could have smiled to see an elderly man wrestling to get a pound coin out of his trolley. In the slow-moving way of dreams, she had time to hear the man say to a woman coming forward to rescue him from his predicament, "How did you know I was married?" laughing with the easy confidence of a man who had turned to women for help all his life.

As they went through the doors at the end of the mall into the car park, she felt the sudden change in temperature.

Bobbie Conway led the way up the ramp to where the cars were lined up. Over the railing she saw cloud slipping off the sun and that a light wind was ruffling the waves in the harbour.

"Don't worry," he said. "I'll bring you back to collect your car."

"I don't have a car."

"You had yesterday."

She realised he must have followed them yesterday from when she and Tommy left the house in Carole's car.

"I came by bus today."

"I'll run you home then. Or nearly. I'll drop you a couple of streets away."

He produced a key and pressed. A light winked halfway along the row; picking out a nondescript family car.

"Is that yours?"

"It's hired. I couldn't live without a car." He laughed. "I haven't been on a bus since I was a kid."

Outside the mall, he circled the roundabout twice as if to give the impression he had changed his mind at the last minute. At the lights he pulled down the stick to signal left, then with a roar of the engine surged straight ahead over the crossing.

"Where are we going?"

She thought that he might not answer, but he said casually, "Tusitala. You know it?"

"Past Morningside Cross on the way to Fairmilehead? I've been there."

"It's got parking. And it's not far from where I'm staying." If she had been going to ask where that was, he anticipated her: "No questions till after lunch."

She couldn't be absolutely sure, but getting to the restaurant seemed to take a long time. Once a row of shops caught her eye for a second time and she had a feeling they might have circled the block. He didn't break his silence, and she sat beside him in a kind of daze, not so much busy with her own thoughts as drifting on the surface of them.

At last they pulled into the restaurant car park and she followed him inside to where a waiter took them down the steps and put them at a table for two by the window.

They studied the menu but she couldn't take it in and when he asked what she wanted, she said, "I'm not hungry."

"The fish pie looks good. Haddock and prawns and a topping of baked potato and cheddar. I'm going to have that." But when she shook her head, he said firmly, "You have to eat something. Tell you what, you like pizza — have that, I was only joking about pizza, it isn't barred. Look they have an oven for them over there in the corner. I'll get you a *quattro stagione*."

He ate with relish and watching him she knew this wasn't a dream and that if she reached out she would feel the reality of his hand.

"I was told you were dead."

"Who told you that?"

He listened intently as she told him about going to the police and about the two detectives, and how the one called Finn had described the body with the burn on its thigh.

"So I was dead? Wishful thinking." And he pushed a forkful of pie into his mouth. "The burn was a strange coincidence."

"I told them about it."

He stared at her. "Why would you do that?"

"They asked if you had any distinguishing marks. It was to help them look for you."

"Do you think they got hold of a corpse from somewhere and faked it to be me? That's horrible."

"Faked?" The idea had never occurred to her. "Some kind of mistake, it must have been. But he said your fingerprints and the corpse's were the same — so it had to be you. I don't understand."

"That's outrageous." He reached across the table and, as if he had sensed her thoughts, took her hand. "You can feel I'm not dead."

But what he'd said sank in. "They were the police! Why would they pretend you were dead? If you can't make sense of this for me, I'll go mad."

"Do you know what a consultant is?"

"Yes, I think so." She looked at him in bewilderment.

"You asked me one time what firm I was with. That wouldn't have been easy to say. The people I work with operate through more than one firm. They've been around for a long time. For sure since before the First World War. How long before I don't know. When I started with them, I worked with an old guy who was

153

their Russian specialist. He was so old the Consultancy wanted to retire him, but the Soviets liked to look a man in the eye when they did business. If they trusted you and they trusted him, they'd do it on a handshake not a contract."

She grasped at the last thing he'd said. "You work in Russia? Isn't that dangerous?"

He smiled. "They're on our side now. And yes, it's dangerous. Not for me, though, I haven't been there in a long time. The Consultancy advises companies and governments all over the world."

"Is that why you're here?"

He paused with the fork halfway to his mouth. "Don't you know why I'm here? I'm here for the same reason I married you. Because I love you." He stood up. "Come on and I'll prove it to you."

He'd said that he was living nearby. It didn't take long to get there.

On the short journey, she spoke once out of the blue, almost as if not aware of saying the words out loud, "I don't know why I didn't tell my father."

"That you'd seen me? You wouldn't be doing him any favours."

"He phoned Lori and spoke to your friend Matt Crais."

"I wish he hadn't done that."

"My father won't give up."

"All I need is a few weeks. Don't say anything to him. It isn't for long. Do that and I promise everything will be all right."

When they went into the house, a mid-terrace with its name on a board in the tiny front garden, a woman was picking up letters from a table in the hall. He nodded to her and Betty assumed she must be lodging there also. When a second woman came from the back of the house, Bobbie said, "Mrs Henson, this is my wife I told you about."

"I'm sorry about your father," the woman said.

When they were in his room, he smiled and said, "Sorry about that. She thinks your father is ill."

She didn't see the point of telling lies, and had a superstitious dislike of a pretence that involved her father being ill. She couldn't see why it should matter to the landlady; and then thought he'd lied to explain why his wife wasn't staying with him. He'd known that he was going to bring her here and that she would come.

She looked round at the furniture, the dressing table, the wardrobe, the chair with the green worn arms. It was all downmarket and shabby.

"I hate this place," she said. "It makes me feel sordid. I don't see why you have to tell lies."

"It's no lie that you're my wife. Or that I couldn't think straight from the moment I met you. Or that I came here because of you. Or that I love you."

He kissed her and then put his arms round her. As the kiss went on, she relaxed against him and he ran one hand down her back and stroked her buttocks.

She pulled away, leaning back from him as he kept holding her.

"No," she said. "What do you think you're doing? I want to know what's happening? Why did you disappear?"

"Later."

As he walked her backwards and the edge of the mattress caught her behind the knees so that she fell back on to the bed with his weight pinning her down, she felt the hardness of his body against her breasts and belly. His lovemaking was urgent and untender. When it was over, she found herself thinking, he *is* my husband, he *is* my husband, yet knew that her legs had opened and she had orgasmed with a force matching his not because of any vows she had taken but because he had won the argument of the flesh.

CHAPTER
THIRTY-ONE

It was Peter Tarleton who precipitated Meldrum into action. With McGuigan he had gone again to speak to Violet Terry. He didn't expect to get more information from her, but was working on the principle that the more he created a stir in the village the better the chance there was of making Croft uneasy.

She'd been at her window again as they came to the cottage, making Meldrum wonder if anything happened in that short stretch of the main street without her being aware of it.

"You've just missed him," she informed them as she opened the door.

"Who would that be?" Meldrum asked as they followed her inside.

"Tony, of course!" The next-door neighbour Meldrum remembered, who came in for a g and t to help celebrate their victory in the quarry inquiry. "He's just gone." She gave a wide smile. "You must wonder why he's in here all the time."

Before Meldrum could offer some careful reply, McGuigan asked, "He's fond of gin?"

"Well, that too," she said appreciatively and laughed.

McGuigan, irritated by her manner, had intended the question aggressively. Meldrum observed how the edges of his ears went red at her response.

"Speaking of gin," she said, "can I offer you a coffee? No point in offering you spirits. 'Not while we're on duty, ma'am,' as they say in the films."

For the police dialogue, she deployed a comic Zummerset accent, so that "ma'am" came out as "mum".

"No thanks," McGuigan said abruptly.

"Coffee would be fine," Meldrum said.

"Have a seat then. I'll only be a moment."

As he sat down Meldrum realised that the armchair with the tapestry back was a good deal less comfortable than it looked. At eye level opposite him, a variety of china figures, a shepherdess complete with crook, an old gypsy in a disreputable hat, two lovers on a bench, were arranged on a shelf. His glance was drawn away by McGuigan who, after a hesitation, had settled into a chair only to have it move back and forward on the fixed base rockers concealed by a flowery drop. "Fucking hell," the sergeant said, not particularly quietly, jumping up and finding himself another seat.

To Meldrum's relief, the coffee in the stark little black and white cup was more than palatable. He took a second sip and said, "Mr Croft confirms your account of what happened the day his wife disappeared."

"Not my finest hour," Violet Terry said.

"I'd like you, if you would, to think back to when Mrs Croft came in and found you with her husband. It must all have happened quickly and I can understand that you would be upset. But in view of what happened later, it's very important to try to work out how she reacted. I hope you feel that it is important."

"Didn't Barry tell you what she said?"

"Not in detail. He said she took it calmly. According to him, there wasn't a scene."

"There wasn't any shouting if that's what you mean. My heart almost stopped when I looked over my shoulder and saw her standing in the doorway. You know what she said to me? Barry didn't say?" He shook his head. " 'The first time Barry and I fucked,' she said, 'I gave him crabs.' That freaked me out. I was still getting dressed as I ran through the hall. I just wanted to get out of there."

"Would you describe her as angry?"

"I don't suppose she was pleased. But she wasn't shouting or anything."

"Was it your impression that she already knew of the affair?"

"I can't imagine how. There wasn't 'an affair'. That was the first time we'd done it together. Mostly my idea, but I imagine he's already told you that."

"No. He didn't say that."

"You surprise me. Men are such pigs. Anyway she must have known he was partial to that kind of thing. That was the gossip anyway. Come to think of it, that may have been why I chanced my arm. No one likes to be overlooked."

Despite Meldrum being the one asking the questions, she'd directed this last speech to McGuigan, who took up the challenge. "It's one thing to hear rumours that your husband may be having affairs. It must be very different to come home and find him in your bed with someone else."

"We weren't in bed," she said. "We were making love on the floor. As a matter of fact we were downstairs. Things were moving too fast for us to make it up to the bedroom."

On the whole, Meldrum found this was a picture he preferred not to dwell on.

"When Mrs Croft didn't show herself in the village," he said, "you said when we talked before that you thought she'd gone off for a few days' holiday. You didn't really think that, did you?"

"Something like that. I'm not pretending I didn't think it had something to do with what had happened. But I didn't assume for a moment that she was breaking up her marriage."

"And now?"

"No! It doesn't make sense. I mean it wasn't serious. I can't imagine she thought it was serious."

"Is it possible that she was angrier than you realised?"

"I don't see how she could have been."

"You said that you got out of there as fast as you could," McGuigan said.

"But what she said to me — that she'd given him crabs, but I wasn't to worry because it was a long time ago. That wasn't anger. I don't know what it was."

"Contempt?" McGuigan suggested.

"Perhaps."

"Maybe," Meldrum said, "she went on like that after you left. It's possible, isn't it?"

But at that something in her look changed, and he got the feeling that she suddenly had seen where he might be going.

"I've no idea," she said.

"How do you think he'd react if she did?"

"He wouldn't like it."

"He'd get angry?"

She said nothing.

"Lose his temper maybe?"

"I can't help you with this," she said. "You should talk to Peter Tarleton."

CHAPTER
THIRTY-TWO

The surface of the water was flat to a casual glance. To Meldrum and the others, however, gathered at the edge, the intentness of their gaze unfolded a dictionary of signs from the wave pulse as the boat's oars beat into the lochan to the spreading rings each diver left as markers to where he'd dropped out of sight into the dark. There was no wind, but the coldness of the air inside the shadow of the quarry did its work in chilling the watchers. They were into the second hour and the boat had made its way along by the wall and back and was making yet another search further out.

"They're not going to find anything," a voice said. It came from one of the group of senior officers and officials in a huddle behind him. Meldrum couldn't place it, but he recognised the bureaucrat's complacent malice directed at someone who had stuck his neck out and got it wrong.

Shortly afterwards, the same voice arriving at his side offered the opinion, "Not looking too hopeful." A heavy man with wings of grey hair attempting to lend distinction to a plump ordinary face. One of the chief constable's little helpers. A more political policeman than Meldrum would have known his name and used it. People liked it if you remembered their names.

Getting no answer, the man broke the silence by asking, "This Peter Tarleton is the same one who sent the anonymous letter that started all of this?"

Meldrum grunted.

"That didn't bother you?"

"I took it into account."

"Not enough it seems."

It would have been satisfying to offer a brief brutal reply, but he hadn't survived so long in the job without acquiring self-discipline. He was saved from the tiny erosion of his self-respect involved in exercising it by an outcry among the spectators. One of the divers had found something. Another joined him, then a third man rolled over the side of the boat to join them.

As the minutes passed, the tension rose and when they broke surface again it became obvious to the spectators that what they were struggling to get into the boat was both heavy and awkward to lift.

CHAPTER
THIRTY-THREE

Peter Tarleton opened the door at the first ring, so quickly indeed that Meldrum took a half step backwards.

"Did you find anything?"

"Can I come in?"

Walking ahead of him, Tarleton didn't stop talking. "All morning, I haven't been able to settle. Up and down. Pacing round the house. I almost came up to the quarry when I heard what was going on, but I felt you might prefer me not being there." He glanced at his watch. "Is it that late? I've skipped lunch."

There was a bottle of whisky and an almost full glass on the table beside the chair in which he settled himself. As he sat down, Meldrum noted that the bottle was half empty, but there was no telling how much had been in it when he started.

"I can fetch another glass," Tarleton said. "Since you're here by yourself, I hope you'll feel free to join me if there's something to celebrate."

"Finding a body isn't anything to celebrate."

"No, absolutely not." He leant forward eagerly. "You have then?"

"First, sir, it would help if you would go over again what you told me."

"About what I saw?"

Before, he'd been reluctant to give an account of what he'd witnessed. It had only been when Meldrum explained that Tony Carr had passed on to his next-door neighbour Violet Terry the odd story he'd been telling, that he'd been persuaded to talk. Now it seemed he'd overcome his doubts.

"It was the Thursday. There had already been some talk about Rachel Croft not being around to celebrate the quarry getting a knock-back. We'd all been involved in the campaign. Even I'd done my bit, which was why I imagine I'd got an invitation that evening to have a drink with Violet, not a woman I care for, and her very *attentive* neighbour. When I came out, it was surprisingly late, after midnight. I'd drunk more than I should have, and decided to take a turn up the hill to clear my head. Walking along the street, I was surprised how many of the lights were already out. It was one of those nights, not a breath of air. By the time I reached the quarry, a poem had come into my head. It sometimes happens like that, not just an opening, but the whole two verses, a perfect little thing." Meldrum offered a silent plea that the man's egotism wouldn't require him to recite it. "I sat on a rock to go over it a few times in my head so I wouldn't forget it. That must be why he didn't see me. I looked up and there he was on the edge of the drop on the other side. Just the shape of a man and he held out his arms and then I heard the splash and knew he'd thrown something in. Something heavy. And then the whole scene was lit up as the clouds came off the moon and I recognised him."

"Can you describe what he'd been holding?"

"Just an impression. As I say, this was before the moon came out. It made quite a splash. And now you've found — you have found her body?"

"A body."

"What do you mean?"

"Just before ten this morning, divers brought up a body bound up in a rubber sheet. It had the limbs and head severed, but it had all been fitted in to make a reasonably neat parcel. Awkward thing to handle though. I doubt if one man could have thrown it that far out from the edge."

"How horrible. Have you identified her?"

"Him. A heavily built male."

"A man? You astonish me. There's not a man missing from the village. Wait! Croft has a thug who drives him around." His face fell. "But I saw him the other day."

"It's too early for forensics. But the consensus among those of us who were there is that the corpse could have been in the water for years."

"Christ!"

Meldrum sat staring at him in a heavy silence. As the moments passed, Tarleton began to fidget in discomfort. Meldrum thought of the body they had found. Let it be someone else's murder.

166

He didn't want the case. What had that bloody bureaucrat offered as his parting shot? *Not a complete waste of time then?*

"Do you want to change your story?" he asked at last.

"Why would I do that? What is there to change?"

"Whatever Croft threw into the quarry — if he threw anything — it certainly wasn't a body."

"Perhaps it was a rock. It seems I misunderstood — but if it was a mistake it was made in good faith."

"Why would he throw a rock in the water?"

"Why does anyone do anything? Impulse. Or getting rid for some reason of one of his wretched antiques. I'm sure if you looked you'd find something."

Meldrum stared back at him blankly. It wasn't a stupid idea; but the divers were gone and he doubted if any request of his for their return would be looked on favourably.

"Anyway," Tarleton said, "it would be worth doing. It might not solve your murder, but if it was anything to do with his business it will certainly have to do with one kind of scam or another."

"Why do you dislike him so much?"

As Meldrum waited for his answer, it was as if he saw the man properly for the first time. In shaving that morning, he had left a fringe of hair along the edge of his upper lip. His tongue smoothed the hair as he licked his lip.

"I'd need notice of that question."

Meldrum waited.

"I mean, I admit freely that I dislike him. Did I tell you he complained about the noise I make repairing bikes? That kind of thing is quite enough to make for dislike. But you're quite right. Why 'so much'? And how 'much' is that? He hasn't stolen my money or raped my wife — no, I'm not, married that is. He hasn't accused me of a crime or tried to blackmail me. He hasn't arranged for me to be beaten half to death. He hasn't done me any insult or injury that I can think of. If you were to take out your policeman's notebook, I wouldn't be able to give you anything to put in it, anything you would understand. But when I think about it 'so much' is a big 'much'. It's really quite a lot. Why does a dog detest a cat? Have you any idea what I'm talking about?"

Doctor Fell, Meldrum thought, but decided against the risk of giving him any satisfaction. He said, "Keep it in your head, no one cares. It's when you act it out, I have to put it in the notebook — and if I can't find the words, we've people who can."

"Psychiatrists?"

"You're not that important, I don't think. But I could put some words in the book — hate mail, malicious accusation, harassment."

"I wonder if you will. I think you'll prefer to concentrate on finding Rachel Croft."

The irritating thing was the element of truth in that. He'd no desire to throw up a smokescreen in which Croft would be concealed.

"There's also, of course, the question of the body that's just been found."

"Oh, but surely," Tarleton said, "that's nothing to do with the village. Anyone could have dumped a body there. Edinburgh drug dealers come to mind."

"You'd better hope then," Meldrum said, "that you're not identified as the man who initiated the search of the quarry."

CHAPTER
THIRTY-FOUR

An unpleasant interview with ACC Fairbairn started Meldrum's morning on the following day. As a result, he found himself immersed in the squalid details of a serious wife assault and with the strong impression that as far as the powers that be were concerned the disappearance of Rachel Croft might well be a non-event best filed away at least for the moment under the routine heading of domestic dispute. The one positive in the working day was that McGuigan was if anything undemonstratively supportive.

It was a relief when the time came to free himself of a caseload which failed to interest him to the point of aversion. The strength of his reaction, of a different order from anything he'd felt before, which had begun by surprising him, by the end of the day was making him uneasy and even apprehensive. It was as if he'd opened a door and was having to struggle to close it again.

They were using a pool car and McGuigan, who'd been behind the wheel all day, had taken him home. He'd been so lost in thought that the car stopping outside his close took him by surprise.

As he opened his door, the engine was switched off. What the hell, he thought, does he think I'm going to invite him up?

"Got lucky there. Not often you get parked right at the door," McGuigan said. "I'll take the chance and get myself a paper."

As Meldrum watched him go into the shop on the corner, on impulse he turned away from the entry to his close and crossed the road to the one opposite. He didn't obviously hurry, but he didn't delay either since he'd have been at a loss to explain to McGuigan or anyone else what he was doing.

At the moment of hurrying into the close, he himself couldn't see where he was going. The lamp in the close had been smashed and the darkness at the end was for a moment impenetrable. At the same moment, a heavy smell filled his nostrils as if someone in the ground-floor flat was cooking meat. He groped his way forward until he touched the banister and, guided by it, began to climb the stairs.

When he reached the first landing the darkness was explained since boards had been nailed over the landing window. On the second landing, the window was dirty but admitted enough light to show the flaking paint and holes like scabs where plaster had been gouged out of the walls. It was only on the top landing that a bulb at either end threw a clear hard light and although the door of one of the two flats was unpainted and scarred the other one had been repaired, painted and furnished with an electric bellpush and a polished brass nameplate. He read the name on each of the plates but neither meant anything to him. For the life of him, he couldn't imagine anyone who settled for living in a place like this being someone the fastidiously groomed Barry Croft would choose to visit. Just in case, he rang the bell on the newly painted door, but got no answer.

Groping his way back down, he decided there was no point in doing any more until he had armed himself with a torch.

He was surprised when he stepped out of the close to see the pool car, a red Ford Mondeo, still parked across the street. Even as he watched, the signal light winked and the car pulled out from the kerb. As it moved away, he thought he saw a woman beside McGuigan but knew he must be mistaken.

The same impulse that had impelled him to explore the close and find it a throwback, still undeveloped in the midst of properties refurbished by developers out for a quick sale, now suggested that he make inquiries in the pub a few doors along the street. After the fiasco of the search of the quarry lochan, he knew that for everyone else Rachel Croft's absence from home was going to be accepted as voluntary, a protest against her husband's adultery. Some time would have to pass before anyone would take it seriously again. The difference between him and the rest of them was that he was sure the man he had seen committing a violent assault outside that pub was Barry Croft: the same Barry Croft whom he'd seen emerging from the close behind him.

He walked along the pavement until he was at the pub entrance. If he'd asked himself at any point on his way along the pavement, he would have said he was just about to cross the street and go up to his flat. He was hungry and wondered what there was in the flat to eat. He could get rolls in the corner shop and there were tins of beans in the cupboard under the microwave and he seemed to recall a pack of pork sausages on the otherwise empty top shelf of the fridge. As he tried to work out how long the sausages might have been there, his feet carried him into the pub.

There were three men at a table in the corner, two men at the bar, a man behind the bar. All of them took a look at him as he came in. His height made him conspicuous and he was used to being checked out, but something in the glance of the bartender made him suspect that at least some of the locals had identified him as a policeman; might even, if they'd seen his picture in the paper, know his rank.

The bartender admitted that he remembered the incident, but didn't know the name of the young man who had been attacked.

"Even though he'd been drinking in here just before it happened?"

"It was a busy night. He wasn't a regular."

Meldrum wasn't in any doubt that he was lying. He ordered a whisky, left money on the counter when the barman "forgot" to charge for it, and took it to a table.

No sooner had he sat down than one of the men at the bar walked over with his pint and joined him.

"Take the weight off my legs," he said. "I can't stand for too long."

Meldrum took a sip of whisky and watched him over the rim of the glass. He could have been any age between the middle fifties and into his seventies. A lean man with thinning grey hair and a mouth like a razor slash in a long dough-white face. "Not a regular, my arse. The boy Hughie was in here every night. He didn't have far to go." He laughed and coughed. "He lives up the next close."

"Did he have a second name?"

"Hughie Mallon. Nice enough boy if you get him away from the crowd. But away from the crowd there's nothing to him. Fancied himself as a fighter. But he's like the rest of them. He's never done a day's hard graft in his life. How could he be a fighting man? My father started as a labourer at fourteen. He wouldn't have needed to chin Hughie — he'd have put him down with the skip of his bunnet. I tell a lie — wi' the *draught* from the skip of his bunnet." And he broke off into the same laugh that ended in a bout of hard coughing. "No wonder the boy finished up in hospital."

"He's in hospital?"

"So I hear."

"Which one?"

Instead of answering, the man looked round and caught the barman's eye. He pointed at Meldrum's whisky glass and jerked a thumb at his own emptied pint.

Turning back, he asked, "Going to take him grapes?"

"Something like that."

174

"He's in the Royal."

Mallon, Meldrum thought. The name he'd just seen on the new brass plate on the door of the flat on the third landing.

He was still thinking about that when the barman came over with the whisky and the pint. Again there was the same turning away as if he didn't expect to get paid; again Meldrum produced a note and held it out. The man opposite looked on with the indifference of a spectator.

Taking a first pull at his pint, he nodded at the departing barman. "Big Hamish can't afford to shoot his mouth off. Doesn't want to look too cosy with your lot. Wouldn't help business and there's some rough folk come in here."

"Doesn't seem to worry you," Meldrum said, genuinely curious.

The thin lips spread in a humourless smile. With his left hand, he touched his back and belly. The long fingers ended in dirty nails bitten down to the quick.

"I'm riddled wi' the big C. See, if somebody kicked my head in, they'd be doing me a favour."

CHAPTER
THIRTY-FIVE

Visiting hour was almost over. As he went along the ward corridor, people were already getting up from beside beds in the small rooms and lifting chairs back against the walls. "Second from the end," the nurse had said. "Near the station where we can keep an eye on him. He's been a bad boy. Tried to go to the toilet in the middle of the night and took a fall. So he's had a second operation and caught an infection. Chances are he'll be left with a limp."

Only one of the four beds was occupied.

He leant in and asked, "Hughie?"

The face turned slowly on the pillow.

"Do I know you?"

He went in and came to the side of the bed, lifting a chair with him. Just before he sat down, he unhooked the notes sheet from the frame at the end of the bed.

"Splintered tibia and broken ankle," he murmured. "That must have been some smack he brought you down with."

"I wouldn't mind more ice-cream," the boy said.

"You've been dreaming." Little wonder, looking at the chart. The boy had the muddy unfocused gaze of someone full of painkillers.

"You knew him, didn't you, Hughie?"

"I did?"

"Whatever you shouted after him, really pissed him off. What was it you shouted?"

"My father was in last night."

"You live with your father?"

"Saw him as clear as you. I think he held my hand too."

"Why not? He'd be sorry to see you in here."

"Don't be fucking daft," the boy said. "He's been dead for years."

"You trying to be funny?"

Meldrum's spurt of temper passed at once as he leant forward and looked into the boy's face.

"Maybe he wasnae here, eh? Awful clear though."

"Forget your father. Think about the man who attacked you outside the pub. You knew him, didn't you?"

"Never saw him before."

"I don't believe that, Hughie. He came out of your close."

The boy shut his eyes. "I'm going to have a wee sleep."

"Still living with your mother?"

The boy's eyelids quivered.

"You have your sleep, and I'll go and talk to your mother. She'll be able to tell me how well she knows him."

Hugh Mallon heaved as if trying to sit up. "Leave her alone!"

"What's going on here?" the nurse asked.

Meldrum sat back and smiled up at her. "Just on?" he asked. "Police — I explained to the other nurse. I wanted to have a word with Mr Mallon about the assault."

"I don't think so. You've got him in a state. Have you spoken to the doctor?"

Meldrum stood up.

"I'll be back, Hughie," he said quietly.

The boy, however, had closed his eyes again, squeezing them tight to shut the world out.

When he got back to his flat, he found a torch at the back of the hall cupboard and went straight out again. The unlit stairs were navigated faster with the help of the torch and he wasted no time in getting to the refurbished door on the top landing with the shiny new brass plate: JC MALLON.

This time when he rang the bell he heard noises within and a moment later a fat old woman in a wraparound apron opened the door.

"Mrs Mallon?"

"What do you want?"

"I'm Detective Inspector Meldrum. I've just been visiting your son in hospital. Could I come inside?"

"What's he telling you?" She took him by the sleeve and drew him along the hall. "You don't want to pay any mind to him. He's just a silly boy. He got into a fight, he'll say anything."

The room she took him into was full of shabby furniture dominated by a new television set with a screen big enough to entertain a small cinema audience.

"Nice," Meldrum said. "You get a great picture."

"S'all right," she said reluctantly, dividing her attention between him and the screen.

"Better than all right." He bent to look at the box under the TV table. "No good having a great set, though, unless you have the programmes. Sky?" He smiled as she nodded grudgingly. "The full package, eh? All the channels. I'll bet you enjoy it."

"Never said I didn't."

"When did you get it?"

She stared blankly. He watched her mind working. At one point she seemed to be on the point of volunteering something then gave up.

"Same time as you got the door done? What else did you get?"

"I didn't ask for anything. Somebody gives you . . . I didn't ask for any of it."

"So who was Santa Claus?"

"Big fellow came to see me. Asked what I'd like. Something to make you comfortable, like, he said."

"He have a name?"

"Don't remember."

"What about 'Barry'?"

"Don't think so."

"You're telling me you don't know anybody called Barry?"

"No."

"I'm not saying there's anything wrong in knowing him. Tell you what. I'm wondering if he might be a relative? You have a relative called Barry?"

"I don't know what you're on about. His name was Kevin."

"Who was?"

"The big fellow that came to the door. Something to make you comfortable, he said."

"And this would be just after Hughie had his legs broken? Am I right?"

"It wasn't anything to do with Hughie. Hughie's name never crossed his lips. I never asked for anything."

Meldrum stood up abruptly. Ignoring her flinch of withdrawal he went out into the hall. There were two bedrooms. In one there was a new bed with a mass of pink bedding. In the other, the boy's, a new player, piles of CDs and a games console caught his eye, the mother's suggestions for her son's homecoming at a guess. Nothing seemed to have been done to the kitchen, unless the big microwave was also new.

When he went back in, she hadn't moved.

"No wonder you thought it was Christmas," he said. "And all given to you for nothing."

"I blame myself." She stared up with faded blue eyes. "I knew fine I shouldn't have had the door done up. But I was tired of the way it looked. I just wanted it to be nice for once in my life."

He sat down again and said softly, "So explain it to me. You've never heard of Barry. That's right, that's what you said? And this Kevin, where had you seen him before?"

"I'd never seen him before."

"Either you're daft or you think I am. Someone you've never seen before turns up on the doorstep and buys you a TV and a new bed and all that stuff in Hughie's room?"

"Hughie'll love it."

"That's nice. Will he not get a surprise when he comes home and sees it?"

"Oh, aye."

"Did Kevin leave a message for him?"

"No." She ducked her head and gave him an upward glance full of stupid cunning.

The thought occurred to him that if he threatened to take away the Sky box she might find her tongue. That might be the worst threat she could imagine. To be left with no distraction from the place she lived and the life she lived and who she was.

With a sigh he got to his feet.

Over his shoulder as he went, he said, "Enjoy your programme," and glimpsed her look of relief at having outsmarted him.

His head was still full of what had happened with the old woman as he stepped out of the close. It was raining again, a thin curtain of smirn that hung like a veil across the street. As he stepped off the pavement, he saw a woman getting out of a car double-parked by the opposite pavement. In the same instant that he realised it was his daughter Betty, he recognised the red Mondeo and the outline of the driver at the wheel. Neither of them had seen him.

CHAPTER
THIRTY-SIX

He closed the street door behind him, holding it all the way so that it shut softly. Noiselessly he paced to the foot of the stairs, then stood for some moments listening before he began to climb. He expected her to be as he'd found her before outside his door sitting on the stone stairs, but he met her coming down from the second landing.

"Oh," she said, startling, then turned and began to go up again with him. "I'd given up," she said. "I tried earlier but you weren't in then either."

As always, once the door was open she made her way into the tiny front room with its distinctively curved outer wall that looked down onto the unending clamour of Leith Walk.

He sat down opposite her and asked, "What were you doing in the car with McGuigan?"

"Nothing," she said, and he heard the authentic sound of her childhood denials of wrongdoing. "I mean I saw him as I came out of the close. You weren't here and I was going to walk around for a bit. He'd been to the shop on the corner for a paper. I asked him where you were."

"I didn't think you knew him."

"Maybe I wouldn't have recognised him, if my head hadn't been full of you. I've seen the two of you side by side in a police car. Once at the lights in Princes Street, you were held up, but you didn't see me standing in the crowd waiting for the lights to change. I'd never spoken to him before."

"You'd only seen him once?"

"I didn't say that. More than once. He's an easy man to remember."

Handsome McGuigan.

"So you remembered him," he said, unsuccessful at keeping the inquisitor's note out of his voice.

"He was surprised you weren't up in the flat. He'd just dropped you. He thought you'd just be a minute. He suggested I wait in the car. We sat for a while. I was embarrassed because I was keeping him from his dinner. We were both hungry so we went for something to eat."

He tried to work it out: he'd seen them pulling away from the close and he'd gone to talk to Hughie Mallon in the hospital, then he'd come back and talked to the boy's mother. How long had all that taken him?

For something to say, he asked, "What did you do? A fish supper in the car?"

"Of course not!"

Why, of course not? McGuigan had more style than that, was that what she was suggesting?

Instead of asking where they'd gone, he said, "It must have been a long meal."

But she was no longer to be diverted. Throwing up her hands in protest, she cried, "Please, stop this and listen to me. I had to see you tonight!"

Still trying to come to terms with her encounter with McGuigan, his response was almost automatic, "Why?"

"Bobbie isn't dead."

"Not dead? Did —" What was his name? The American detective. "Finn? Did Finn phone you?"

"I've seen and talked to him. Bobbie's in Edinburgh."

Despite the shock, his mind moved in the routines of long habit.

"What does he say happened? Why'd he disappear?"

She appeared to be struggling to find words.

"He didn't say? He didn't have any explanation?"

"I tried to make sense of it. I lay awake all last night thinking it over. In the morning all I could think of was coming to see you."

"Tell me then."

She looked at him helplessly.

"I can't help until you tell me." He waited. "Either tell me or tell the police in Phoenix."

"He doesn't want to do that!"

"One of you will have to tell them." At the moment, all that he cared about was that she kept on the right side of the law. If anything was wrong, he didn't want her drawn into it.

"I'm seeing him tomorrow. If I tell you where we're meeting, will you be there? If you listen to him, you'll know what to do."

As he tried desperately to calculate what would be best, he saw her eyes fill with tears.

"Please, Daddy," she said.

CHAPTER
THIRTY-SEVEN

The face lit when he pressed the button, and he tilted the alarm to read: 5.30. He'd been lying awake, but it was too early to get up. He'd been told that Betty and her husband had arranged to meet at half twelve. He lay trying to decide what to do. It was a measure of his difficulty that he considered phoning in sick. With what? What was severe enough to keep you at home one day and be back at work the next? It was impossible for him to imagine being off for more than a day. There was so much to do. He hadn't reported sick for any reason in a long time. What had it been for that time? He lay counting the scars on his body. It must take courage to be a surgeon and cut. To be cut all it took was to breathe deeply and sink into sleep. He looked at the alarm again: 5.36.

By half eleven in the morning, Meldrum was tired, an unusual feeling for a man of his physique and temperament. He had gone to work, of course, and spent the morning going through the motions of investigating one of those assaults which is serious in its results for the victim but otherwise without interest, since the assailant was quickly identified, his crime the product of alcohol and the intelligence level of a humanoid chimpanzee.

To hours of sleeplessness broken by dozing made uneasy by dreams, he'd added a constant underlying strain as he tried to find some way of keeping his promise to Betty. At intervals, he felt McGuigan's eyes on him and knew the sergeant was waiting for the storm to break. Perversely, he stuck to the business in hand and refused to show any curiosity about the previous night.

The solution to the problem of the promise he couldn't break was abrupt and unpredicted. As they came to a halt among the other police vehicles at St Leonards, he said, "You get the paperwork started. I won't be long till I'm back." He waited for the sergeant to move but, when he didn't, heard himself going on, "I want to talk to Barry Croft again. It would be better if I did it on my own."

What was it Billy Ord, his first boss long dead of cancer, the old superintendent who'd taught him the tricks of their odd trade, had said? *Never explain, never apologise*. It worked, though. The normally difficult McGuigan had got out of the car without a word. Perhaps he had a bad conscience.

As soon as he walked into the restaurant, he saw Betty at a table on the lower deck by the window. To the waitress who'd come forward, he said, "It's all right. I see my friends are here."

The man had his back to the room. He was wearing a leather jerkin and had a full head of very black hair.

"Can I join you?" Meldrum asked.

As the man looked up, Meldrum saw that his eyes, widening with surprise, were a very pale shade of luminous blue.

"Don't tell me," he said.

Before Betty could respond, Meldrum sat down.

"I thought better of you," the man said to Betty.

"This is my father," she said.

"Like in the song," he said looking at Meldrum.

"What song would that be?"

"Her heart belongs to Daddy. Some women are like that. It doesn't make for a good marriage."

"Is a good marriage what you're planning to have?" Meldrum wondered.

As he waited for an answer the waitress brought a menu.

"I can recommend the fish pie," the man said.

"That would do," Meldrum said, handing back the menu.

"I think you've just spoilt my plan for the afternoon," the man said.

"What would that be?"

"Same as yesterday." He smiled across the table at Betty. "We were going to screw our brains out."

"Bobbie!" she said.

Looking at her, though, Meldrum was in no doubt about what they'd been doing yesterday.

"You know I'm a policeman?" Meldrum asked.

"They haven't passed a law against a husband screwing his wife?" Bobbie said.

Keeping his temper, Meldrum concentrated on the man's smile. Very white teeth. Very even. American dentistry.

"Please," Betty said. "I don't want it to be like this! I haven't told my father anything. I wanted you to tell him."

At that moment, the waitress brought the main courses for Betty and her husband, some kind of pie in a server for him and a pizza for her. As the man poked under the piecrust, lumps of meat showed through thick brown gravy.

"Beef and ale pie, they call it," Bobbie said with a smile. He took a forkful up to his mouth. Chewing he said, "Mushrooms in there too. That's not bad." He nodded at Betty. "She's stuck on pizza. She ate better Stateside. Do you have a Mexican restaurant in the city, sir?"

Meldrum grunted what could be taken as confirmation.

"I'm going to take her to a Mexican restaurant. Get chicken or beef wrapped in a tortilla. Cream. Guacamole. Be just like when we were in Phoenix, eh? That's the last pizza I'm going to let her have. I'd be ashamed to buy you one next time." And he laughed displaying white even teeth. "Or a Japanese restaurant. That would be good too. We ate well in Phoenix. Why not? After all it was our honeymoon."

Moments later Meldrum's fish pie came, and he began to fork up the mashed potato-and-cheddar crust. They ate in a silence Meldrum was determined the man would break first. When, however, Betty began to show signs of distress, he gave in.

"You've something to tell me?"

Bobbie nodded and, intently chewing, continued to excavate his pie.

"Why did you disappear? My daughter had a phone call saying you were dead."

"All in good time. Let's finish our meal and go back to my place. We can talk easier there."

"No!" Betty said sharply.

That same white smile. "We don't have to use my room, honey. Though the bed'll be made, of course. No, there's a sitting room for guests. This time of day we'll have it to ourselves."

When Betty looked at him, Meldrum gave the smallest of nods. He needed whatever advantage he could find, and there should after all be an advantage in finding where Bobbie Conway was staying.

CHAPTER
THIRTY-EIGHT

It was the most depressing room he had ever sat in, and he had the unhappy feeling he would remember it for the rest of his life. The furniture, five imitation-leather easy chairs, a scatter of side tables, one laden with magazines, an undersized television, was presentable enough. It had somehow, however, the air of having been bought as a job lot, and a glance showed the magazines to be not only out of date but the kind of golf and motoring publications that found their way into dentists' waiting rooms. It would be a sad fate to be alone there, and it was hard to imagine it being shared.

"Consultancy," Meldrum said in a tone of careful neutrality. It was the first word he'd spoken in ten minutes, and had been produced since he felt some kind of response was needed for Betty's sake. Conway had just described the man he'd worked with when he began his career, a Russian expert "so old the Consultancy wanted to retire him, but the Soviets liked to look a man in the eye when they did business. If they trusted you and they trusted him, they'd do it on a handshake not a contract." It was the kind of detail Meldrum associated with falsity and as he listened his gloomy concern for his daughter grew like a weight in his chest.

"Don't let the word give you the wrong idea. You won't find us in an office tower in any downtown. It's more of a loose arrangement. And some people you'd see in *Forbes* magazine might be part of it and people in firms you'll never have heard of and politicians you know from the headlines. We advise, we go and look, we go in and help. In some ways, it's like what mercenary soldiers do." He gave a smile that had plenty of teeth but not much humour. "You could call us the mercenaries of capitalism. So consultancy isn't the ideal description. It might even be —" He paused in search of the right word.

"Misleading?" Meldrum suggested.

"Exactly. But it's what we call it. You talked to Matt Crais?"

Thrown by the change of direction, Meldrum had to think for a moment.

"The guy who invited me to the wedding," Conway insisted. "Where Betty and I met."

"I spoke to him on the phone."

"He'd give you some bland runaround, but he's part of it. I've known him off and on for ten years, but we were never close, not what you'd call real close. That's why when he invited me to his wedding, I knew they were on to me. Inviting me to his wedding was a mistake." He glanced at his wife. "Luckiest mistake of my life, though. I knew that as soon as I saw Betty."

Meldrum too glanced at Betty and looked away at once for there was a response in her face that he didn't want to see.

He asked, "On to you? What does that mean?"

"I'd committed to giving evidence at the trial. I'd been promised no one would know until the moment I walked into court."

"Trial? I've no idea what you're talking about."

"I'm talking about the money that went astray in Iraq. Not millions but billions of dollars. It's hard even with massive incompetence to lose that much — and little bits of one-firm-at-a-time fraud wouldn't cut it. For what happened, special advice, special expertise, was needed. I'm talking about the Consultancy."

Of course you are, Meldrum thought, his face carefully expressionless. Somewhere a long time ago, he'd been told of an American psychiatrist who cured a schizophrenic by joining wholeheartedly in his delusion, the theory being that there wouldn't be room for both of them in a one-man-sized fantasy. Drawing a hint from that, he determined to take what he was being told at face value in the hope of exposing for Betty what nonsense Conway's story had to be.

"I don't understand," Meldrum said, "if this conspiracy —"

"Consultancy," Conway interrupted; Meldrum's sharp glance catching not the hint of smile.

"If it's been around for as long as you say, it should have been in court before this."

192

"Money's a great way of staying out of court. And it's always had friends in high places."

"All right, if it's that powerful —"

"Don't be in any doubt about that."

"Then why now? What's changed that it could be in trouble?"

"I've asked myself that. Some kind of split at the top? Somebody in the Administration covering his back? How would I know? I'm a cog in the wheel, low man on the totem pole."

"If you're as unimportant as that, why should your evidence matter?"

"You know better than that. Your father knows better than that," he said to Betty. "When you're giving evidence, it's not how powerful you are, it's what you know. It won't only be me, there'll be others, like pieces in a jigsaw puzzle. But I've been told if I don't turn up in court the bit that matters will be missing. That's why two Federal Marshals were in town for Crais's wedding. They were there to look after me." The remarkable pale eyes had been holding Meldrum's gaze. Now he looked again at Betty. "You know that's true. You've met them."

"Finn and his partner!"

Meldrum tried to combat the conviction this seemed to carry for her. He asked, "You're claiming that the detectives my daughter met in Phoenix were your Federal Marshals?" He made no effort to keep the scepticism out of his voice.

But it was Betty who said, "I knew they were different. They weren't like ordinary policemen."

"If they were looking out for you, why did you run away?"

"I was advised I should take off. Don't ask who gave me the tip. I won't tell you and anyway the name wouldn't mean anything to you."

Despite his self-control, Meldrum's voice rose as he asked, "Why the hell did you have to involve my daughter?"

"I don't blame you for being angry. But think about it. They found me so quickly because Betty was with me. On my own, maybe they wouldn't have. Maybe I wouldn't even have gone to Phoenix. I didn't marry Betty to help me hide." He got up and sat on the arm of her chair and said as she looked up at him, "I married Betty because I fell in love with her."

Looking at her face, Meldrum knew that he had lost the chance to make her see the truth; for the moment, he promised himself, for the moment.

"For your own sake," he said quietly, "I'd advise you to get in touch with the Phoenix police. As far as they're concerned, you're a missing person who deserted my daughter."

"Betty told you about the man who came to the flat looking for me!" Conway protested. "I knew he had to be from the Consultancy. Since they'd found me, I'd no choice but to run. There was no way I was going to put Betty in danger by taking her with me."

"So why are you here?" Got you, Meldrum thought. It seemed so obvious to him that the man could have no answer to that.

"Because I couldn't stay away." He ran the tips of his fingers down Betty's cheek and along the line of her jaw. He told her, "Missing you was driving me crazy."

Meldrum had the illusion as he watched that her skin shivered under Conway's touch.

CHAPTER
THIRTY-NINE

He could phone the Phoenix police himself, he thought as he drove down Lothian Road. There was the mystery of the body they'd found and identified as that of Wilbur Conway. "They"? Had the finding and identification of that body really been done by the Police Department? Who was James Finn? Meldrum's profession which instructed him to contact the police was at odds with the uneasiness of his instinct that there was something wrong out there in Arizona. He disliked doing anything until he was sure of his ground. "Give me four weeks till the trial," Conway had asked. "I'm safer here than going home." Perhaps in that time he could persuade Betty that they were dealing with a confidence man. He needed time to save her from herself. He forced his mind away from the last image of her standing in the hall of the boarding house with Conway's arm around her.

He had been driving automatically and so when he spotted a parking place and wrenched the wheel round to slide into the space, he took a moment to recognise the bright arch of the entrance opposite. He'd told McGuigan that he'd been going to interview Barry

196

Croft again; and the lie had led him to the place where he could turn it into a truth.

It was only on his way up to the second floor that he realised there had been no new development to justify his interviewing Croft again. Even as he tried to put his thoughts in order the escalator hurried him upwards.

It was a relief when the manageress, the same woman to whom he'd spoken on his first visit, told him that Barry Croft wasn't in the shop. "No," she said, "we're not expecting him later. Not today. Wednesday's his day for meeting people."

I wonder what kind of people he meets? Meldrum asked himself and looked at her in silence until she made an unexpected response.

"For a minute, when I saw you," she said, "I thought you'd come about Mrs Hodge. But then I knew someone like you wouldn't be dealing with it. I did think, that was quick!"

"Dealing with what?"

That morning she had caught one of the cleaners committing theft. She had tried to contact Mr Croft but had got no answer. On her own initiative, she had contacted the police, and had given the details to two policemen who had promised to get back in touch.

"And this Mrs Hodge, did they arrest her?"

"I don't know what's happened. She'd walked out before they arrived. I certainly wasn't going to try to stop her! I don't know what Mr Croft will say when he hears about it."

It was a question that intrigued Meldrum also, not least since one of the names he'd glimpsed by torchlight on a darkened landing had been HODGE.

Hours later, having worked what was left of the afternoon and fended off McGuigan's curiosity about his supposed interview with Croft, Meldrum played his torch on the nameplate and confirmed that his memory had not deceived him. It was on the first landing with the boarded-up window and the broken lights. He put his finger on the bell and kept it there until the door was opened.

"Police," he said at once and as the woman backed away made his way into the flat, following her into the front room. Again there was the odd mixture he'd seen upstairs of old furniture and new; including a television with an outsize screen. This time he leant down and switched it off.

Into the silence he said, "You know why I'm here."

"I haven't done anything wrong."

She was fifty if she was a day. Her hair was full and too black, the shade suggesting a home kit for dying. She wasn't exceptionally plain, but unlike the Violet Terrys of this world the largest feature on her face wasn't her mouth but her nose.

"I've been to the shop," Meldrum said. "I'm told you left before the police arrived."

"She shouldn't have done that. I told her Mr Croft would sort it out in the morning."

"Barry," Meldrum said.

She kept control of her expression but her eyes widened.

"Mr Croft," she said.

"So how will he explain in the morning? What will he say?"

"It was a present."

"Mr Croft will say he gave you an expensive piece of jewellery as a present?"

"No."

"No? He'll deny giving you it?"

"It wasn't him."

"How many rich men do you know?"

"I don't know any rich men!"

"So you got the jewellery from Barry Croft?"

She sat down as if her knees had given way under her. Her brows were pulled together in puzzlement. As she spoke, she wrung her hands together in her lap.

"Somebody else gave me it. But it wasn't expensive. It looks nice but it's not real. It's imitation. That's what I told her." And then to his surprise she said, "I'll show you."

When she came back, a first glance persuaded him, but he took his time, holding the stones up to the light, checking the settings, since he wanted to be sure.

"I'm not a jeweller," he said, "but I'd take a bet this was real."

"Are you kidding me?" she cried. She took it back from him and turned it in her hands. In contrast to what she was holding, he was conscious of the red coarseness of her hands. He had not a shadow of a doubt that she'd been ignorant of the value of the present she'd been given. "Why would he do that to me?"

"Are we talking about Barry Croft?"

But on that point she kept a stubborn silence.

"Why did the police not take this away with them?"

"Nobody's been here but you. I've been out all day."

"I'll give you a note of my name. If they come, tell them I've taken it."

Again he wondered, with even more curiosity than before, what Barry Croft would say in the morning.

CHAPTER
FORTY

Croft headed north as if he was going into Edinburgh, but after five miles took the turn to the left. The road that climbed into the hills took a sharp curve to the south so that when he came to a stop hard against a farm gate he knew he was siting above the village. When he got out, it was dark, the half moon lost in low heavy cloud cover. It took an effort to lift the old rucksack he'd taken from the boot over the gate, and his breath began to come heavily as he set out over broken ground to the edge of the quarry. He had weighted the rucksack with stones so that it would sink in the water and it pulled him to one side until he cradled it in both arms and carried it like a child.

His intention had been to throw it over at once and get back to the car. It would be foolhardy to hang about, though the road was rarely used even in daylight and there was little chance of anyone coming along at two in the morning. Despite common sense, however, he found himself down on his knees fumbling with the straps until he had the top thrown back. The dress was white and the blood that had come from her mouth and nose showed black against it in the dim light. Her watch was under it and he had pushed in her handbag and the underwear she had been wearing for they had buried her naked. As he fumbled with the clothes, he imagined that he caught the scent of her body and shuddered as he held her underpants against his face.

He had been lucky. If he had thrown the rucksack into the water the night of the burial as he had intended, then it would have been there for Meldrum's divers to find and he would now be in jail accused of murder. At the last moment he had been unable to get rid of her clothes, however, and instead had taken the shovel to the edge of the quarry and thrown it over in a fit of revulsion.

Now the clothes she had died in were gone, and she had gone into a grave under the earth anonymous among rows of others.

BOOK FIVE

DON'T MISS ME TOO LITTLE

CHAPTER
FORTY-ONE

Croft found having the Russian there almost unbearable. Just after the fall of the Soviet Union, he'd taken a van and made a trip to St Petersburg where he'd found the Russian through a contact in the trade and made the return trip with a variety of items up for grabs in the new confusion, shrewdly chosen and worth a small fortune. Like every other piece of trade with that benighted city in that wretched country, though, things had quickly turned sour; and the last thing he needed in the present circumstances was to have the man turn up out of the blue and ask to stay. "Just for two nights. I'll be going to London on Saturday." He was about fifty and had put on weight, stones rather than pounds by the look of him; not a tall man, it seemed a fair bet that he measured nearly as much round the waist now as he did in height. Even sitting down, his lips hung open as he panted softly for breath.

"I'm not in the market for icons," Croft said.

"Suppose I told you I have three Andrei Rublevs and two by Dionisius."

"I'd be sceptical."

"And you'd be right." He laughed with what might have been real amusement, though it faded quickly into wheezing. "But I was close at one point," he said wistfully. "I had all of an iconostasis from a monastery in Georgia, which enjoyed special protection from that atheist Stalin. I thought my fortune was made but I was told I could have the collection or my head but not both."

"Who told you that?"

"You wouldn't have met him. He was a great man for about seven years. Not any more. Since Putin our great men tend to come and go - go more than come, maybe." He lifted his head as the storm battered a squall of rain against the window, then looked again into the fire. "Can I stay?"

"It's only the middle of the afternoon."

"I've come a long way. I did the last stretch without a break. Forty hours of driving."

"That was stupid."

"I'm not an old woman. Can I stay?"

"Till tomorrow morning."

"I wouldn't be here if the man I came to see hadn't been out of town. I don't have to be back in London till Saturday."

"You'll have to leave with me in the morning. I'll be away by eight."

"Don't you wonder why I came to see you? Believe me, it could be a piece of luck for you."

Before Croft could answer, however, there was a ring at the outside door. For some reason, the sound startled them, it seemed almost equally. Like conspirators, they sat staring at one another until a second ring brought Croft to his feet.

206

The Russian as he waited strained his head forward, patting his forehead with a white handkerchief as he listened for voices. As two women came into the room, he struggled to his feet.

"Oh!" The older woman stopped abruptly. "I didn't know you had a visitor."

"Just till the morning," the Russian said smiling at her.

"You're a friend then?"

"A business friend."

Coming in after them, Croft said to him, "These are my in-laws. You'd be bored. There's a little sitting room upstairs. Why don't you wait there?"

Looking at the quite remarkable breasts of the younger woman, a redhead with a trailing scarf knotted at her throat, the Russian nodded regretfully. He went into the hall and marched upstairs, before turning on the landing and coming down again. For a fat man, he moved very quietly. He waited until he heard a woman's voice raised above normal then turned the handle and let the door settle open a fraction. It was something he had done before; mostly it went unnoticed; if it didn't, he was a man without embarrassment.

The older woman was speaking. ". . . imagine why. What kind of quarrel would prevent her getting in touch for so long? I can understand a few days —"

Croft's voice interrupted her. "She has plenty of money. You know that. If she wants to stay away for a bit, what's to stop her?"

"What did you quarrel about?"

"Nothing important."

"Nothing important! I'm sorry, Barry, but surely that can't be true. You two have always got on so well. Has she ever done anything like this before?"

"We've quarrelled. We're not saints."

"Perhaps she's been kidnapped." It was the younger woman, the one with the red hair and the extravagant length of scarf. Her voice was carefully low in tone, a voice studied for effect, not least when being ironical. "Do you think I'd be here if I hadn't been kidnapped? To be honest, I don't much mind where Rachel is! Mummy only told me in the car we were coming here. If I'd had the nerve I'd have opened the door and jumped out!"

"Did you feel you needed company, Maggie?" Croft asked. "I'm disappointed in you."

"Of course not. Sylvia is being silly. Sometimes she talks wildly. It's because she's an artist."

"I don't know why you didn't come by yourself," he complained. "I've always thought we got on well."

"It's because she's afraid of you," Sylvia said, her tone a touch lower and more thrilling. "From the way she talks, I've always sensed that."

"Nonsense!" her mother cried. "You can be such a silly girl! It's not true. I've always . . . Dear Barry, you were so kind to me when Ken died."

"If you speak of Daddy," the younger woman cried, "wasn't I heartbroken?" There was a brief silence, then she said, "I was the one who was close to Daddy." Her voice had so shed its affectation that the fat man wished he could see inside the room.

Again for the listener there was an infuriating spell of silence, before Croft said, "Anyway she's not here. You can see that for yourself."

"Can I see her room?"

"For God's sake!"

"What harm could it do?" The older woman's voice sounded high and thin as if he'd startled her. More calmly, she went on, "I could tell something by the clothes she's taken. A man never notices such things."

If there had been a flash of temper from Croft, he had mastered it at once. His voice came quietly, "I don't think there's any need for amateur detective work. She's gone off. She'll come back when it suits her. And no, you can't go upstairs."

"Perhaps we should go to the police," Sylvia said.

The other two responded more or less together. As the mother was saying, "Oh, I'm sure not," Croft said, "Do what you want."

"The police have already been to see me, Sylvia," the mother said as if anxious to prevent her from making a mistake.

"And me." Her daughter sounded grim. "All the same, you could go and see them. They might be glad to hear from you."

Croft said, "What the hell is it to do with you? You haven't spoken to Rachel in years."

"I didn't say I would go. Mummy would go."

"You asked me if there had been a quarrel." His voice was fainter. Perhaps he had turned to speak to the mother. "The police know why she walked out. She caught me fucking one of our neighbours."

"Poor Rachel."

"You don't sound surprised."

"Don't let it break up your marriage. People let that happen too easily now."

"She took it well. Went upstairs, packed a case and walked out. Come up and look if you want to."

Taken by surprise, the Russian hadn't enough time to get upstairs. Instead he made the front door with little trotting steps and slipped outside.

He walked to the gate and looked up at the hills wreathed in grey mist. The wind had dropped but tired and hungry he shivered in the damp air and wondered about clambering inside his van to sit out of the cold. He had slid open the side door when he heard voices.

The two women were coming from the house. Conscious of Croft watching in the doorway, he knew that he needed an excuse for being outside. The van dipped as he got in and lifted a painted panel from behind one of the seats.

As he carried it to the house, the younger woman stared at him curiously.

On impulse, he turned it towards her.

"Here," he said. "You're an artist. Look at this."

She broke stride and came closer as he held the icon out to her.

"What is it?"

"Sylvia, please," her mother said. She sounded as though she might burst into tears.

"This isn't traditional icon," he said. "Look at the right hand of Christ the Redeemer. You know what he's doing? What the Americans call giving the finger. This is an icon by a young man who's only twenty-two. A young man who believes in nothing. He's been bought by — you wouldn't know the name — believe me, one of our very richest men. He is going to be famous. He'll like that. It's what he wants to be. Famous and rich."

The woman stared a moment more, then said, "I'm afraid it's not really my kind of thing."

He watched as they got into their car.

"Stupid woman," he said.

He turned at a sound behind him. Croft was gone. Hardly believing what had happened, he began to ring at the bell and then, cradling the icon against him, to bang on the door but it stayed shut against him until he gave up and set off again on his journey.

CHAPTER
FORTY-TWO

Being divided and obsessed at the same time was new to him. More often than not, a case that really involved him took over his life. It was an experience he'd observed in other detectives and even discussed with a few of them. But this time there was the thought of Betty and the mess she had got herself into, constant under everything like a pulse beat measuring time.

"Thanks," Bobbie Conway said. "I needed to get out. And anyway my landlady might not have been pleased if we'd stayed in. You do know you look like a cop?"

"I need to talk to you."

"Fine. What are you going to do? Just drive around?"

"Not in Edinburgh." Meldrum remembered how Betty had described watching McGuigan and him caught at the lights in Princes Street. "We'll take a run. Don't worry, I'll bring you back."

"As long as you haven't brought a spade in the trunk." Conway laughed softly. "Those hills look cold to be buried in."

"Don't talk nonsense."

"Hey, I didn't mean to offend you. I was just kidding."

As they went up Colinton Road, Meldrum realised he'd started to go too fast. He raised his foot and the indicator settled back under forty.

Conway broke the silence. "Maybe you make me nervous," he said. "You're a pretty intimidating guy."

"I've no interest in you. I just don't want Betty to be hurt."

"We're married all right. Don't make any mistake about that. I've got the wedding certificate to prove it. You should have asked. It's in my case."

"Why did you marry her?"

"Same reason she married me. It's what people do when they fall in love."

"Love," Meldrum said, surprising himself with the venom he put into the word. "You met her one day and married her the next. Love takes longer."

"Not for everybody. You never hear of love at first sight?"

As they left the city behind, the hills crowded close on the right.

"If we keep on this road," Meldrum said, "we'll come to a village. I was called out there not long ago. A man's wife disappeared."

"You find her?"

"We're looking."

"Not very hard, eh?"

"My colleagues think she's in hiding somewhere."

"Cops," Conway said dismissively. "She's probably run off with somebody else's husband."

"No. He killed her."

"You think?"

"I know."

They drove in silence the next few miles. Ahead of them the hills folded back one behind the other. From the flat land below, in a certain light they could be seen as a range of mountains.

At last, Conway said, "I wonder how many people are buried up there."

"It's poor soil. You'd have to work hard to get a spade into it."

"Are you trying to frighten me?"

Meldrum glanced at him in surprise. He didn't want to question Conway until they got to the inn, and had talked about Croft's case only because it was in his head all the time.

When he didn't get an answer, Conway began to whistle. "Recognise that? 'The Black Bear.' It's a pipe tune. My father was in the army. Before he got shot, he killed men in the desert and in Italy." He began to whistle again, and interrupted himself to ask, "You ever kill anybody?"

Meldrum tugged the wheel and they went into a road on the right. He knew if they went on it would take them up to the reservoir, but within a hundred yards they were pulling into the park at the side of the inn.

It was a quiet place, busiest at the weekends in fine weather. Now seated with coffees they had the tables at the back to themselves.

"I'm listening," Conway said.

214

"You tell a good story. I've met men who could tell a good story. Sometimes they even believed it themselves. Mostly they were con men."

"You don't believe Betty that a man came to our flat in Phoenix looking for me?"

"I'm counting that as one of the only two things I can be sure of."

"What's the other one?"

"Something made you go on the run." He held up an open hand and folded down first one finger then another. "A man came looking for you. That frightened you into running away. Two facts. And an unlikely story."

"What would you think was a likely one?"

"You've stolen money. You've run up gambling debts. Something to do with drugs. I'm a policeman, I go for simple explanations."

Conway sipped his coffee, pale blue eyes intent and unwavering. "You don't trust anybody. Your job's taught you to watch your back. So stick to the book. Pick up the phone. Talk to the police in America."

"You've been reading my mind."

"But you're also smart. Something about those guys in Phoenix doesn't sit right with you."

It was true. Not because I'm smart, Meldrum thought; maybe because I can't think straight for worrying about Betty.

"I'm only asking you for a little over three weeks," Conway said. "Like I told you before, I feel safe here. In three weeks I go to America for the trial. If everything goes right, then I can get on with the rest of my life. And that means looking after Betty and the kid."

"I won't let Betty go to America." Only after he'd spoken, did Meldrum realise how much he'd conceded.

Conway smiled. "Before the trial? After the trial? Ever?" he asked. "Could you really stop her doing what she wants?"

CHAPTER
FORTY-THREE

There weren't enough hours in the day. Like everyone else, his caseload was too heavy and now he was driven to keep after Barry Croft in his own time. When he phoned the hospital and learnt that Hughie Mallon had signed himself out, he took the torch and went visiting. The only consolation was that crossing the street from his flat wasn't far to go.

When Mrs Mallon opened the door she flinched at the sight of him.

"You shouldn't be here worrying him. He's not well enough to see you."

From the lobby behind her, he could hear the television, reminiscent of the decibels from a low-flying jet. Rather than struggling against the noise, he shook his head at her and went into the sitting room. When he switched off the set, the contrasting silence came with a mild shock.

"That's not right," the mother cried behind him. "You're the police, not the bloody Gestapo."

"Hello, Hughie," Meldrum said to the boy lying on the couch. "Couldn't keep away from the home comforts, eh?"

"He'd a hell of a time getting up the stairs," the mother said. "Big Hamish and one of the regulars had to give him a lift up. They were both pechan by the time they got here. Big Hamish said he was a stupid wee cunt for coming home before he was ready."

"He wouldn't be far wrong there," he said.

"Why don't you keep your fucking mouth shut?" the boy suggested to his mother.

"Big Hamish the barman," Meldrum said. "Who was the regular who gave him a hand?"

"Nobody."

"Tell you who it wouldn't be," Meldrum said. "The guy with cancer."

"Poor Peter Cross?" the mother said. "He was in my class at school."

"Face like a well-skelped arse," Meldrum said. "Doesn't look as if he's got long to go. He was the one told me about Barry Croft coming here."

"Barry what?" she said.

"You can tell that old shite, I'll sort him when I'm up," Hughie Mallon said.

The mother looked at him in alarm. "Don't even say that. He'd hurt you. He's hurt a lot of people."

The news didn't come as a surprise to Meldrum. "Right enough, son," he said. "I'd leave him well alone. Anyway, what would be the point? He's already told me how you spotted Croft visiting Mrs Hodge."

"How would he know that?" the mother cried. Although the boy told her again to shut her mouth, his heart it seemed was no longer in it.

218

"He was picked up by car, of course, so you couldn't follow him," Meldrum said. "It must have been frustrating. There you were with a nice chance to blackmail somebody who was obviously worth a bob or two but you didn't know who he was. And you were too stupid to ever find out. No wonder you lost your rag that night. What did you do — ask him if he was screwing her?"

"The old whore," the boy muttered.

"That what you called her? And then he broke your legs."

"He's a lunatic."

But now the mother was the one urging silence. "Tell him you're no' well. He's just raving, mister. It's all these tablets they gave him."

"Turned out well, though, didn't it, Hughie? Your mother got a telly out of it. Pity you'll walk with a limp the rest of your life." He bent and laid a hand on the plaster on the right leg. "And that it'll hurt every time the weather's cold." He straightened again and looked down at the boy who had his eyes fixed on his legs. "Do you want to let him get away with that?"

"You want a statement," the boy said at last. He spoke softly without lifting his head. "I'll give you a statement. I don't know anything. I've seen nothing. I'm saying nothing." He glanced up, a quick look and away again. "Legs are bad enough. Next time it could be my fucking arms."

Meldrum sighed. A stupid boy, but not unfortunately a complete half-wit.

CHAPTER
FORTY-FOUR

On leaving the Mallons, he'd intended to go in and talk to Mrs Hodge, but persistent ringing brought no answer. Either she was out or didn't answer late at night. Giving up, he'd made his usual solitary supper and gone to bed.

Next morning, just after he'd finished a case conference he had a surprising visitor.

"He knows the strangest people," Sylvia Lenzie said, settling herself into the chair in front of his desk. "He had some kind of foreigner there who was selling obscene pictures."

"How do you know that?" McGuigan asked. Meldrum thought obscene pictures a red herring, and regarded the sergeant's interest as his way of expressing a generalised scepticism about the value of spending more time on Barry Croft.

"He showed me."

Sensibly, McGuigan decided not to pursue that.

"I'm sure you didn't come to tell us about pictures," Meldrum said. "To be honest, I'm surprised you went to see him at all. If I understood you correctly, you've been at odds with your sister for many years — I seem

220

to remember you said you hadn't gone to her wedding."

"I'd never set eyes on the man until yesterday. My mother persuaded me to go with her — well, kidnapped me would be nearer the mark. I didn't know where we were going when I got into the car. But when I saw how worried she was —" She leant forward. "No. Do you know what it was? I saw that she was afraid to go and see him by herself. When I understood that, it made such a difference. Until that moment, I'd taken it for gospel all that stuff about how well she got on with him and how kind he'd been to her after Daddy died."

"You thought your mother was afraid of Croft?"

"She didn't have to put it into words. I'm an artist. I feel some things."

Meldrum looked at her sceptically. "Why was she so anxious to see him?"

"Oh, come on!" she said. "Do I need to spell it out? Why did you come out to the art exhibition to see *me*? Because you believed something might have happened to Rachel. And I sent you away with a flea in your ear. I'm sorry now that I did that. I'm here to tell you that I've changed my mind. When I talked to you before, I hadn't seen him. I hadn't been to his house. I hadn't been in their bedroom. I could *feel* something was wrong. There was evil in that room. Something had happened there." Her voice deepened thrillingly. "I found myself looking for a bloodstain on the walls."

There was a protracted pause. McGuigan broke it by asking matter-of-factly, "Did you see one?"

"Of course not," she said dismissively.

"So you don't have anything except a feeling," McGuigan said.

Conscious of the sergeant's glance, Meldrum didn't have much choice about taking up the point. "We've already interviewed Mr Croft," he said. "He's been quite frank about the circumstances of his wife's going off, and we've no reason to disbelieve his account."

Contempt dripping from every syllable, she said, "I should have thought being caught in the act of adultery was rather more than 'circumstances' whether he was frank about it or not."

"How do you know about the adultery?"

"He was quite shameless about admitting it. He told us that Rachel caught him making love to a neighbour."

"Did he seem angry about that?"

"As I said, shameless. He didn't seem angry."

"Our difficulty," Meldrum said, "would be the lack of motive."

"You don't call adultery a motive!"

"For the injured partner perhaps. But that would be your sister in this case, and we know that Croft hasn't been murdered."

McGuigan made a little humming noise. Meldrum recognised it as something he did when struck by an idea and paused to give him a chance to speak. He said, "By going away and staying away, though, she must have known that suspicion would fall on him. Maybe she's doing it to punish him." His slight boredom had been replaced by an alert interest. There was nothing McGuigan enjoyed more than his own cleverness.

Meldrum let him enjoy his moment, though the obvious objection had occurred to him at once that the anonymous letter which had drawn their attention to her disappearance hadn't been written by her but by Peter Tarleton.

"Another possibility," he said, "might be if the man caught committing adultery was in love with the woman and wanted to get rid of his partner. That doesn't seem to be the case here."

"I don't see how you can be sure of that!"

Meldrum shook his head. "I'm afraid that's not something we can discuss with you. I'm sure you understand."

"I'm sure," said Sylvia Lenzie, who although a lady sometimes allowed herself the freedom due to the artistic temperament, "I bloody well don't!"

CHAPTER
FORTY-FIVE

Although before her abrupt departure, Sylvia Lenzie made no secret of how unsatisfactory she found the interview, her appearance as a concerned relative had the effect of allowing Meldrum to justify a second call on Violet Terry.

A comparatively mild dry day in Edinburgh had given way to blustery rain by the time they got to the last stretch before the village. It always rains here, he thought, the damned place has its own climate. Hell must be full of the damned, places for the damned. The rooms and circles of hell. Any area would do. Fill any location with the damned and the walls and soil would soak up weakness, wickedness and stupidity and make another place of the damned. Another damned place. Luckily, he didn't believe in hell. For some reason, he thought of an old joiner he'd been apprenticed to as a boy. See the Plymouth Brethren, the old man had said, they don't smoke, they don't drink, they don't go to the pictures, they don't watch television; what do you think they do? Commit adultery! Too bloody right, it's all they've got left!

When Violet Terry came to the door, she was wearing sunglasses with big frames and broad sidepieces, which she touched with a forefinger, explaining, "I have an eye infection."

When they were seated, she asked, "Has something happened? I didn't think I would see you again."

"If you don't mind," Meldrum said, "I'd like to go back over what happened the day Rachel Croft disappeared."

"She hasn't been found then?"

"No."

"That's a relief, I suppose."

"She hasn't come home?" Meldrum asked.

"Oh, no. The village would know. You can't keep any secrets here."

"When you said she hadn't been found, what were you thinking of?"

She stared at him and then looked to McGuigan as if for an explanation.

"I don't know what you mean."

"I was wondering," Meldrum said, "if you thought she might be dead."

"That's too horrible even to think of. I don't know why you'd even suggest such a thing. I told you she was very calm, unpleasant to me but calm; my God yes, quite calm. I was surprised to hear she'd gone off, I didn't even expect that; my biggest worry was how to behave next time I met her and now you're talking of suicide. I honestly don't think she cared much, certainly not that much."

"Yet she did go," Meldrum said, seeing a way into what he'd come to ask her. "Is it possible that Barry Croft was angry and that's what made her decide to go off until things had cooled down? When you described for us what happened that day, you concentrated on how calm she was."

"She was. And unpleasant."

"Yes. But if we think about Croft instead, how did he seem to you?"

"I imagine he got a shock. I know I did."

"How did he look? Did he say anything to her?"

"I don't think so. He just lay there while she said that stuff about giving him crabs the first time they slept together, but not to worry since it was a long time ago. I was horribly upset, I just wanted to get out of there as fast as I could."

"He must have been upset too. Don't you think?"

She shook her head. "I don't know. What I felt at the time was that what we'd done didn't matter to him. As I was walking home, I kept imagining them laughing at me together."

While Meldrum was thinking about that, McGuigan intervened. "Have you spoken to Mr Croft since?"

"No," she said promptly, but there was something colourless in her tone, which made both men feel she was lying.

Outside they were about to get back in the car when Meldrum saw the note that had been folded and pushed under the wiper blade.

"What is it?" McGuigan asked.

Meldrum passed it to him.

Together they crossed the road at an angle to the front door of Peter Tarleton's cottage.

"I won't say it's a surprise," he said.

226

"I take it this is yours," Meldrum said, showing him the note. *I have to see you*, it said, and was signed with the initials PT.

"Come in," he said. "I'd really rather you weren't seen by anyone."

This time he took them to a small room at the back of the house. Two upright chairs sat on either side of a table large enough to hold an open chessboard with pieces set out as if for a game in progress. McGuigan took one of the chairs, turning it to face into the room. Meldrum sat in a shabby green leather easy chair, leaving their host to take the rocking chair set beside a second table upon which there sat a rack of pipes.

"I'm beginning to feel," Tarleton said, "the sooner this business is settled the sooner we'll all be able to sleep easy in our beds again." He took a briar pipe from the rack and began to suck on the dry stem. Like a baby with a comforter, Meldrum thought. "I don't regret writing you that letter, but I doubt if I would do it again. Did you see her face?"

"Miss Terry?" Meldrum guessed.

"Of course!"

"I'm not sure what you mean."

"But you must have seen! She's been beaten up."

"She was wearing dark glasses," McGuigan said as if making an admission.

"There you are! She's got two black eyes!"

"Perhaps she had a fall," Meldrum suggested, his innate caution preventing him from jumping to the conclusion which would have best suited him.

227

"You don't believe that," Tarleton said. "We're peaceful people in this village," he went on. "This is too much for us," he said plaintively.

"Are you accusing someone?" Meldrum asked.

Tarleton stared at the carpet and made little smacking noises with his lips as he sucked on the pipe stem.

"How can I do that? I wasn't there when whatever it was happened. All I can do is tell you about her face. Go back and ask her. Wouldn't that be the thing to do? I always felt safe in this village. It was like a haven. You read such dreadful things in the papers. But horrors like that belong in the city. They have no place here."

Aye right, Meldrum thought, no woman ever got beaten up in the country. He'd heard much the same thing said by someone about being in a nice house in the suburbs — you had to be in a slum for the worst to happen. He stared impassively at the little man sucking on his pipe.

"I'll tell you a strange thing," Tarleton said. "I've begun to feel sorry for Croft. I think he's one of those men who is addicted to women. There's a story by Aldous Huxley about a man like that. It gets him into dreadful trouble, but at the end when the poor wretch sees a woman below on the terrace, never mind how foolish he knows it is, he can't resist the temptation. Common sense, self preservation, everything should stop him, but he goes down the steps to join her."

228

And Meldrum, normally a man who kept his imagination firmly in check, perhaps because of what had gone through his head earlier had an image of Croft going down a flight of moss-covered stone steps into a garden of flames.

CHAPTER
FORTY-SIX

Betty felt the tension rising between them. Sooner or later, she thought, he's going to want to take me upstairs. An unbidden image came to her of them on her bed in the room next to the one in which Tommy was sleeping.

"I'm disappointed," Bobbie said. "I was looking forward to meeting your mother."

"She and Don are at the theatre. They've got season tickets. Didn't I tell you that?"

"You mean before I got here tonight?"

"At the boarding house. I'm sure I said."

"Was that when we were lying together after we made love?"

She nodded reluctantly.

"You go a little crazy when we make love. And after you come, you don't know which end is up". He smiled. "If you know what I mean."

"It's just that I'm sure I told you."

His smile thinned and disappeared. "I'd hate it if you were telling me I was wrong."

It was a new experience: that little shiver of discomfort that ran down her spine. She had never had cause to be afraid of the men in her life. She had always been sure of her father's love and her husband Sandy had been the gentlest of men. It had to be just discomfort, not fear. All the same, she was sure that she had told him, and had the feeling now that he might have sat in his car until he had seen her mother and Don Corrigan leave.

To distract him, she said, "I had a phone call from Lori Allingham."

"She enjoying wedded bliss?" He put his arm around her shoulder and cupped her breast.

"She and Matt are coming here."

"What?"

She winced as his hand tightened on her.

"You're hurting me."

He released her slowly, as if someone was breaking his grip one finger at a time.

"Did she say why? No, doesn't matter. Did she say *when* they were coming?"

"They're coming for a second — or a late — honeymoon. I'm not sure which she said. They're catching a plane tomorrow."

"They could be here tomorrow?"

His voice was quiet and under control, but it rose a little on the last word.

She spoke quickly, as if he'd accused her of something. "No! They're going to London first, but they're going to come to Edinburgh before they go home."

"Did she say London first?"

Had she?

"That was the impression I had. I'm sure she said that."

"Unless she was lying."

She looked at him in astonishment. "Why would she lie about a thing like that?"

His astonishment matched her own. There was a difference, though, she thought. I would never look as if I despised him.

"I told you Matt Crais works for the Consultancy. You think that doesn't matter or something? I'm supposed to be happy that he's coming here?"

"I'm sorry," she said. She'd been stupid. She couldn't understand why she'd been stupid. She wasn't normally stupid. She felt her eyes fill with tears.

"Hey!" he said, "You going to cry?"

He kissed her. After a moment, she felt him grip her by the back of the neck as he pressed her head back.

"Seeing you cry is hot." He kissed her again until he felt her respond. "I should bully you more often," he said, and slid his hand along her thigh until he could get between her parted legs, not kissing her this time but watching her eyes as he stroked her.

When the bell rang, she might have ignored it, but something in her, which had shied away from the word "bully", made her push him away and go to answer.

In the little porch between the two doors, she paused trying to calm her breathing.

When she opened the door, one of the two men who had stood back to study the house front stepped forward again.

"Can we come in, Mrs Croft?" James Finn asked.

The shock of astonishment slowed all her reactions. Later she would be grateful for that.

Even as the question was being asked the two men were moving in as slowly and calmly as if they had been invited. She had the sense that they had practised the same procedure often before. The three of them moved towards the living room, whose light spilt out into the hall. When they went in, the room she had just left was empty. She moved back to the couch and sat down to hide the trembling of her legs.

"James Finn. I spoke to your father on the phone," Finn said.

The big man said softly, "Wally Perzynski. We met in Phoenix. You made me a coffee."

She looked up at them. "How could I forget? That was a terrible time."

"I think we appreciated that," Finn said. "Though we couldn't do as much to help as we'd have wanted to."

"You said my husband had been found dead."

"But you know he isn't." It was a statement, not a question. "Is that because you've seen him?"

She stared up at him, not able to think of an answer.

Perzynski asked, "Have you seen your husband?"

"You told me he was dead. Why would you do that?"

"Mistakes happen," Finn said. "Forget the past. It's what happens next that matters."

"We're here to look after your husband," Perzynski said. "I'd guess you know why. Hasn't your husband told you why?"

"Why would policemen come all this way? I don't think policemen would do that."

"Mrs Croft, does that matter?" Finn shook his head. "Let's not be foolish. We're not the bad guys, and there are bad guys. In my opinion, you know that. Let's say you've seen him. Let's say you love him. I believe you love him. Best thing you can do is tell us where he is."

"I don't know," she said.

When the door made a noise brushing the carpet as it swung open, all three heads turned towards it. After a pause, a small boy came in rubbing his eyes. At sight of the two strange men, he stopped and then gathering his courage ran to his mother.

"I can't sleep," he said. "Will you come up and tell me a story?"

"Not just now," she murmured, holding him tight against her.

"First husband's boy?" Perzynski asked.

"Fine boy," Finn said. "You must be proud of him."

At her wits' end, she heard herself saying, "Why don't you talk to my father?"

Finn considered the idea. "Maybe we should do just that. Tell you what. We'll leave you to put the boy back to sleep. Come on, Wally. We'll sort this out in the morning."

All the time she was soothing the boy with a story, she listened for her husband, imagining him outside the bedroom door or wandering about what she thought of as Don Corrigan's house. When at last Tommy fell asleep, she came down expecting Bobbie to be in the living room. Finding it empty, she searched in every room downstairs and then, telling herself she was being foolish, all the rooms on the upper floor. It took a long time to persuade herself that he was gone.

CHAPTER
FORTY-SEVEN

It was late when Meldrum got back to the flat, so late that he hesitated about going over to try to see Mrs Hodge. If she hadn't opened the door to him on the previous occasion, she might be even warier about doing so at this hour. He made a pot of coffee and a ham sandwich, and tried to make up his mind while he ate supper. It had been an unsatisfactory morning. Violet Terry hadn't answered her door when they went back to talk to her after Peter Tarleton had raised the possibility she might have been beaten by Croft. The rest of the day had been taken up with a court appearance and the paperwork on a serious assault. He chewed mechanically on the dry sandwich, getting up once in search of a tomato but finding none in the fridge. Faced with the prospect of a couple of hours to kill before he could go to bed, he settled for trying Mrs Hodge again.

To his surprise, the door opened at the first ring.

When she saw him, however, outlined against the darkness of the landing by the light from the lobby, she tried to close the door again.

He held it effortlessly, an open palm against the door panel, "Were you expecting someone else?"

"It's late."

"I took your necklace back."

Perhaps because of what he'd said or because she had tired of pushing against him, she gave up and led the way inside.

"Do you mind putting the television off?" he asked in the sitting room.

Grudgingly, she pressed the mute button on the remote, leaving the set on so that as they talked pictures flowed and reshaped on the giant screen.

"You hadn't been to work. Did you go in today?"

She shook her head without looking away from the television.

"There's no problem with the necklace apparently. The manageress was apologetic. According to her, it was all a mistake."

"I told you that."

"So you did. Barry wasn't there when I called, but he must have been the one who sorted it all out. Don't you think so?"

Her gaze remained stubbornly fixed on the screen.

"When I was there anyway, I asked the manageress how much she thought the necklace was worth." He watched as Mrs Hodge stole a look from the corner of her eye. "What do you think she said?"

"A few pounds?"

"And the rest. Why do you think Barry gave you a present like that? He must think a lot of you."

As she sat dourly silent, he studied the grey at the roots of her very black hair and the way the jut of her nose took a curve off the moving screen as she turned her head up to him.

"Does it give you pleasure to torment me?" she asked.

"Not for a minute," he said and hoped that was true, for it was certainly the case that he had been bored and wasn't any more. Yet even the suggestion was enough to deflect him, though instinct told him something was here to be uncovered, and he was about to go when the doorbell rang.

When she started up, he knew who it had to be and was past her and down the lobby in three long strides.

As he opened the door, he saw Croft, the smile curdling on his face, holding out his hand with the necklace hung from the crook of his forefinger.

Deftly, Meldrum unhooked it and carried it back inside.

Mrs Hodge stood where he had left her, and going behind her he was clasping the jewellery around her neck as Croft came into the room.

"There's a coincidence," he said. "We were just discussing how much this might be worth."

"That's a lie," she said. "It was him, not me. I never said a word about it being worth anything."

"Don't upset yourself, Netta," Croft said gently. "He has no business to be here."

"Is he not a policeman?"

"Oh, he is. But he has no business to be here, and he knows it."

Meldrum taking a step or two back cocked his head to one side as if in admiration.

"That's a bonny necklace," he said. "Any woman would be glad to have it. Wait a minute!" He made a face as if a thought had just struck him. "Would she be your auntie, by any chance?"

"No, she fucking well isn't!"

But before Croft could say anything else, the woman had fumbled the necklace free and was holding it out to him.

"Take it."

"No."

"I don't want it," she said.

"Aye, but I want you to have it."

Taking it from her, he laid it around her neck. As he clasped it, his eyes never left Meldrum's.

"I'll tell you what this lady is," he said. "She's my friend."

"You must be in line for an employer of the year award," Meldrum said.

"I don't work there any more," Netta Hodge said. "I'm not going back." She turned and looked at Meldrum. "Does that satisfy you?"

Meldrum shrugged. "Nothing to me either way."

Ignoring him, Croft told her, "You were the one that wanted to go on working."

"Well, I don't, not now."

"That's all right with me. All I'm saying is, if you wanted to you could."

"And have those posh bitches whispering behind my back?"

"I'll make sure they don't."

238

"I know you'd try. I liked my wee job, but it's ruined now."

She began to cry and he took her in his arms.

Looking at Meldrum over her head, he said, "Would you mind leaving us now?"

CHAPTER
FORTY-EIGHT

Dinner was good and plentiful, though Finn denied himself the platter of oatcakes and wedges of cheese with which Perzynski rounded off his meal. Afterwards they had coffee and brandy before going through to the bar. By the time the evening was over, they would have spent something over a hundred pounds between them, how much over depending on how long it went on. Later they would adjourn to two of the best rooms in the hotel. As Finn was fond of saying, no one was richer than the man with a no-questions-asked expense account. Generous at home, abroad and working in a foreign currency it went almost unquestioned.

Despite which, Perzynski was far from happy. His bulk overflowing the chair, one meaty thigh supported by an ankle on the other, he sipped whisky and grumbled steadily. There had been a time not so long ago when Perzynski went in for being the strong silent type. As he'd relaxed, he'd started to make more conversation. Finn didn't find it an improvement.

"How are we supposed to work with bad intelligence?" he asked rhetorically.

240

"I was thinking it over," Finn said. "It's my opinion Bobbie Conway was there. I suspect he went out the back door as his wife let us in at the front."

"He's not living there." Perzynski gathered up a handful of nuts and dribbled them into his open mouth. "We were *told* he was living there."

"We'll find out where he is tomorrow."

"I hate fuck-ups."

"He hasn't any reason to hide from us," Finn said. "We're his best friends. Fuck, we're his only friends."

"So why did he run away?"

"Love's young dream?"

"My ass."

"More like her ass," Finn said. "She has a nice ass."

"It would look cute on your face," Perzynski said. "But I'd still like to know why he ran."

"So ask him tomorrow."

"If we find him."

"We'll find him."

Perzynski leant up on one ham and eased the release of a long, almost silent fart. For a big man, he had good muscle tone.

"We're running out of time," he said gloomily.

After a time, on the pretence of going to the toilet, Finn slipped out of an entrance into the narrow street that ran along the side of the hotel. As he walked, he fished his mobile out of an inside pocket. Listening to the number being rung, his eye took in the big shabby black car parked on the other side. As he watched, a man approached it, bent to ask the woman something and then ducked his head and slid inside. Not a pick-up, Finn thought. Something about the way the man scuttled into the car suggested the woman might be a Domme collecting a first-time client. Whores everywhere, he thought; it was the way he saw the world.

The voice at his ear sounded a cautious, "Yes?"

"Mr Smith?"

"The weather's fine here. How is it with you?"

"Sunshine and clouds." The preliminaries over, he went on, "We didn't manage to collect the parcel today. I'm hopeful for tomorrow."

"As long as you have it for me when I get there."

"I'm hopeful of that."

"Your partner's not a difficulty?"

Surprised by the question, Finn took a moment to answer. "He's restless. But he's a restless guy."

"Maybe I should speak to him."

"That wouldn't be a good idea."

"I've been thinking, it's too big a risk having an honest man around when we undo the parcel."

"My partner wouldn't be interested."

"Not even if I offer to pay twice as much for him as I did for you?"

"For some people, it isn't about money."

After waiting for a reply, Finn realised he'd been terminated.

Fuck you very much, he thought. Have a nice honeymoon.

He never ceased to be amazed at how stupid clever people could be.

CHAPTER
FORTY-NINE

ACC Fairbairn was unimpressed.

"Not a chance," he said. "With what you've got, there's not the slightest chance of you getting a warrant to search Croft's house."

It had been a long shot.

"The necklace was worth thousands," he said. "And we could have the manageress as a witness to that. Doesn't that prove how he feels about Netta Hodge?"

"Did I mention," Fairbairn wondered, "that I once met Croft's wife at a dinner? She was a strikingly good-looking woman. Can you imagine going into court and putting your cleaner on the stand? A defence lawyer like Donald Finlay would make mincemeat of the idea of any man killing a beautiful wife to marry someone like that, and Croft has enough money to get the best. Sorry, it's not going to happen."

"So we just wait?"

"You had your chance when you put divers on the budget. And found nothing but a corpse well past its sell-by date. Giving us another mystery to put on the books was the kind of publicity we could do without. Unless of course you've solved that one and I haven't heard yet?"

"Farquhar's got it. Nothing much seems to be happening."

"After a result like that, it really isn't a good idea to push your luck."

His eyes strayed to the papers on his desk as a sign that they were finished. When Meldrum had stood, however, and turned to the door, Fairbairn said, "*Nostalgie de la boue.*"

"What?"

"It's a French phrase," Fairbairn said with satisfaction. "It means 'yearning for the mud'. It just came to mind there. It struck me how appropriate it was."

Meldrum stared at him for a moment then, rather than showing he was baffled, turned again to leave.

"I was thinking of your cleaner," Fairbairn said. "Some men pick a woman who's beneath them. It gives them a sexual thrill to use a woman who is their inferior."

Meldrum let the silence lengthen till Fairbairn began to look uncomfortable, then he said, "It doesn't always have to be about the kinky stuff. My impression is that Croft was fond of her."

"Don't worry about it. Either way, your average jury wouldn't give it the time of day. There's nothing to be done about Croft for the moment."

"There's one thing. We could go and see Violet Terry. A neighbour claims that Croft beat her up."

"Is she the one Croft was with the day his wife caught them?"

"That's the one."

244

Meldrum, who'd made something of a study of the ACC, watched the wheels go round as Fairbairn calculated the angles.

"Can't see that it would do any harm. Be discreet and don't throw any accusations around."

CHAPTER
FIFTY

"To be honest with you," Violet Terry said, "I'm beginning to feel sorry for Barry."

"Peter Tarleton said the same thing," Meldrum said.

"You astonish me. Why would he?"

"Because he can't resist women."

She frowned. "Any women? How unflattering!"

Seated in the front room of her cottage, they had already gone through the business of her assuming at sight of them that Rachel had "been found", that wonderfully ambiguous phrase which covered the notions of alive or dead.

"Why are you feeling sorry for him?" Meldrum asked.

He was conscious of McGuigan more or less openly studying her face. She was still wearing the glasses that hid her eyes, but there did seem to be a thickening at the top of the bridge of the nose. He wondered, if the make-up was washed off, would there be the distinctive colours of bruising?

"It's gone on for so long," she said. "Of course, he bears up well."

"You feel he puts a good face on it?" McGuigan asked.

"Oh, yes," she said, seeming to accept the phrase as innocent. "But he must be under an enormous strain. People are gossiping, you know. And s-h-l-t's like Peter Tarleton don't help."

"I take it then," Meldrum probed, "you've seen something of Croft?"

"Not really."

"How can you have formed an opinion on his behaviour then?"

"What do you mean?"

"I don't understand how you can know he's bearing up well unless you've seen and talked to him."

"I met him walking. I like to walk on the hill."

"No hard feelings?" McGuigan asked.

"I don't know what you mean."

"I was taking it that you hadn't seen him since his wife walked in on you both."

"Oh."

Oh, indeed, Meldrum thought. But then, McGuigan hadn't been there when Fairbairn was issuing his diktat on the need for discretion. Settling back, he decided to let the DS make the running.

"Miss Terry?" McGuigan asked as she sat silent.

"He was nice."

"Nice?"

"When I met him. He didn't mention — mention what had happened. We talked about his wife's disappearance. He said it was no one's fault. That she'd been building up to doing something like that for some time. And that he was sure she'd be home soon. I remember exactly what he said. 'I'll be sitting one evening and the door will open and there she'll be.' He said to me, 'I can't tell you how much I'm looking forward to that.' I was very touched."

"You thought he was being sincere?" McGuigan asked.

"Oh, yes. I was almost in tears."

"This was when you met him out walking?"

"On the hills, yes."

McGuigan thought for a moment. "You weren't in his house?"

"God, no. I'd be too . . ."

To break the silence, he suggested after a moment, "Embarrassed?"

"Ashamed," she said.

McGuigan rubbed a nail along his lower lip. Meldrum had seen him do it before during interviews. Here it comes, he thought.

"Would you mind taking off your glasses?" McGuigan asked.

To Meldrum's surprise, she didn't argue. It occurred to him that people more often than you might expect were capable of offering a surprise. Very slowly and with a steady hand, she lifted the glasses from her face. Her eyes were swollen, the bruises around them going from black to yellow. Either she's had a fall, Meldrum thought, or she's been slapped, perhaps punched, in the face.

"I blame myself," she said.

"Yes?" said McGuigan. Not a masterstroke, but at that stage he didn't think he needed one.

"I was quite keen." She made a face at her own schoolgirl euphemism. "I wanted him. I knew it was stupid, being in the same village. But I couldn't help it."

"And then his wife caught you."

"What?" She stared at him. "He isn't married."

It was the men's turn to be baffled.

"I'm talking about Tony," she said.

Meldrum was chary about spreading the inquiry to Violet Terry's next-door neighbour. If Tony Carr made a formal complaint, he could imagine how unhappy that would make ACC Fairbairn. On the other hand, he didn't feel that he had a choice. If there was still a chance Violet Terry was lying and had been assaulted by Croft, they had to find out.

Fortunately, instinct told him almost at once that Carr wasn't going to complain. Tony Carr was about thirty, certainly younger than his neighbour with whom he had shared the celebratory gin and tonics after the quarry victory. Despite his comparative youth, his hair was thinning and when he bowed his head a circle of pink scalp shone under the lights. When he understood the purpose of their visit, his mild brown eyes widened and became moist.

"I didn't think she would be so vindictive."

"Is that an admission, sir? Did you assault Miss Terry?"

"Did she say I did?" If intended as a piece of cunning, it was ineffective. His eyes never left McGuigan's lips as he waited for a reply.

"She has severe facial bruising."

"It was a slap!" He bowed his head. "And then another one."

It was what they had come for, and more or less ended Meldrum's interest in the affair. Unless Barry Croft had also been there and holding her down, he was indifferent. It seemed as if every promising lead to Croft was going to end in disappointment.

It was McGuigan then who asked, "What did you quarrel about?"

"We're friends, you know. We've been friends for a long time. Ever since I came to live here. But being on the committee — about the quarry, you know — we had got into the habit of having a drink after the meetings. We never did that before. I haven't much of a head for drinking. One or even two was all right. Too many and I got silly."

When he'd tired of waiting, McGuigan said, "Silly?"

"I tried to kiss her and she refused. I'm afraid I lost my temper."

"I see," McGuigan said.

Meldrum rather supposed that he did. Remembering Violet Terry's *I wanted him*, it was easy to believe that the interested, only too solid reality of her might have been too much for Carr. At a guess, Meldrum decided, and reckoned it shared by the sergeant, he couldn't get it up.

"Are you arresting me?" Carr asked.

"No," McGuigan said.

Meldrum added, "From what she said, Miss Terry won't be pressing charges."

250

"Oh, God." Carr blew his nose on a very white handkerchief. "I haven't been sleeping," he said.

Nothing to do now but get out of here, Meldrum thought, and got to his feet.

"I don't know how I'll ever be able to face her again."

"I think I'd avoid gin," McGuigan said.

They were at the door when Carr dropped his bombshell.

"Has anyone else said to you that they saw Rachel Croft in the village the day before yesterday?"

CHAPTER
FIFTY-ONE

Croft wasn't at home and when Meldrum phoned the shop from his office to say they were coming to see him, the manageress informed him that her employer was away for the day attending an auction in Stirling.

What now? he thought, and for a moment contemplated finding the location and going to the auction. He ran over all the sensible reasons why not: he had other things to do; it would keep; he had to stop obsessing about Croft.

The decision, however, was still in the balance when McGuigan rescued him with the information that he had visitors.

"We've spoken on the phone," the first man in said, holding out his hand.

Introducing himself as James Finn, he was a little shorter than Meldrum, but was dwarfed by his companion Wally Perzynski, who was the biggest American Meldrum had ever seen apart from a military policeman stone-faced on the other side of a fence watching anti-nuclear demonstrators at the Holy Loch.

"That was from Phoenix," Meldrum said, trying to come to terms with his surprise.

252

"We've already had a meeting with your chief constable," Finn said. "I asked if I could speak to you since we've already been in contact."

"Not very satisfactorily," Meldrum said.

By this time they were all seated. As Meldrum wondered about telling McGuigan to leave, Finn pre-empted the idea by saying, "We're here about your son-in-law. Do you know where he is?"

"He isn't buried in Phoenix then?" Meldrum asked. In theory the most conformist of men, when authority took his compliance for granted theory and practice might briefly part company, at least until common sense brought them together.

"Forget about that," Perzynski said. "Your boss knows why we're here."

"I'm sure he does."

"No reason why you shouldn't," Finn said with a smile. Letting the smile fade, he said, "There isn't, is there?"

Meldrum stared at him in silence.

Shrugging, Finn said, "We're federal marshals. Wilbur Conway is due to give evidence in a federal court in Houston on the seventeenth. He shouldn't be in this country at all. We're here to take him back."

"You have a warrant for him?"

"No. We're not looking for extradition, nothing like that. We just want to talk to him. I'll tell you something in confidence. He came to the authorities of his own free will. He was the one who wanted to testify."

"So why did he run away?" Meldrum asked.

"We want to talk to him about that."

Perzynski said, "For sure it wasn't just to get married. We've seen your daughter."

"Ignore him," Finn said. "He's not being disrespect-ful. It's just that running away was such a bad idea. There has to be another reason."

"My daughter," Meldrum said, "has nothing to do with any of this. Is that understood?"

"We just want to talk to him."

"Is that understood?"

"Absolutely," Finn said. "We never thought she had. Can I ask you again? Do you know where he is?"

"It must be important if you've chased him all the way here."

"He's an important witness."

"For an important trial?"

Finn nodded. "It's a big company."

"Just the one?"

As Meldrum registered Finn's hesitation, Perzynski said impatiently, as if brushing aside a stupidity, "Of course."

Time for common sense to take over. Meldrum took McGuigan with him as a witness if one was needed. He drove with an eye on the mirror and led the two Americans in their hire car to the boarding house where he'd talked to Conway.

Following Finn's suggestion, he stopped a few blocks away.

"Does this place have a back door?"

"I imagine so. But it's in the middle of a terrace. You want to wait until we put a guard on it?"

Finn chewed his lip. "Fuck with it," he said. "We go in fast and he won't have time."

As they crossed the road, he spoke softly to Perzynski. The four men hurried up the path and Meldrum pressed the bell. When the door was opened, the big American shocked them by pushing past the woman who'd answered and heading straight down the hall, presumably in search of the back entrance.

"Don't be alarmed, lady," Finn said, taking charge as of right. "Police business. We're looking for Mr Conway. Is he in?"

"Mr Conway?" She was a spare woman of sixty with a thin precise Edinburgh voice. As she spoke, she turned to look down the hall in search of Perzynski. "Where does he think he's going?"

"Don't worry about him. Where's Conway?"

"Mr Conway is no longer a guest here," she said. "His wife's father died, and they've gone back home."

"Is that the truth? We need to look."

"No," Meldrum said, "we don't."

"You willing to take the responsibility?"

"That's enough," the landlady said, looking in alarm from one to the other. "I want you all to leave now or I'll call the real police."

"Collect that idiot from the back door," Meldrum instructed McGuigan. "One thing before we go." He held up his warrant card and let the woman read it over. "Did Mr Conway leave a forwarding address?"

Out in the street, Finn said in disgust, "Forwarding address? Christ."

"It was worth asking," Meldrum said quietly.

Perzynski's complaint rumbled deep in his chest. "So he's gone? What a fuck-up. Did you know he was gone?" he asked Meldrum.

"Don't be stupid," Meldrum said.

"I tell you, if you hadn't been with us all the time, I'd have had you down as making a phone call."

"Why would I have done that?"

"You tell me."

"Gentlemen," Finn said, "let's cool it. I apologise for my partner." He held out his hand, which Meldrum shook briefly. "What can I say? We've come a long way. Let's go, Wally. We'll be in touch, Inspector."

CHAPTER
FIFTY-TWO

"Bit of a coincidence Conway taking off just when these guys arrive looking for him," McGuigan said. "Unless, of course, he got the tip they were here."

They watched the car with the two Americans turn the corner out of sight.

"Wonder how?" the sergeant speculated. "I wonder if they went to see your daughter."

"She's got nothing to do with it."

"It would be the natural thing for them to do."

"Leave it."

They went back to the car in a silence that lasted until they had driven out of Edinburgh.

Finally, McGuigan asked, "Can I ask where we're going?"

"I phoned Croft's shop," Meldrum said. "He's in Stirling at an auction."

"This isn't the road to Stirling."

"We're not going to Stirling."

"Thank Christ for that," McGuigan said. "If he's in Stirling, why are we going to his house?"

The hills on their right, they were following a stretch of road that had become familiar since they had started to investigate the disappearance of Rachel Croft.

"We're not."

As he spoke, Meldrum was turning into a narrow road that led downhill on the left. It was the one they'd taken the first time they had gone to the small town in search of PC Harrison, who'd received the anonymous letter about Rachel Croft's disappearance.

McGuigan ran through the possibilities. Through gaps in the hedge, he could see a great pool of water at the near edge of a field. There had been a lot of rain recently and the ground was sodden. "Kevin Roche?" he asked.

"If we can't get Croft, he's the next best thing."

"Fine," McGuigan said.

They ran past Harrison's little sub-station and headed through the housing scheme until its neatly tended gardens were interrupted by the tangle of tall grass and weeds outside Kevin Roche's flat, half of the ground floor of a four-in-the-block.

After a long press of the bell, McGuigan turned a jaundiced eye on the front garden.

"Idle big sod," he said.

After a repeat pressure on the bell, he offered a second opinion. "He's out."

"Maybe not," Meldrum said. "His bike's leaning against the wall along there."

Cursing himself for missing that, McGuigan put his thumb on the bell and kept it there.

This time there were sounds from inside, and in a moment the door was opened.

"What happened to you?" Meldrum asked.

Roche slouched in the doorway with his head lowered. One meaty hand, livid with split knuckles, supported him by gripping the doorframe. When he looked up, they could see both eyes were full of blood and his left cheekbone, a congealed mass of bruises and blood, gave every evidence of being broken.

"Can you come back later?" he asked in a subdued growl. "I'm feeling rough."

"Needs to be now," Meldrum said.

Roche went inside without further protest. He looked as if he'd just climbed out of bed; the vest he wore was rucked up and the pyjama trousers sagged giving them a view of the crack of his behind as he led the way.

In the tiny living room, he started to let himself down carefully, gave up and half fell into a chair.

"You should get a doctor," Meldrum said.

"I just need a rest," he said reproachfully.

Meldrum was having an internal debate. Although his main interest was in Rachel Croft, it seemed wrong to ignore the fact there had either been an accident or a fight. If the latter, there was the possibility that a trained fighter like Roche could have inflicted serious damage on someone. Perhaps that was why he didn't want a doctor.

As he came to this conclusion, he heard McGuigan say, "You look as if you've been in a fight."

Roche grunted.

"Is that a yes?"

Another grunt.

"You been to the police?"

259

"What for?"

"If you've hurt somebody," McGuigan said, "it's better to go to them, instead of them coming to you."

"Ah, *fuck!*" Roche said, and astonished them both by putting his face in his hands. After a while, he took them away again, but he spoke without raising his eyes from the floor. "If you must know," he said. "I'm the only one hurt. I was walking back from the pub and a bunch of kids started being cheeky to me. I mean *kids*, fourteen-year-olds, something like that. A crowd of them. If I'd hit one of them, I'd have killed him. I didn't want to hit any of them. Next thing I knew I was down on all fours. One of them must have got behind me and hit me with a baseball bat, something like that. They kept on hitting me till I passed out." He pulled the vest up to show a towel wadded against his side and held with a length of soiled bandage. "I got stabbed as well."

"Sure none of them were hurt?" McGuigan asked. "You're as well telling the truth now. It'll be easy enough to find out."

"Something's gone wrong with the world," Kevin Roche said. "They were like a pack of fucking wolves."

"If they're as dangerous as that, go to the police."

Roche gave a painful smile. "That would look good, wouldn't it? Beaten up by a bunch of kids. A couple of days in the house, I'll be fine."

As the big man shook his head, Meldrum thought that the injured hand might well have come from trying to ward off blows.

"Suppose they kill somebody?" he asked.

"I told *you*. You're the police, aren't you?"

"We've more to do," McGuigan said. "Tell the uniform guy — the one that was here before."

Right enough, Meldrum thought. Get yourself killed and then maybe it'll be a job for us.

He said, "We're here about Rachel Croft."

"I told you already. I took her into the bus station."

"That was the day she disappeared. We've a witness that says she's back again."

"God almighty!" Blood drained from Roche's face.

"What is it?"

"I moved the wrong way," Roche said, putting a hand over the wound in his side.

"Rachel Croft was seen this week. She was in a car being driven by you."

"That's not right. No way."

"The day before yesterday," McGuigan said.

Roche's face went slack with what looked like relief. He even managed a smile. "That wasn't Mrs Croft. Somebody needs their eyes tested. That was — what's her name? — friend of the boss', one of these ones that call themselves Ms — what's her name? Wilkie, that's her."

"Carrie Wilkie?"

"Ms Wilkie."

"What colour are her eyes?" Meldrum asked, then thought it a question wasted on Roche.

The big man said at once, "Green. You see eyes like yon on a cat."

"What car were you in?" McGuigan asked.

"The boss's car."

"Not Miss Wilkie's?"

"She didn't have it with her."

"So how did she get there?"

"Boss brought her, I suppose."

"According to our witness, it was early in the morning."

"So she was there all night," Roche said. "Wouldn't be the first time."

CHAPTER
FIFTY-THREE

He'd decided against anywhere either of them might be recognised. In the car, he'd wondered about going all the way to Haddington, but since pensioners had been given free travel on the buses it had become a favourite destination for a short jaunt from Edinburgh. Instead, spotting a café, he pulled in to a tiny parking area just off the main street in Musselburgh.

There were half a dozen tables, none of them occupied. At one time it was the kind of place that would have stunk of cigarettes, but since the smoking ban there was nothing to offend his fastidious nose. He ordered two coffees and sat trying to keep a smile of contentment off his face as he looked at her.

"You certainly know how to treat a girl," Betty said.

"It's out of the way," McGuigan said.

"You mean we're not likely to run into any of your colleagues."

"Or any of your friends."

"I'm not sure I've many of those left." She made a face. "I'm sorry. Didn't mean that the way it sounded. I'm not really sorry for myself."

"You've had a hard time." He hadn't meant to say that, and very particularly he hadn't meant to say it in that special gentle tone which few people had ever heard him use.

They sat in silence, each of them bewildered by what was happening.

"It's a bit like that place we were at before," she said.

There wasn't any doubt as to which place that was, since they had only sat together once before on the night when she'd gone to her father's flat to tell him that Bobbie Conway was in Edinburgh.

"Did my father ever ask you about taking me for something to eat while I waited for him to come back?"

"Not really." An unexpected smile lit his face. "Dealing with your father, it's useful to be a detective. It lets me work out where we're going."

"Are you laughing at him?"

She seemed not so much shocked as startled by the idea.

"Only inside. And only when it's a choice between that and jumping out while the car's still moving."

"He's not an easy man."

"No." Not easy on anybody, he thought, not even himself.

"But he's a good one."

He was about to make some kind of joke, when he saw how intently she was watching him. It was as if his opinion mattered to her.

"This job," he said, "doesn't make it easy. But I think he tries as hard as anyone."

"I'm glad you're with him," she said.

It was one way of looking at a relationship that for much of the time felt more like a penance than anything else.

"One good thing's come out of it," he said. "I met you."

"You know I've a little boy," she said. "And I'm married. I don't know why this is happening."

"You're the kind of woman I disapprove of," he said, and again perhaps it was meant to sound like a joke, but he saw her wince and knew she understood it was true. All that's changed, he wanted to tell her. Everything's changed.

After a moment, she said, "I'm Bobbie's wife. I'm not going to change that."

"I know," he said. "How could I want you to? We're not that kind of people."

He waited for her to say she'd thought he disapproved of the kind of people she was. When instead she said quietly, "It's impossible, isn't it?" he knew they were in a place he had never thought to find himself.

After a while, she asked, "What made you want to be a policeman?"

He'd been asked that question before. Asked by friends, asked by guys he ran with on the street when he was still swithering about taking the plunge. Asked by women, meaning want-to-go-to-bed or have-you-no-ambition? Asked once by a lawyer, who'd told him people became policemen either because they were guilty about something or because they needed a job that gave them power over other people. Rich clown, he'd thought, have you never heard of unemployment? and wished he could ram the silver spoon up the man's well-upholstered arse.

He couldn't remember ever giving an answer that wasn't flippant or evasive.

"My brother came to see me the other day," he said. "He'd brought the paper in case I'd missed seeing this bit about a soldier killed in Iraq. A guy called Collie Harper. A bomb at the side of the road. Blew up as the lorry passed, but he was the only one killed. Three of them injured, bits blown off, but Collie was the one that was killed." He felt her watching, but kept his eyes on his hands folded on the table as he talked. "Collie's father used to beat his wife. He'd hit her so often she'd gone soft in the head. Every weekend the neighbours would hear her screaming. Collie spent all the time he could at our house. My mother was more of a mother to him than his own ever was." He fell silent. "You don't want to hear this stuff."

"Go on."

"My big brother had a hell of a soft heart. What went on at Collie's house got too much for him. He and three pals got hold of the father and gave him a hiding. They overdid it. I should have been there. I'd have gone if my brother hadn't kept it from me. I was so angry with him. But when I saw him in jail, he said, 'You were the brainy one. I didn't want to spoil your life.'" He rubbed a hand over his lips as if to hide his words. "He was the one who always wanted to be a policeman."

"So you became one."

266

He grinned. "Well, I wasn't smart enough to be a brain surgeon."

Not smiling, she said quietly, "It's all right. You don't have to make a joke of it. Not with me."

"No," he said with a sigh, relieved of all the life he had led till then.

CHAPTER
FIFTY-FOUR

If things hadn't gone so extraordinarily differently with McGuigan, Betty would have told him. Because of the turmoil of her feelings, however, telling him would have felt like a betrayal of Bobbie Conway, who was, despite everything, her husband. And so she let McGuigan drop her in George Street in the belief that she was meeting her mother later in Jenners. As she was about to get out of the car, he touched her lightly on the shoulder. It was the only physical contact they'd had.

In a daze, she made her way along the crowded pavements until she crossed Princes Street and went down to where the buses gathered. And there, sure enough, behind a tourist bus, she found one that would take her out to the airport.

She'd been afraid of being late, but the Arrivals board indicated more than an hour's delay and she had time to have a coffee and work herself into a state of anxiety before the passengers began to emerge. The usual trickle of specialists in making a fast exit was followed by the main body of passengers, and there somewhere in the middle of the stream she spotted Mr and Mrs Crais. Lori and Matt. Oddly enough, though she'd only had the briefest of words with him at the wedding, he was the one she recognised first, a tall lean American with a straggle of blond hair, wearing jeans and a plaid sports shirt, his jacket slung over the bar of the trolley he was pushing.

Lori embraced her. "It was so great of you to meet us," she said. "I'm sorry it was such short notice. Wasn't it lucky I had your home number?"

Blonde, of a colour almost to match her husband's, with a wide grin of white teeth, she looked as cheerful as a new bride should, though still a shade too sharp-featured. As a matter of fact, when she'd phoned the first time, Betty had been puzzled as to how she'd known the Corrigans' phone number. If, as Lori assured her, it had been among all that lazy afternoon's talk they'd exchanged on the porch in the house at Bethesda, she had no memory of it.

After he'd kissed her, Matt said, "I hope we can get all the stuff in the car. Lori doesn't travel light."

That was what began the fluster that ended with her inviting them to dinner at her mother and stepfather's house, for she had to explain that she hadn't come in a car. She'd planned to, of course, only to learn as late as that morning that her mother's car was having its MOT. And after she'd explained what an MOT was, she'd said she planned to get a taxi to take them to their hotel.

"Absolutely not," Matt said. "I'll get a hire car. I'd have needed to get one anyway if we were going to take in the sights. You can come back to the hotel and join us for dinner."

At which point she'd issued the invitation to dinner, which her mother had suggested that morning, an offer she'd had no intention of making until she heard it spilling from her lips.

It was when they were coming back from the Hertz desk that she happened to glance into the little lounge where she'd had coffee while waiting for the plane. Lori was saying something and she managed to smile and answer and next moment they were going through the exit doors. She had been granted no more than a glimpse of the man at a corner table who had looked up and then bowed his head. Perhaps it had been the swiftness of that response, though, which convinced her. Whatever the reason, she had not the slightest doubt that she had just seen the man who'd come to their flat in Phoenix, in a different life it seemed, in search of her husband, Wilbur Conway.

On the way into Edinburgh, Crais drove and the two women sat in the back. Lori did ask about her marriage, but when Betty hesitated she changed the subject and the rest of the journey passed in giving directions and remarking on the sign for the zoo and the fine façade of a church, and as they neared the hotel, exclaiming at the image of the castle set above the city.

She went up with them to their rooms and they had coffee and biscuits brought up. Then Crais said he needed a shower.

"I'm just fine," Lori said. "Betty and I have a lot to catch up on."

No sooner were they alone than she leant forward, brushing back the fall of blonde hair in a gesture Betty remembered. "Girl talk," she said. "I let it go in the car, but what's happened with Bobbie? He's not really dead, is he?"

The shrewd thing would have been to say that yes, he was, but Betty was superstitious enough to hesitate before confirming something so tempting to nemesis.

"So he's not?" Lori said. "God, I'm so glad. Right from the get-go after your father phoned, Matt said he wasn't sure it was true, but he doesn't tell me everything. He's not here, is he? Bobbie, I mean."

And when Betty couldn't think what to answer, she went on, "Will we see him at dinner?"

"He's not at my mother and stepfather's house."

"So when are we going to see him?" Lori cried, so freshly, so enthusiastically, that Betty was reminded of her surrounded by a sweetness of bridesmaids.

"He's away at the moment."

"We'll be here for at least a week."

"He might be longer than that."

Dinner that evening began badly and got worse. For one thing, some function having been cancelled, Don Corrigan was there. He began by treating them to a gratuitous analysis of the prospects for Hilary Clinton if she got her chance to fight for the presidency. This led him on to a survey of tertiary education in America, a sector that was apparently (leaving aside a handful of institutions) so debased by the attempt to offer a university education to everyone and by the influence of fundamentalist Christians on the teaching of science that it could only lead to the decline of the United States as a great power.

The response of Matt Crais to all this was sparing but courteous. Betty's discomfort was compounded by the way her mother, who had been a head teacher for much of her working life, was confined by Corrigan as an educational administrator and a man, not necessarily in that order, to the role of admiring supporter. Things took a disastrous turn, however, when Lori, less adept perhaps at concealing boredom than her husband, turned the conversation to Wilbur Conway. Corrigan, who had belatedly learnt of his son-in-law's supposed death, now learnt that in fact he was alive. He didn't take the news well.

By the end of the evening, Betty, in addition to everything else she had to think about, had come to the conclusion that she had to move out as soon as was humanly possible. I'll go back to the States with Bobbie, she thought, and this time I'll take Tommy with me.

CHAPTER
FIFTY-FIVE

A number of phone calls didn't find Croft at home. Next morning, Meldrum went by himself to the shop only to be told by the manageress that her employer had contacted her after the auction in Stirling to say that he was going to take a break for a few days.

"Where?" Meldrum asked.

She had no idea, since he had said that he planned to tour around, making overnight stops where the notion took him.

"It's not like him," the woman said, "but, of course, he's been under a strain."

"Business hasn't been good?"

"Oh, nothing like that. I meant about his wife, but you know about that or I shouldn't have mentioned it."

"What about her?"

Looking uncomfortable, she said quietly as if afraid of being overheard, "She's left him. Hasn't she?"

"Who told you that?"

But she refused to be more specific, leaving the impression of a small world where gossip flourished, and the favourite game was Chinese whispers. Who could tell, perhaps this particular rumour had come from one of the cleaners who'd been a friend of Netta Hodge?

However, when he raised her name, the manageress frowned and said, "Mrs Hodge? She no longer works here."

Later in the day, having held a case conference with the team that had been set up to deal with an indecent assault on a mother and daughter returning late from a hen night, he'd phoned Carrie Wilkie and, finding her at home, had arranged to go with McGuigan to talk to her.

She gave him the same chair again so that he found himself looking out through the patio doors at wreaths of mist slipping over the tops of the Pentland Hills as the afternoon drew to a close.

"We've been to see Kevin Roche."

"Ah," she said.

"I imagine you can guess why we're here."

"I can guess," she said, "but it doesn't persuade me that who I sleep with is any of your business."

"That wasn't the first time," Meldrum suggested, ignoring her doubts as to whether or not his curiosity was legitimate and reasonably sure of an answer, since people usually did answer if questioned with enough conviction.

"Which time would that be?"

"Put it a different way," Meldrum said, "have Croft and you been lovers for a long time?"

"Put it this way," she said, "that wasn't the first time."

274

"How soon after his marriage did you two become lovers?"

" 'Lovers' again," she said. "I don't think we were ever lovers. I enjoyed him. He was wonderful in bed. And Barry, in the right mood, would sleep with anyone."

For obvious reasons, the plain, socially deprived Netta Hodge came to Meldrum's mind, and that brief distraction left a pause which McGuigan filled. "Would you mind telling us how long after his marriage you went to bed with him?"

"A few months, but of course we'd had intercourse before he married Rachel. Not in bed though. In the kitchen of the flat he had then. On the table, in fact."

Mouth slightly open, McGuigan looked as if it should have been his turn to say, *Ah*.

Meldrum rescued him. "I'm sorry if this is embarrassing for you," he said, carefully avoiding any hint of irony. "But I'm sure you understand that Mr Croft's private life does have a bearing on why his wife may have disappeared. Did his wife know that you slept with her husband?"

"We were very old friends."

"I take it that means yes. Did it bother her?"

Feeling herself fully in command by this time, she said lightly, "Rachel accepted Barry as he was. Otherwise the marriage would never have lasted."

"She accepted his affairs. Not love affairs, as you say. Just encounters for casual sex. So why should she disappear because she caught her husband having sex with Violet Terry?"

He waited for an answer. She opened her mouth, then closed it again without a word.

"Perhaps," Meldrum said, "we wouldn't have known about Violet Terry if you hadn't mentioned her. Why did you tell us to talk to her?"

She started to speak then stammered to a stop. Her confidence seemed to have gone for the moment. Perhaps, Meldrum thought, it had dawned on her at last that Croft might after all have played some part in the disappearance of his wife.

With a visible effort, she pulled herself together and said, "Because she had such a thing for him. She couldn't hide it. We used to joke about it." Her green eyes widened on them. "It never occurred to me that she might actually have had sex with him that day."

"That's two of you had him," McGuigan said. "Do you know the names of any others?"

She shook her head firmly. The two men looked at her sceptically, but lost in her own thoughts she said, "I'm not saying there wouldn't be. I know him too well not to think that." And added, "Poor Barry."

Isn't it strange, Meldrum thought, how many people feel sorry for him?

CHAPTER
FIFTY-SIX

He hadn't been a churchgoer for a long time, but Wally Perzynski had had a religious upbringing.

Later that day when they were looking over Edinburgh from the path under Arthur's Seat, he recalled how Jesus had been taken up into a high place by the Devil and tempted with the riches of all the Kingdoms of the world. Man shall not live by bread alone, and bread transmuted out of stone remained stone. *Retro me, Satanas.*

First though, they'd breakfasted, he and Finn, with the happy couple.

"What a great coincidence," Finn said. "You two holidaying here. I couldn't believe my eyes when I saw you coming in."

"I've been making an attempt to persuade Lori to try the porridge" Crais said.

"I don't think so," she said, sipping at her orange juice.

"It tastes different in Scotland," he told her.

"Coffee, toast and a poached egg," she said.

"The egg's her concession to being on holiday."

"You wouldn't like me if I was fat," she said.

"No one would like you. They don't have fat people here," Crais said.

Finn laughed. "You haven't been here in a while."

"Not like back home, though."

"They're getting there."

"God bless America," Crais said.

They fell silent for a moment as Wally Perzynski came back from the buffet with his second plateful.

"What's that you've got?" Crais asked. "The black stuff at the side?"

"That's black pudding," Finn said, doing the talking since his colleague's mouth was full. "They make them with blood. I read that somewhere and the guy on the server said it was true when I asked him. Wally thinks he was kidding. And that's haggis. And sausages — they do pork, beef and venison. And scones made out of potatoes. All of it fried."

"Don't forget the eggs," Wally Perzynski said. "Fried too," he explained jocularly.

"Haggis?" Lori asked.

"There's probably blood in that as well," Finn said.

"Don't listen to him, honey," Crais said. "He's just having fun."

"Anyway, the coffee's not bad. I don't know how I'd've survived if it had been," she said.

"This is Lori's first time in Europe."

"If that's so, you got to see Princes Street," Finn said. "Let me show you."

"Well . . ." Crais hesitated.

"He's got calls to make," Lori said.

278

"I won't be more than an hour," he said. "People in Paris. I should have done it before we left. I'm so damn sorry, I could cut my throat."

"Can you believe he'd do that to me?" She looked at her husband fondly, though, so it didn't seem she was too bothered. "On our honeymoon trip?"

"So punish him," Finn said. "I'll show you where to spend his money. Haven't been here for a couple of years, but I know this city well. Wally and I have to meet a guy for lunch. Till then we have a free morning."

"What about you, Wally?" she asked. "Are you going to join us?"

Busy wiping egg off the plate with a piece of folded toast, Perzynski took a moment to answer.

"That's all right," he said finally. "You two go."

"Wally," Finn explained, "isn't made for shopping."

Wally nodded and went on chewing.

After the other two left, Crais and Perzynski lingered over coffee.

On their second cup, Crais suddenly asked, "Who are Finn and you having lunch with?"

Perzynski stared at him. "Why would you want to know that?"

"The name Wilbur Conway came to mind."

"Why would that be?"

Perzynski glancing up under heavy lids, a crumb of egg sitting at the corner of his mouth, seemed half asleep, and suddenly, to Crais' eye, dangerous.

"Let's not talk here," he said.

"Your room or mine?" Perzynski asked.

"I've a car. You can be private in a car."

After a thoughtful moment, the fat man nodded.

Half an hour later, they were sitting high up on the road under the summit of Arthur's Seat, looking beyond the panorama of Edinburgh church spires giving their thumbs up to the past to where the waters of the Forth glittered in the distance.

Perzynski had listened in almost unbroken silence while Crais made his pitch.

Nearing an end, Crais was saying, "Do you know the profit we made last year? We could buy a country with it: every field, every house, factories, every damn thing they've got that's for sale. In fact, you'd be surprised if I told you the presidents and prime ministers and kings and princes we already own."

"I don't surprise easy," Perzynski said, and it was true he had a low opinion of foreign kings and the great men he'd come across at home in the way of business.

"Think of nights on the beach with an orchestra playing. Think of ranches and riding night and day on your own land."

"I'm a city boy," Perzynski said.

"Think of any damned thing you want, stuff you've wanted all your life, stuff you dreamt about when you were a boy, a horny boy. It's yours. Don't tell me you don't want it."

"And you can give me it."

"All you have to do is reach out your hand."

"We'd have to work out an arrangement. It's not something you could put on paper."

"We've done it before. There are safe ways. We wouldn't ask you to trust us."

280

"A house on Malibu beach," Perzynski said. "And all that horny stuff."

"The best chef money could buy. And your own plane to fly in the caviar."

"You certainly know how to pitch to a fat man," Perzynski said.

CHAPTER
FIFTY-SEVEN

Lying in bed that morning, before going down for the breakfast at which Finn and he had feigned surprise at meeting one another, Crais had listened as Lori described Betty Conway's parting words to her.

"You must have wondered what was keeping us when I went to get my coat," Lori said, stretching like a cat that had been stuffed with cream. Being wakened and made love to while she was half asleep was still a novelty she enjoyed. "She was so pissed off she couldn't hide it. He really embarrassed her."

"You'd be embarrassed if he was married to your mother. The guy's a total asshole."

"What with you being an expert," she'd said throatily as he slid a hand down the smooth length of her back and fingered her, the word being father to the deed.

After a brief interlude, he'd taken up the subject again. "Can't be easy for her with her husband taking off as well."

"Oh, I think she must be in touch," Lori had said. "She says she's going back to the States with him."

Later, after breakfast and his talk with Perzynski there was nothing to do but wait to see how things panned out. There was always the danger, of course, that the fat man would report direct back to Washington, but he was pretty sure he wouldn't do that right off the bat on his own. It was a risk worth taking and, if the worst seemed likely to happen, Finn had assured him he had a contingency plan.

Meantime, the best thing he could do would be to follow up the lead Lori had given him that morning.

Back at the hotel, he persuaded her to let him keep their lunch appointment on his own. It involved some bribery but he was good at that, which was one reason for her agreeing. Another was that she knew he had no interest in Betty Conway. British women with problems and small children weren't his type. In the background, too, was the unadmitted knowledge that coming abroad might have something to do with his work, about which she had decided some time ago it was better not to be overcurious.

"Where is this place?"

"She wrote it down for me. It isn't far from the hotel, she said."

In fact, Randolph Place was only ten minutes' walk away and when he went up the stairs in La P'tite Folie Betty was already sitting at a table in the corner.

"Where's Lori?" she asked.

"Too much shopping," he said. "She's lying down in the room. Thank you," to the waitress as he took a menu. "A blinding headache. Did you know she had migraines?" And as Betty nodded, went on, "I hope you can put up with me on my own. Have you decided what you'd like?"

"It was nice of you to come," Betty said. "I'm sure you'd rather be with Lori."

"She's not great company at the moment. An hour's sleep'll fix it, she says. I think I'll have the soup and the roast beef." He laid the menu aside.

"I'd like the salmon salad followed by the blanquette of chicken."

After the waitress had taken the orders, they sipped glasses of wine and talked. As she got over her initial uneasiness, she began to relax and find him good company. When he mentioned the previous evening, she found herself saying, "I hope you didn't find my stepfather too hard going."

"He's a man of strong opinions," he said solemnly and when she smiled responded with one of his own.

"He's not always as bad as that," she said, feeling a need to defend him for her mother's sake.

"Americans bring out the worst in a lot of people."

"Oh, I don't think he's political at all." When he laughed, she went on, "He's not waving banners about Iraq. Not that waving banners would be his style. The truth is, he admires power. Believe me, he's on your side."

"Lori tells me you've had about enough of living at home."

She grimaced involuntarily at the word "home". It had never been her home. With her first husband Sandy she had had a home, and before that one with her mother and her father, but that had been a long time ago.

"They've been good to me since Tommy was born," she said.

"But you're thinking of going back to the States with Bobbie?"

At this moment it came back to the forefront of her mind that this was the man whom her husband had spoken of as his enemy. What he'd described, though, was so far outside her experience, she'd almost managed to shut it out of her thoughts. Now all the wariness she'd suppressed came flooding back.

"It's one option," she said.

"So you know where Bobbie is?"

"No, I don't."

"But he's been in touch with you?"

Lying was difficult for her, and so she said nothing.

"I wish you would trust me," he said. "I don't want to have to hurt you."

"Hurt me?" She was shocked, but not afraid. How could he hurt her in this pleasant room surrounded by people laughing and talking as they ate?

The waitress bringing the main courses provided a slight distraction from what he said next. Had he really said that he'd invited someone to join them for lunch?

"I hope you don't mind," he said and, following his gaze, she half turned to see the man who'd come to the flat in Phoenix looking for her husband.

Naturally that recognition was followed at once by its rejection. She stared at the man as he took the third place set at the table: a plump middle-aged man with wispy brown hair and a nose and mouth that seemed too small for his face, a man you wouldn't look at twice across a crowded room or passing him on the pavement. When he spoke, it was with an American accent. Matching his appearance, his voice was light and unemphatic.

"You may not remember me," he said. "People often don't."

"You were the start of a nightmare for me."

"I'm sorry you feel like that. I was only doing my job."

"What for God's sake is your job?"

Her voice had risen. Without doing anything so ostentatious as moving his head, the man at the next table let his eyes slide across to look at her.

"Mr Oliver," Crais said, "is a private detective. He came to see me just before Lori and I left for Europe. I was able to tell him it was my belief Bobbie Conway was here."

"Why would you *do* that?" she asked, forcing herself to speak quietly. "Is this something to do with the trial?"

"My client isn't interested in any trial," Oliver said. "She's not a vindictive person."

"I've no idea what you're talking about." Bewildered, she looked from one man to the other.

"Tell her who your client is," Crais told him.

"I'm employed by Mrs Conway."

"Is this a joke? I'm Mrs Conway."

"I'm afraid not," Oliver said softly.

CHAPTER
FIFTY-EIGHT

Don't get mad, get even. It was the slogan Crais had offered her, but it didn't fit. For one thing, she couldn't help feeling a whole mix of emotions, one of which was certainly anger. How could she not be angry at what Oliver had told her? The anger, though, in part was at herself and bled into a feeling that was akin to shame. For the first time since the death of baby Sandy, she stood back from things, saw herself from the outside. It was like escaping from a room where she'd been bedridden for an endless time and walking out into the fresh air. The death of her child, the loss of restraint, the drinking, the casual sex, the unpinning of everything that made the person she had always been, all of that she now understood had culminated in meeting with Conway, being seduced by him. It felt as if her breakdown had gone on long after her time in hospital. Now at last it was over. It had to be over. More than anything now, she wanted to go back to being herself again.

They were eating the evening meal, when she felt the mobile drumming against her heart.

When she took out the phone, Corrigan frowned across the table at her.

Bobbie said, "Betty?"

"Yes?" She stared at the food on her plate, avoiding the outraged look she sensed was focused upon her.

"Are you alone?"

"No."

"I want to meet you tonight. Remember the place you and Tommy were having lunch and I joined you?"

"I'm not sure it'll be open."

"There's a restaurant at the side of it. I'll meet you there in an hour. OK?"

"Yes."

When she put the phone away, Corrigan said, "That is unacceptable. I don't want you to do that ever again, while you eat at my table."

Her mother said nothing.

The cinema programmes at Ocean Terminal had started. The walkways were quiet like evening streets in a town about to come under curfew. As she passed the open space where she'd lunched with Tommy, the high glass wall showed the harbour and the distant twinkle of lights.

The restaurant at the side, though, was reasonably busy and she saw Conway at the back sitting at a table for two, not looking towards the door as if expecting her but staring out through the glass into the darkness. At sight of him, a stab of rage took her by surprise.

"Sorry," she said as she sat down. "It took me longer than I thought."

"Your stepfather?"

"He was in one of his moods. I needed to borrow Mother's car, and that made him angry with her."

288

"You want something?" He hadn't waited for her arrival, but already had a plateful of food in front of him.

"Just coffee. I've eaten."

He chewed thoughtfully, then said, "You'll be glad to get away. Sooner the better, that right?"

"That's right."

"We'll send for the kid soon as we're settled," he said.

"That would be good." She clenched her fist in her lap.

"Your mother could bring him out. Give her a break from the old man."

"She'd like that."

He gave a wide smile. "I'll just bet she would."

As he looked down again at his plate, she saw McGuigan come in and sit at a nearby table. Conway would only have to turn his head to see him.

"It isn't your birthday?" he asked.

"Nowhere near."

"Pity. I've brought you a present."

He slid a long envelope from his pocket and laid it on the table.

"Open it."

Inside, she found two plane tickets.

"Memorise the flight number."

"I won't forget."

"Look at the date."

"Tomorrow?"

"Why not?" He held her gaze. She felt the force as if for the first time of those pale beautiful eyes. "The sooner we go, the sooner we can send for the baby. A new life can't start too soon."

"No, it can't." She was afraid he would see the effort it took to say the words. "Why does it have to be tomorrow?"

"I'm not going back with anybody but you," he said. "I don't need federal marshals. I'll work out what to do when we get back home."

"Federal marshals?"

"Finn and the fat guy. Especially the fat guy. Forget them. You can come with me now. Spend the night, we'll go to the airport in the morning."

She didn't want to say no, she wanted to scream it. "No," she said quietly. "I have to see Tommy. Explain things to my mother. Get clothes."

"Come back anyway, just for an hour," he said. "It's been too long. I need to make love to you."

Her skin crawled at the thought of being touched by him. She couldn't think of any excuse that wouldn't alert him something was wrong. She had a nightmare vision of being taken away by him, passive, helpless.

"Don't look away from me," he said. "Keep your eyes on me. The policeman who was with your father is watching us. Don't look! I've just said something funny — smile and nod at me. Didn't you see him following you?"

"Oh, God, no."

The distress in her voice must have seemed genuine to him.

"I'm going to get up and go to the toilet," he said. "I already checked it out. There's another way out of the corridor. Sit here and act natural."

She nodded and even managed a smile. "Do you still want me to come to the airport tomorrow?"

His eyes went blank. It was as if he withdrew from her as he thought.

"You'll have to make sure you're not followed. Arrange for a taxi to pick you up at the back of one of those shops in Princess Street. Take a taxi to the front of the shop, walk through and pick up the other one."

"With my luck it'll be gone," she said, and then cursed herself for raising objections.

Perhaps that was all right, though, for he smiled as if her seeing the difficulties was the passing of some kind of test.

"You'll manage. You're a smart woman. At the airport, find the nearest seat to the booking desks for our flight. I'll join you when I'm sure you don't have company. You understand?"

But already he was standing. She watched as he walked to the door for the toilets. Even then, she didn't turn her head to McGuigan but sat watching the door and then after a time looked out at the darkness until she saw him as if in a mirror walking towards her.

"Thank God you were there," she said. "I didn't know if you would come."

He laid his hand on her cheek. It was the second time they had touched.

"I'll always be there," he said.

CHAPTER
FIFTY-NINE

Nature and experience had made Wally Perzynski a careful man. There was no way he was going to be alone with Finn when he told him what had happened that morning in the car with Crais on the road above Edinburgh. He had thought of getting in touch with Washington, but that would amount to an accusation and he wasn't sure enough for that. He liked Finn as much as anyone he had ever worked with and it was hard not to trust him. The truth was you could be cautious and still have a weakness for trust, something to do perhaps with getting on too well with your father.

It had been nagging at him that Conway would be in danger until something was done about Crais. As they sat at the end of the day drinking in the hotel bar, he was still running over the arguments in his mind, which distracted him from a story Finn was telling about a Cuban exile in Florida who'd tried to pimp his mistress to him in exchange for information on an ongoing investigation.

"She was just so hot," Finn said. "Not just ass and tits, she was a beautiful woman and smart with it. She had an MBA from Coggin College at UNF."

"Did you fuck her?"

"Fuck her? I'd have married her if she hadn't been in love with the little Cuban guy. Shit, he wore high heels. Women, go figure!"

Looking at him over the rim of the glass as he drank, the arguments running in his head like hamsters chasing one another round a wheel, Perzynski said, "I'm going to gamble it isn't true that you fucked her."

"You'd lose," Finn said. "But —" he interrupted himself with a big warm belly laugh. "But the guy got no information out of me!"

That carried conviction for Perzynski. This was the Finn he knew. A guy who cut corners. An operator. But when the chips were down, a guy you could trust.

"I've been propositioned," he said. With the admission, he was conscious of his bladder being full. It ached as if he was about to testify in court. "If I don't go a place, I'll piss myself."

When he came back, Finn had bought another two malts.

He raised one in a toast and said with a cheesy grin, "In the hotel?"

"What?"

"Some woman propositioned you?"

Perzynski knocked back the whisky. It didn't often happen that he felt so nervous.

"Crais."

"What about him?"

"He offered me a hell of a lot of money to help him make sure Conway never got to the trial."

"How much?"

"Does it matter?"

"It's interesting."

Perzynski studied him. At last he said, "I'll tell you what interests me more."

"What would that be?"

Before Perzynski could answer, Finn's mobile rang. He flipped it open and listened. After a brief conversation, he slipped it back in his pocket.

"That was the cop."

"Meldrum?"

"He's found Conway, who's going to the airport tomorrow to fly home. We're invited to the farewell party."

"At the airport?"

"I've got the flight details. I'll phone and get us tickets."

Perzynski wiped his forehead with a large white handkerchief. He had begun to sweat heavily.

"You think," he asked, "that he's going back to testify?"

"It would be the smart thing for him to do," Finn said.

"Crais'll want to stop him."

"Well, he's asked you."

Perzynski shook his head. He moved it very slowly as if it had become insupportably heavy.

"There isn't enough money in the world. I couldn't do that to my father."

"I know," Finn said. "I told him it was a stupid idea."

As he took in the significance of what had been said, Perzynski's eyes widened and his mouth fell a little open.

Finn took a small empty phial from his pocket. Shielding it from the room in his palm, he held it up so that Perzynski could see it.

"Crais gave me it. I was supposed to use it on Conway."

The stupid thing was that none of that surprised Perzyinski. Part of his mind had been struggling to tell him it made no sense for Crais to leave his arrangements till the last minute. He gathered his legs under him and tried to stand up. When he fell back in his chair, the peanuts that he'd dribbled down his front rolled from his lap on to the floor.

At the bar, Finn motioned discreetly. To the barman, he said, "Would you get an ambulance? I think my friend's just had a stroke." He spoke softly, since it was a good hotel and he didn't want to cause a disturbance.

By the time they got to the hospital, it was after midnight.

The first thing the young doctor asked was how long the patient had been unconscious, then he wondered about diabetes.

"No," Finn said. "Not that I know of. I never saw him take anything."

"He's very overweight," the young doctor said in the faint tone of moral indignation British doctors used about fat.

"I loved the guy," Finn said, "but he was his own worst enemy."

CHAPTER
SIXTY

Meldrum's heart went out to his daughter as he watched her on the CCTV screen. She had been sitting there for more than an hour. To her father's eye she seemed forlorn and vulnerable. She had a case at her feet. He hadn't seen her pack it, since they couldn't take any chance of Conway watching the house. Its weight was designed to prove to anyone who lifted it that she intended to take the flight.

"It's getting tight," McGuigan said.

His voice sounded strained. What's he got to worry about? Meldrum thought irritably. He'd only involved the DS at the last minute, explaining that Betty had been in touch with Conway the previous night and that the American was planning to leave the country.

"There he is," McGuigan said.

They both watched as Conway, who seemed to have come from nowhere, picked up Betty's case and added it to his own. Pushing the trolley, the tall man and the woman by his side walked quickly towards the nearest desk.

"Couldn't we stop him now?" McGuigan asked.

"You know better than that."

What's wrong with him? Meldrum wondered.

All the same, it took all his own self-discipline to wait until the couple walked back from the desk and started up the stairs.

It was a considerable relief when they hurried the length of the queue, showed their warrant cards and came on the little group standing just the other side of the security checks. The couple was standing between Finn and another man.

Conway, it seemed, still didn't understand what had been happening for he was saying to Betty, "It's too bad you were followed, but don't feel bad. These guys are professionals." Seeing Meldrum, he said, "Here's Daddy come to see you off."

"I'm not going," she said.

As if the words ended a spell, she turned on her heel and headed back out into the concourse.

Conway took a step after her, but was stopped as Finn laid a hand on his arm.

"Time to go home," Finn said.

"I'm not sure you could make me," he said. "I haven't done anything."

"You don't count bigamy?" Meldrum asked. It wasn't entirely uncalculated; though he was angry, he also needed to have it confirmed.

Finn frowned and said to Conway, "Don't worry about it. Testify and all that stuff will be taken care of."

Two young women broke step in passing at the impact of Conway turning the full force of his smile on Meldrum.

"There you go, Dad," he said. "Looks like good things happen to bad people."

"Let's go," Finn said.

But Conway hesitated. "Where's your fat friend?" he asked.

"Wally Perzynski's in hospital. They don't think he'll recover consciousness. But we're still going back. I had to get the Consul up in the middle of the night to sort it out."

The nondescript man accompanying Finn introduced himself, "Ted Oliver. I'm going back with you." He said it as if making an apology.

"Let's go," Conway said.

Suddenly it seemed all his reservations were gone and he was laughing as the three of them moved off.

Watching him go, Meldrum felt a great weight lift off his heart.

BOOK SIX

WORTHY TO BE REMEMBERED

CHAPTER
SIXTY-ONE

Meldrum loved trees. As a young man, before chance had taken him into the police, he had worked as a carpenter. There had been an old journeyman who had taken him under his wing and off site, when they weren't pushed to compromise jobs by hurrying to make some link in the chain of slap-up housing schemes, he had shared his craft of making furniture in an outside shed, working with the grain of walnut and beech and ash. Slow work that took its own time, the time it was meant to take, sharing a common passion, not talking much, very occasionally accompanied by the murmur of the old man reminiscing, stories that ended often enough in a bout of coughing as his emphysema grew worse.

Sitting on the bench in the Botanic Gardens, he could recall the varied scent of wood shavings curling back under the stroke of the plane, long slants of sunlight finding their way in through a dusty window, an old man's voice, a sense of being at peace. He watched Tommy playing on the grass at their feet and let new contentment fuse with that of the lost past.

"Thank God, he's gone," he said. "No obligations to him, no ties. You can get on with the rest of your life."

"It's funny to think I was living in sin."

"Only legally."

"Never thought I'd hear you saying that."

"Sometimes the law is an ass. Don't quote me on that."

"Promise." She mused, "It's strange all the same. I wonder if I'd have enjoyed living in sin if I'd known that was what I was doing."

"Doubt it."

"Oh," she said affectionately, "just because you've always been a saint."

If that was how she saw him, he was happy to leave it at that. He scooped the little boy up onto his knee and pointed.

"That's an ash. You can tell because the buds are black. The black ash. And that's a sycamore — see the shape of the leaf — that's what we call palmate. And over there — the leaf on that one is a lot bigger — it's a horse chestnut."

Betty laughed. "He doesn't understand a word you're saying."

"Och, but it's going in all the same. I'll keep going over it. And one day he'll be telling me. You'll see."

"Right enough," Betty said, "he seems happy enough to listen."

After a dull spell, the sun had come out. Three young women strolled towards them. The middle one had undone her coat and his eye took pleasure in her. As if cued by their laughter, a blackbird began to sing.

"I'm very proud of you," he said. "It was brave of you going to meet him by yourself."

"It wasn't like that." She hesitated. "I've got a lot to tell you. Just not now. I've used up all my stock of courage for the moment."

"You don't have to worry about him any more. He won't come back to this country. You've seen the last of him."

The sun warm on his cheek, he fell into a daydream. Surely she would let him help her with the rent of a flat. He would teach his grandson and love him. Of course, sooner or later Betty would have to meet someone else. He couldn't bear for her to be lonely. In the meantime, though, there was something to be said for being the only man in her life.

CHAPTER
SIXTY-TWO

As he crossed the road, it occurred to Meldrum that perhaps the curious Hughie Mallon had recovered enough to hobble his way downstairs for a drink. He swerved to the right and walked along to the pub. Passing the group of smokers, he went inside. At nine in the evening it was too crowded for him to be sure at a glance. He started over to the bar, but had taken only a few steps when he saw the man who'd told him about the boy Mallon in the first place. In the crowded bar, he was sitting at a table alone. Cancer or not, it seemed his reputation was enough to clear himself a space. He looked up as Meldrum stopped beside the table.

"I'm looking for Hughie Mallon."

The face narrow as an axe blade tilted from one side to the other.

"I take it that means he's not here?" Meldrum asked.

The man gestured with the hand that wasn't holding the pint. Warily, Meldrum bent closer to listen.

A voice like the rustle of dry leaves whispered, "I feel fucking awful."

When he switched the torch on in the close, he realised the batteries were almost gone. He followed the pale light up the stairs and on the landing ran his fingertips along the wall, finding the door as much by touch as sight. There was no answer when he rang, but he kept his finger on the buzzer until he heard the noise of movement inside.

"God's sake!" Netta Hodge protested.

"Is he here?"

She turned without a word and went back down the lobby. It was only as she bumped the wall on one side and then the other that he realised how drunk she must be. In confirmation, there was a bottle of whisky and a glass on the table beside the chair she'd fallen into.

"Do you mind?" he asked, bending to switch off the television.

"Would it matter?"

"You can put it on again after I've gone."

"I'll have missed my programme."

"What were you watching?"

When she laughed, she looked less haggard.

"Got me there, you bastard."

He picked up the bottle. "Bunnahabhain single malt. Did that come from Croft?"

"Wasted on me — you think I don't know what you're thinking? Want to join me?" She laughed again to see his tongue unconsciously wipe across his lips. "You'll get a glass in the kitchen."

To his surprise there was a crystal whisky tumbler in the cupboard. Croft again, he thought. He brought it back together with a small milk jug he filled with water from the tap. He poured himself a glass and added the same again of water.

"One for me," she said. "Forget the water."

As he held the whisky in his mouth and felt it warm in his chest, he thought that he was better off than alone in his flat. Nice to be sociable, he thought, and smiled at his own stupidity.

"I thought he might be here," he said.

"He's been and gone."

"Tonight?"

"Last night."

"Nobody's seen him for a while. He was at an auction in Stirling, and phoned the shop to say he was taking a holiday."

"I wish he'd let me alone," she said. "I liked my wee job."

"So where's he now?"

"Back home, I suppose."

"I've been trying to contact him."

"Maybe he's not answering the phone. He wasn't all that happy when he left here."

"Why was that?"

She lifted her hand with the forefinger extended and let it waver in front of her face, before making a face of concentration and managing to press it against her lips.

"You want to go to bed with me?" she asked.

"I don't think so."

"Have another drink."

Nobody ever got the clap from a single malt, he thought, and poured another glass for himself and one for her.

"I was brought up by the nuns," she said.

"That right?"

"Maybe I'm lying."

"You lie a lot?"

He took another sip of the whisky: two acquaintances having a nice comfortable conversation.

"One New Year," she said. Her head nodded forward and it looked as if she was off to sleep, until it jerked up again. The hand holding the glass had kept steady; not a drop spilt. "One New Year, I'm talking about years ago, I was in Glasgow. In Bath Street. I just wanted my hole. I was taking them up the lane. Not charging for it. I was just awful happy. I wasn't a bad-looking woman in them days."

"Spread a little happiness," he said, and grinned into his drink.

"Then this boy, had a good build on him though, a good-looking boy, just young, asked me —" She made a face. "Not a chance. I told him, you've learnt that in the army. All those young boys. It's a right shame, so it is."

"You're right there."

"Would a girl out a convent do that?"

"You said it yourself. Not a chance." He yawned and stretched his legs.

"My father was a farmer." Before he could comment on that, she said, "I wish I'd never met him."

"Your father?" Meldrum had seen too much, listened to too many life stories, for anything to surprise him.

"Now you're being stupid! Barry Croft. He sat in that chair you're in and started crying. I've lost my job, but that's not the worst of it."

Meldrum was careful to stay slouched, his long legs stretched out in front of him, but every nerve in him had tightened with the instinct of a hunter.

"He told you what happened to his wife," he said quietly.

"He didn't mean to do it."

"He lost his temper. He's got a terrible temper."

"That's right."

"When he loses it, he just wants to do damage."

"You know then?"

"I don't know what she said that pushed him over the edge."

"She was at the shop one morning before it opened. Looking for money I expect. I mean, she didn't know, not until she saw me, then she knew. Don't ask me how. Maybe the way he looked at me. He told me later it was my imagination. But after she caught him with that woman, she started laughing at him. She told him he'd stick his prick in anything."

"Even somebody like you?"

"He didn't say that."

"No," Meldrum said. "He wouldn't say that to you. He's fond of you."

"I wish to God I'd never met him."

"Did you tell him that?"

She blew out her lips in scorn. "Do you think I'm stupid? He's just told me he's gone mental and killed his wife!"

"Did he say what he'd done with the body?"

"All he said was he couldn't have managed on his own."

Meldrum let out a long sigh. "That'll do it," he said, and set down the rest of his drink untasted.

When she staggered up, he thought it was to stop him from going, but when she caught up with him at the door she pulled something from her pocket and held it out to him. He recognised the necklace.

"I told him I didn't want it. That cow Dinney already got me fired. She could see me in jail for this. I tried to tell him, but he wouldn't listen. She doesn't just want to run the shop, she wants him between her legs. Here, here, here, please, mister, you take it."

CHAPTER
SIXTY-THREE

It all took time and he was driven by the feeling that what they had was running out. Fairbairn as usual was sceptical but too cautious to put up much resistance. If anyone was going to carry the can, it wouldn't be him. The procurator fiscal passed on the written details to a local sheriff, John Twomey, an old acquaintance of Meldrum's, who grumbled about the time but made out the arrest warrant. When he had it in his hands, Meldrum rang McGuigan's house. He needed somebody with him he could rely on. The phone was answered on the third ring. "Hello?" he asked into the silence. After a brief pause, the phone was put down. What the hell? Meldrum wondered, but there was no time to brood on it. DC Sharkey, a redhead with a sense of humour that had never amused Meldrum, was the best he could do at short notice.

Traffic was light and he ignored the speed limit, peering grimly ahead as the wipers battled a storm of rain.

As the speed rose, Sharkey asked plaintively, "He's definitely there?"

"I think he's tired of running."

"Chances are he'll wait for us then?"

Getting no answer, Sharkey sank back. The rest of the way they drove in silence.

As they came into the village, the headlights picked out the figure of a woman walking towards them. The car was stopped so abruptly that Sharkey was thrown forward into the belt until it tightened on him and forced him back. Next moment, the door was opened and he was alone.

Violet Terry watched the coatless figure hunched against the downpour as it hurried towards her.

"I suppose I should be glad it's you and not some mad rapist."

"You're out late."

She looked around.

"Sleepy hollow. All the lights are out."

"You've been at Barry's."

"He was lonely," she said.

"So he's there."

He was turning away, when she said, "He's not alone."

His first thought was that Kevin Roche was there, and he'd made a mistake by not coming mob-handed.

"That's why I came away," she said. "Orgies aren't my thing. He must have known she was coming. But he had to have me while he was waiting. I think he's mad."

Again Meldrum turned towards his car. As he did, he saw that he had neglected to dip his lights. The mainbeams swept ahead like searchlights coring out the dark. How bloody stupid, he thought, and then: if he's in bed, he won't be looking out of the window.

Even at night there was traffic through the village and he paid no attention to the oncoming vehicle until Violet Terry caught him by the arm and said, "That's his car!" In the same instant, it had rushed past them.

He ran back across the road and scrambled in.

"What's wrong?" Sharkey cried as he wrenched the wheel and spun the car back in the direction they'd come.

"It's Croft."

"What the hell does he think he's playing at?"

High on sex and running for it. Fuck him! Meldrum thought and pressed the pedal to the floor.

He roared up to the crest of a rise and the lights ahead had vanished as if a curtain had been drawn.

"A side road," Sharkey shouted, caught up in the excitement of the chase. "There must be a side road."

And there it was. Meldrum stamped on the brakes and swung the wheel round. Stiff branches from the roadside hedge rattled along the length of the car on his side. Next moment he saw Croft's lights and knew they were still in the hunt.

Even set at double speed, the wipers could hardly clear the screen. He knew he was driving too fast. The car was driving him. He was trying to work out where the road might be going. They were heading back in the direction of the village, but they must be higher than that. Some road south, heading perhaps for Carlisle and the border? The road glimmered in the lash of the rainstorm. He knew he was driving too fast.

He heard Sharkey give a kind of groan and came to his senses. Using all his willpower, he forced his foot to ease up slowly. He braked for a corner and the wheels locked into a skid that he fought to correct, pumping the brake, turning the corner as he gentled the wheel, letting his breath go as the car straightened.

It had been just in time. That had been his last chance. Instead of the road turning again, it went on through the hedge. In the glare of their lights, they watched as Croft's car went straight ahead. At the last moment, its brake lights flared and then it tipped up by the nose and was gone.

Next moment they were off the road and on to the mud path that shone in the lights. He braked and braked again and slowly the car seemed to stop. He wrenched on the hand brake. "We're still moving," Sharkey whispered. As if the car had become his body, he felt the unturning wheels *move* under him.

"Get out," he said, and kept his foot pressed on the brake until Sharkey was out. Only then did he open the door on his side and roll out on to his knees.

He fell forward on to hands and knees and felt the vomit rise in his throat. Slowly like an old careful man he got to his feet. The sleeves of his jacket were wet with mud.

The car was stopped about five feet from the edge. He took a step towards the brink and felt the mud slither under his shoes. With that he began a slow retreat that only ended when he was back at the hedge. Standing in the rain, he looked up and saw the long yellow scar where the mud had slid free taking half the hill with it to smash through the hedge and tumble into the quarry.

Using his mobile to call for help, his voice was steady, but when he tried to put it back he couldn't find the opening to his pocket and still had it in his hand when the cars came.

CHAPTER
SIXTY-FOUR

Meldrum belonged to a generation that didn't stay off work or accept the need for counselling. His only compromise was to crouch in his office drinking innumerable coffees while the rest of the team, including McGuigan but not Sharkey who'd called in sick, were out on inquiries. At intervals, someone would appear to tell him he should go home.

The phone call by the time it came late in the afternoon had a hallucinatory quality.

After a perfunctory exchange of greetings, Finn said, "Poor Wally. What is it you guys say, The best laid plans of mice and men?"

"Wally Perzynski?"

"He died in the middle of the night. Didn't you know?"

"I've been busy at this end," Meldrum said.

"I'd arranged with the Consul to let me know. They'll make all the arrangements."

"Has the cause of death been established?"

"I wouldn't worry about it."

Irritated, Meldrum said, "That's what I'm paid for."

"To worry about Wally?"

"To look into sudden deaths."

"It was sudden all right." He sounded relaxed and even cheerful. "The Consul reported it to your procurator fiscal as soon as he heard. They got two pathologists to do the autopsy. Natural causes." He chuckled. "The fat man dug his grave with his knife and fork."

The ache behind Meldrum's eyes grew worse, so that he had to rub a hand across his forehead.

"Thanks for letting me know," he said, though he couldn't see what it had to do in particular with him.

"I'd have phoned anyway to let you know about Wilbur Conway."

"What about him?"

"Damnedest thing. He's dead too." There was a pause. Meldrum pressed the phone against his ear. Rubbing his hand against his forehead, he could hear a siren, police perhaps or ambulance, sounding from outside the room Finn must be in. "You there?"

"Yes."

"He was found by the maid. He'd died in bed. Far as they can tell he'd had some kind of stroke."

"Like Perzynski."

"Isn't that the damnedest thing?"

"He wasn't fat," Meldrum said, and realised how stupid that sounded. He tried again, "Conway didn't look like the kind of man who'd have a stroke."

"I wouldn't argue with that. He looked like a fit son of a bitch. But know what you're forgetting?"

"What?"

"He'd been under a strain," Finn said, and Meldrum had the unwanted image of him smiling.

316

"He won't be testifying at the trial then." Stupid, he thought, stupid again.

"That's for sure. Anyway, I thought — professional courtesy — I'd phone you. Even apart from the personal angle. You can tell your daughter he didn't suffer. Wouldn't want her to have a bad conscience. Not with her being so helpful and all."

There was nothing to say to that. At last, Meldrum heard the phone go down at the other end.

Time to give in. He made his way along the corridor moving at half his usual pace. When the lift doors opened, he was about to step inside when he heard a voice calling him. He debated pretending to be deaf, but turned and groaned inwardly to see Fairbairn bearing down on him.

"Going home?"

Meldrum grunted agreement.

Fairbairn studied him. "It's all very well being a hard bugger," he said. "But there's nothing hard about giving yourself pneumonia. Stop off at your doctor on the way. That's an order."

In the lift he tried to remember if he had ever heard Fairbairn swear before.

To his surprise, John Melrose, the expert on e-fits, was waiting in the car park to offer him a lift home. It crossed his mind fleetingly that he could ask to get dropped off at the doctors' surgery, but then he decided that Fairbairn was only covering his back in case he was found dead in bed. There's a lot of it about, he thought, not sure if he meant chest trouble or caution.

After Melrose had driven off, he went into Leith Walk and found a chemist shop, where he bought ibuprofen and a bottle of cough medicine. It took a long time to climb the stairs to the flat and once in he took three tablets and a slug of the medicine and fell into bed having managed only to get his trousers off.

Some time in the middle of the night he started up in bed telling himself that he had to go and tell Betty about her husband, then with relief he remembered that she wasn't married after all and went back to sleep.

CHAPTER
SIXTY-FIVE

When Meldrum wakened, the sheets tangled round him smelt of stale sweat and the faintest trace of urine. Sunlight was slanting in through a gap in the curtains and when he checked the alarm on the shelf beside him he was shocked to see that it read ten o'clock. He made it to the bathroom and emptied his bladder for what seemed like quarter of an hour. He soaked a towel and scrubbed himself with it, stuck his head under the cold shower and got dressed. It was only when he phoned in to apologise and say he'd be late that he learnt he'd slept for thirty-nine hours.

Ravenously hungry, he bought filled rolls at the corner shop and ate three of them on the way to work.

By that time McGuigan and most of the others weren't available, Sharkey was on sick leave, and so when he set out to interview Kevin Roche he had to content himself with DC Campbell — a raw-boned, acne-cheeked newcomer to the squad.

Fortunately the DC was a smooth competent driver and he was able to sit back and shut his eyes till they got into the scheme when he was needed as guide for the last bit.

When Roche came to the door, he was unshaven, his eyes were red and sunken, his nose was running and he could be heard coughing as he came along the hall. He looked the way Meldrum felt.

"I can't talk," he said. "I'm a sick man."

"You've no choice," Meldrum said.

"Just you then."

The DC began to move forward assuming they were going to strong-arm their way in, but Meldrum stopped him with an outstretched arm.

"Wait here."

Without waiting for a response, he went in, pulling the door shut behind him. As he went through the lobby, he said over his shoulder, "You should be in your bed."

"I would be if you hadn't hammered on the door." Plaintively he said, "I've got flu."

"It's a bad time of year." In the kitchen, Meldrum put on the kettle. While he waited for it to boil, he spooned coffee into two cups.

"How long have you been ill?"

"Got bad last night."

Meldrum poured the coffees and put them on the table. He sat down and waited till, after a hesitation, Roche followed his example.

"You won't have heard the news then."

"What news?"

"Middle of Monday night, they pulled a car out of the quarry. It had gone over from the top road. Barry was dead in the driving seat."

"You bastard," Roche said on a sob.

Meldrum gathered his legs under him ready for anything, but Roche sunk his face in his hands.

After a while, Meldrum said, "You're going to have to talk to me."

Roche spoke with his head still bowed so that Meldrum had to strain to hear him. "Oh, Christ, if only I'd been there. He wouldn't have done it if I'd been there. I wouldn't have let him."

"He didn't commit suicide. It was an accident."

Roche looked up. "You said he went into the quarry."

"He did."

"How the hell could he go into the quarry by accident?"

"Part of the hill came away because of the rain. He drove through where the hedge had been smashed."

"He was too good a driver for that."

"So he was going too fast."

A thick ribbon of snot had gathered under Roche's nose. He wiped at it with the edge of his hand. "I can't get my head round it being an accident. I blame you. The boss said you'd get him sooner or later."

"It was an accident." Meldrum said it quietly as a statement of fact.

"You can't be sure."

"He might have killed himself deliberately. I don't think he'd have killed Carrie Wilkie. She was beside him in the passenger seat."

"God almighty! Is that true?"

"I was there."

They had rigged floodlights at the edge of the water, and their glare had flashed from the side of the car as the crane fished it up from the depths. No one had expected the body of the woman to be in the car. When it had been eased out, her hair had trailed on the ground and when he had gone close he had seen that her green eyes were open. He had been there, and for the rest of his life would wish that he hadn't been.

Then Roche, the boxer who'd taken too many headshots and never been all that bright, surprised him by echoing something said by Violet Terry. "If he'd been able to keep his zipper shut, he'd still be here. Bloody women!"

"You include Netta Hodge in that?"

"Who?"

"Don't play silly buggers. You bought furniture for her flat — including an enormous television."

"What about her?"

"Barry confessed killing his wife to her."

Roche gaped and sighed. "Aye, it would be her. Could you understand what he saw in her?"

"She wasn't my type."

"She wasn't anybody's type," Roche said bitterly. "Old whore."

Jealous bloody clown, Meldrum thought, and said, "That wasn't the way he saw her," but the raw look of deprivation on the man's face made him ashamed. There wasn't anything sexual in Roche's feeling for the man he called Boss. What he'd lost was his hope for the future.

"You shouldn't have helped him to hide Rachel's body," he said. "That makes you an accessory to murder."

"What does it matter?" Roche asked.

322

CHAPTER
SIXTY-SIX

The morning sun was low so that their shadows stretched between the headstones. The nearest church that had served one village now drew its congregation from three, and the cemetery had fallen out of use. At the farthest end of it, a narrow triangle of grass lay between a grave and the lee of a broken wall. According to Roche, this narrow space had been just wide enough to take the body of Rachel Croft.

Now two gravediggers were carefully stripping the turf off and laying it aside on the path.

Roche said softly to them, "Careful. She isn't buried deep." The police officers gripped his arms reflexively as he turned to Meldrum. Sounding apologetic he explained, "He wasn't in a fit state. I had to do most of it myself." He'd already confessed to the sequence of events. The summons from Croft, wrapping the body and lifting it into the boot, the digging of the makeshift grave, shovelling earth through the breach in the wall, replacing the turf. "He cried all the time."

As the spade slid into the earth, he whispered, "Other end. I put her in wrong way round. Her head's at this end."

Gradually, the sailcloth she'd been wrapped in came into view. The bundle was lifted out and laid gently on the grass of the adjacent grave. Once the presence of a body had been verified, it would be put on the stretcher and taken to the van for passage to the mortuary. Later that morning, Mrs Lenzie or Sylvia, perhaps both of them, would be required to identify it. Later still, the remains would be subjected to the final indignities of the autopsy.

At the last minute, Roche indicated there was something concealed behind the old headstone and with his manacled hands pulled a board up out of the soft earth. In the centre it showed the image of a bearded Christ. None of them could read the strangely shaped letters around the edge. "It's Russian," Roche said. "It means something like she was worth remembering." One of the officers wrapped it in cloth and it too went off for forensic examination.

It was a long day and the excitement that had kept Meldrum going ran out suddenly so that he was exhausted by the time he got to the Corrigans' house. Too tired to get out, he sat and tried to gather his resolution for the task of telling Betty about Conway's death. His eyes closed and his breathing slowed. He saw the bundle in the cemetery stretched out on the grass of an old grave. All the years that Rachel Croft had been married, she must have thought she knew all that there was to be known about her husband.

He forced himself out of the car. As he went up the path, his jaws stretched in an enormous yawn. Denying tiredness, he told himself it was nerves.

Grateful for small mercies, he was glad that it was Carole and not Corrigan who opened the door.

With that in mind, he mouthed more than said, "Come to see Betty," and went in without waiting for an answer.

The noise of the television led him to her sitting room on the right of the hall. The door of Corrigan's study on the other side was closed.

As he bent and switched off the television, he had a sudden vision, not of Netta Hodge but of the set she'd be sprawled in front of, double the size of this one. No doubt at some point she would hear of Croft's death and learn that for her too a place had been reserved among the ranks of the bereaved.

"I'm sorry. I shouldn't have switched off without asking you."

"What on earth are you doing here?"

"I need to talk to Betty."

"Don't you know?"

Before he could ask "know what?" (already with one part of his mind complaining that he was always the last to know) Corrigan put in an appearance, hair ruffled up as if he might have been taking a nap at his desk.

"What the hell do you think you're playing at, letting him in here?" he asked his wife. "Didn't I tell you if he showed his face I'd throw him out?"

What a hero, Meldrum thought, and could hardly contain his fury until he saw, as Carole looked at her husband, that there was something in her responding to Corrigan that should not have responded to him. She had met the wrong man and been changed, and Meldrum admitted it to himself for the first time. If he had seen that truth before, it had been blurred by bad conscience and his own guilt. Now, however, something moved in him. Once, as a young man, he had walked the fields with a farmer who'd shot a limping fox. Picking it up by the scruff of the neck, the man had told him that the fox had gnawed off its own leg to get out of a trap.

When Carole spoke at last, she said, "He's here to see Betty."

"Don't you know?" Corrigan asked. "Your precious daughter's gone to live with her fancy man."

"What is he talking about?"

"His name's McGuigan. Betty says she loves him."

Corrigan laughed at that, an ugly sound. "Don't ever come looking for her here again. She took her little bastard with her. As far as I'm concerned, they're both dead."

When Meldrum stepped close, he had to look down to see Corrigan's white face and felt how good it would be to punch it. He could feel the impact tingle up his arm as if the punch had already been delivered. At once, however, even before Corrigan's venomous whisper, he knew that he wouldn't, the habit of self-discipline was too deeply engrained. "Do it!" Corrigan pleaded. End your career, he meant. Slowly Meldrum shook his head.

Restraint, all the same, came at a cost. It was as if some fragment of his self-respect crumbled away.

326

Control himself against such provocation too often and how many fragments could he afford to lose?

"That's her left her husband," Corrigan tried again, "like a bitch in heat."

But it was too late, and as Carole made no objection to what was being said Meldrum finally relinquished her and with that acceptance came the hope, unadmitted but there, of some new and better life. Even a three-legged fox could survive at least for a time.

Stepping back, he said, "It's my belief she might be happy," and was content to leave it at that.

Also available in ISIS Large Print:

The Judas Heart

Ingrid Black

Marsha Reed was just another aspiring young actress trying to make it in Dublin. But now she's found fame for the wrong reasons — as victim of a brutal murder, her body left tied to her bed.

With former FBI agent Saxon now living in Dublin, the murder squad have the perfect expert to call on. Particularly when it turns out Saxon once knew the victim. However, Saxon is already in the middle of another, more personal, mission — tracking down her ex-colleague, Agent Leon Kaminski, who seems to be hiding out in the streets of Dublin. It's not the first time he's gone missing — but it's the first time since his wife was murdered . . .

Soon enough, it's clear that Saxon's hunt for Marsha's killer and her search for her old friend are heading disturbingly in the same direction . . .

ISBN 978-0-7531-8036-5 (hb)
ISBN 978-0-7531-8037-2 (pb)

The Sporran Connection

Peter Kerr

The droll Scottish detective, Bob Burns, is once again aided by his game-for-anything forensic scientist lady friend, Julie Bryson, and abetted by keener-than-smart rookie detective, Andy Green.

When Andy becomes the unwitting recipient of a drop of £100,000 in used notes, the trio become enmeshed in a web of murder, intrigue and Caledonian skulduggery, as the action shifts to Sicily, New York and a remote Hebridean island. The arrival of a Sicilian blacksmith as the island's new laird leads to some hilarious misunderstandings as the line between the good and bad guys becomes increasingly blurred.

After many a Highland shenanigan, including a vital kilt-raising stunt by Andy Green, the mystery is finally solved . . . or is it?

ISBN 978-0-7531-8028-0 (hb)
ISBN 978-0-7531-8029-7 (pb)